FIREFIGHTER UNICORN
FIRE & RESCUE SHIFTERS 6

ZOE CHANT

Copyright Zoe Chant 2017
All Rights Reserved

🎕 Created with Vellum

The Fire & Rescue Shifters series

Firefighter Dragon
Firefighter Pegasus
Firefighter Griffin
Firefighter Sea Dragon
The Master Shark's Mate
Firefighter Unicorn

Fire & Rescue Shifters Collection 1
(contains Firefighter Dragon, Firefighter Pegasus, and Firefighter Griffin)

Series available in Kindle ebook, paperback, and audiobook.

All books in the Fire & Rescue Shifters series are standalone romances, each focusing on a new couple, with no cliff-hangers. They can be read in any order. However, characters from previous books reappear in later stories, so reading in series order is recommended for maximum enjoyment.

CHAPTER 1

When I find my sister, Ivy Viverna thought grimly as she flew through the cold night air, *I am going to kill her with my bare hands.*

This was, unfortunately, a distinct possibility. As a wyvern shifter, Ivy was the most venomous creature on Earth. And thanks to her unusually powerful inner animal, she was *always* venomous. Even in human form.

At the best of times, Ivy's briefest touch would give someone an instant, agonizing rash. This was most definitely not the best of times. If she'd been in human form now, the storm of fear and anger currently churning in her gut would have had deadly poison sweating from the palms of her hands.

As it was, she had to be careful to keep her sharp-toothed jaws clamped tightly shut. She couldn't risk any of the boiling acid rising in her throat dripping out over the buildings and streets below.

Spit. Kill. Destroy. Her inner wyvern was a blaze of fury in her soul, urging her to rip apart the entire city of Brighton until she found her sister. *Rescue! Defend!*

Ivy shook her horned head, trying to suppress her beast's snarls. Wyverns were the smallest of all the draconic breeds, but like all dragons they had a bone-deep need to hoard treasure, and an equally deep instinct to defend it. Anyone who stole from a dragon soon regretted it—briefly.

Ivy's treasure wasn't cold gold or unfeeling gems, though. Her treasure was flesh and blood. *Her* flesh and blood.

Her sister.

Other dragons have it easy. Their treasures don't skip merrily away while their backs are turned. At least she left a note this time.

The note had been written in purple glittery pen. Hope's messy handwriting, always ridiculously girly, had sprouted heart-dotted i's and extravagantly curling loops of excitement. The exclamation mark situation had gone critical.

Got a ride to the party!!!! See you there?? If not, don't wait up!!!! Love you!!!!!!

Hope had signed her name with a little smiley face in the o.

Ivy could *murder* her little sister sometimes.

Well, technically she could murder Hope all the time. She had to work very, very hard to make sure that she didn't.

And right now, Hope sure as hell wasn't helping.

Ivy narrowed her eyes, trying to pick out the apartment block she sought. She wasn't used to flying over Brighton, and it was hard to recognize neighborhoods from the air. She tried to spend as much time in human form as possible. The less she reminded other shifters of her existence, the better.

One building caught her eye. It rose at least ten floors higher than any of the structures around it, thrusting up into the air defiantly. It had a wide, flat roof terrace, illuminated by dozens of red LEDs. The bright lights marked out a wide circle bisected by a cross, something like a helicopter landing pad.

This landing pad wasn't intended for human machines, though.

That has to be it.

Beating her emerald green wings hard, Ivy landed in the circle. She dug her talons into the graveled surface of the roof terrace, finding her balance before folding her wings. Unlike larger dragons, wyverns had two legs, not four. She was built for speed in the air rather than agility on land.

Her arrival hadn't gone unnoticed. Two hulking brutes straightened up from where they'd been lounging on either side of the open door leading into the building. They were both dressed in artfully ripped designer jeans and leather jackets that strained across their broad shoulders. Ivy's shifter senses prickled at the unmistakable aura of feral energy exuding from them.

Ivy's long, scorpion-barbed tail instinctively curved above her back, ready to strike as the two shifters sauntered forward. She hissed in warning.

The two men stopped in their tracks, eying her arched tail warily. "Shit," the smaller of them muttered. "I told Gaze this was a bad idea."

"Take a chill pill, freak," the other man said to Ivy. A snarling wolf-head tattoo on the side of his neck marked him as a member of the Bad Dogs, a local pack with a particularly vicious reputation. "You may think you're a big deal, but if you start something you're sure as hell going to regret it."

Ivy let her scaled lips wrinkle back from her foot-long fangs. Acid dripped from her jaws, sizzling as it hit the ground. She had the pleasure of seeing both men flinch.

Stay back, puppies, Ivy said telepathically. *I can obliterate you with a single breath. Now where is my sister?*

She had the unmistakable sensation of her mental demand bouncing unheard off the men's skulls. Shifters could generally only talk in animal form to others of the same general type—cats to cats, wolves to wolves, and so on. It was one of the reasons packs and crews usually tended to be formed of similar types of shifter.

As a wyvern, Ivy herself was a mythic shifter, one of the rarest of all the shifter groups. Although Britain had an unusually high population of mythic shifters, they were still uncommon. It wasn't too surprising that neither of the men could hear her.

Ivy concentrated, pushing her wyvern's endless anger down to the bottom of her soul. Her scales tingled as she shrank back into her human skin.

Both men's taut shoulders relaxed. Ivy was no lightweight, but in this form both men had at least six inches and a hundred pounds of muscle on her. They clearly thought they now had the advantage.

They were idiots.

"Huh," the shorter man muttered, staring at her curiously. "It's just a girl."

Ivy aimed her sharpest scowl at him, yanking off one of her gloves. "Who can still kill you with my little finger. Stay right there."

"Like either of us would want to touch you even if you weren't a monster," the tattooed man sneered, his eyes flicking dismissively down Ivy's curves. "Anyway, you got an invite. That means you're safe...for now."

"I'm not here for the party." Ivy's fist clenched on her glove, her bare hand still raised and ready. "I just want my sister. Go get her."

He jerked his thumb at the half-open door behind him. "Go get her yourself."

Ivy switched her glare to the smaller man, but he just shoved his hands in his pockets, leaning casually back against the wall. It was clear neither of the men was going to move a muscle. No doubt they were under orders from their alpha to make sure she went inside.

Ivy bit back a curse. When the mysterious party invitation had arrived last week, she'd known it had to be some sort of trap. No one invited a wyvern to a Christmas party. Not even an all-shifter Christmas party. She'd *told* Hope it was a trap.

And her stupid, *stupid* sister had happily bounced straight into it, and now Ivy had no choice but to take the bait.

Lifting her chin, she strode between the two men, heading for the doorway into the apartment complex. It led to a stairwell, the bannisters decorated with twining boughs of holly. Festive music and laughing voices drifted up from the penthouse apartment below.

Ivy grimaced, but jammed her hand back into her glove. Much as her wyvern screamed that she needed to be ready to defend herself, she could hardly walk into a crowded room with bare skin exposed. Her entire body was venomous, and she couldn't risk hurting anyone.

Tugging at the sleeves of her thick denim jacket to make sure every inch of her arms were safely covered, she headed down the stairs. The sounds of revelry got louder, making her wyvern's hackles rise. Her inner beast was on hyper-alert, its protective fury making Ivy's stomach churn. She was unpleasantly aware of a wet stickiness starting to fill her gloves. In her agitated state, her venom would be deadly enough to kill instantly.

She had to find Hope and get out fast. And pray that no one tried to get in her way.

Taking a deep breath, Ivy pasted her very best *I-give-zero-shits-about-anything-especially-you* expression onto her face. Then she strode into the party.

Thankfully, it was loud and raucous enough that her appearance didn't immediately attract attention. A couple of nearby Bad Dogs gave her a professional once-over, but didn't move in her direction. Ivy had a moment to scan the room.

Her sense of unease deepened.

What the hell is this?

The luxurious, open-plan penthouse was packed with a wild assortment of shifters. Ivy picked out the distinctive heads of the Smile Time crew, their hair shaved and dyed into spots and stripes to match their inner hyenas. She was pretty sure that the trio of women in slinky, short dresses shaking their asses on the dance floor were snake shifters from the Cold Blood gang. And if the pack of red-headed men in the corner yelping encouragement as one of their number attempted a keg stand weren't foxes from the Urban Vermin pack, then Ivy herself was a bunny.

Regardless of species, every shifter in the room had one thing in common. They were all members of some of the less-domesticated—and less law-abiding—groups in shifter society.

Exactly the sort of shifters that she'd sworn she'd never associate with again.

"Ivy! Ivyyyyyy!"

Ivy winced at the familiar, ear-splitting shriek. When Hope was excited—which was way more often than any sane person should be—she could reach a pitch high enough to stun bats.

"'Scuse me, coming through." Hope's running commentary cut through the crowd at waist-level as her wheelchair shunted startled shifters aside. "Beep beep! Pardon me—oh, I'm so sorry! Was that your foot?"

A massive hyena shifter swore viciously, clutching at his leg as he rounded on his unexpected assailant. "Why you little-"

"Sister," Ivy finished for him, stepping forward. She met his angry gaze coolly. "*My* little sister."

The hyena's eyes widened as he took in her green-streaked hair. Ivy had deliberately adopted the dyed, asymmetric haircut in order to stand out. It helped to have a distinguishing feature that other shifters could use to describe her to each other.

The wide, acid green stripe in her dark hair was her own version of a wasp's black-and-yellow warning: *Don't mess with me.*

The hyena shifter swallowed his growl, his face paling. Like most shifters in Brighton, he'd obviously heard about her. Without another word, he hobbled away.

"Sorry again!" Hope called after the retreating thug. "Can I get you a—oh, you're gone. Well, I guess you have shifter healing anyway." Hope swiveled her wheelchair round to face Ivy, a beaming grin splitting her thin face. "Ivy! You came!"

"Briefly," Ivy growled. She reached for the handlebars of Hope's wheelchair. "We're leaving. Now."

Hope spun her wheelchair out of reach with a practiced flick, evading Ivy's grasp. "Nuh-uh. There's someone here that you have absolutely *got* to meet."

She's seventeen years old, Ivy thought in despair. *And she still has all the survival instincts of a toddler on a sugar high.*

"For once in your life, listen to me," Ivy hissed, her hands sweating in her gloves. "We have to get out of here. Can't you see what sort of people these are?"

Hope lifted her chin, her mouth setting in a stubborn line. Despite the fact that Hope was blonde, thin, and beautiful, for a moment it was uncannily like looking into a mirror.

"Yes, I can. They're people who have to cope with powerful,

dangerous inner animals, in a world that's not made for them. People shunned and feared even by other shifters, just because they're different." Hope folded her thin arms across her chest. "Remind you of anyone?"

Ivy clenched her fists, matching her sister's glare. "I'm not like them!"

"But you could be," said a deep, amused voice from behind Hope.

A tall, broad-shouldered man sauntered out of the crowd. He was wearing tailored black dress pants and a fine white shirt, the top few buttons undone to show off a hint of the deep crease between his hard pecs. Wrap-around designer sunglasses hid his eyes.

"Gaze!" Hope squealed, clapping her hands. "Ivy, this is who I wanted you to meet! Gaze, look, this is my sister!"

"So glad you could join my little party after all, Ivy Viverna." The man flashed brilliantly white teeth at her. "I'm Gaze."

"Never heard of you," Ivy said, eyeballing the distance to the nearest exit.

The man chuckled, not looking in the least offended. "Then I've been doing my job right. But in any case, I've heard of *you*. I've been looking for an opportunity to meet you for quite some time."

Out of his sight, Hope was silently mouthing something that looked suspiciously like the words *your, true,* and *mate*. She was practically bouncing in her wheelchair, her green eyes alight with excitement.

Ivy repressed the urge to groan out loud. Of all the disastrous attempts Hope had made to set her up, this definitely ranked somewhere in the top five.

For all she knew, of course, Gaze *could* be her one true mate. Shifters typically didn't recognize their mate until they made eye contact, and Gaze's eyes were completely concealed.

Not that it mattered. Finding her true mate was top on Ivy's list of Things Not To Do. What would be the point, when they could never touch?

Gaze, for his part, seemed to be fascinated by her. His chin dipped a little, as if he was taking her in from head to toe. Even hidden behind his sunglasses, she could feel the heat of his appraisal.

"You are an elusive woman, Ivy. But I very much hope to be seeing more of you in future." His voice dropped to low, thrilling murmur. "We have *so* much in common."

"Yeah, no." Ivy sidled closer to Hope, trying not to be too obvious about it. "I don't think so. We're leaving now."

"But you've only just got here." Gaze rested a hand on the back of Hope's wheelchair, and Ivy swallowed the possessive snarl that rose in her throat. "And Hope doesn't want to leave yet, do you, sweetheart?"

"No way! I haven't even danced yet, and Betty promised to introduce me to her whole pack!"

Betty? Who the hell is Betty?

Before Ivy could ask, Hope did a transparently fake double-take. "Oh look, there they are now!" She pointed across the room at a group of teens in black leather lurking in a corner. "I'll just leave you guys to it, shall I? I'm sure you'll have tons to talk about!"

"Hope!" Ivy made a grab for her, but Hope was too fast. She zoomed away, heedless of the shifters she scattered.

"Can I offer you a drink?" Without waiting for a response, Gaze turned on his heel, starting to stroll away.

Ivy had no choice but to follow. The milling partygoers moved aside for Gaze a lot more willingly than they had for Hope. Even the toughest, most brutal-looking gang members gave way to him with respectful murmurs.

Who is this man?

Ivy couldn't even tell what sort of shifter he was. With the scents of so many different kinds mingling in the air, mixed in with the fumes of mulled wine and the tang of evergreen boughs, it was impossible to get a good whiff of him.

His easy dominance told her one thing, though. Despite the powerful creatures all around—hyenas, vipers, even the hellhounds of the Bad Dogs—Gaze was the most dangerous person in the room.

"Who *are* you?" she asked warily, as he led her to the gleaming kitchen area of the vast open-plan penthouse.

"A broker, of sorts. I make connections. Bring people together for mutual benefit." Gaze extracted a bottle of champagne from one of the many ice buckets clustered on the black marble counter. He let out a deep chuckle as he poured. "And you could call this a staff party. All the shifters here are…private contractors, shall we say, who do business with me. Very profitable business, I might add."

Ice ran down Ivy's spine. "Let me guess. That business isn't exactly legal."

Gaze smiled behind his sunglasses, pushing a glass of champagne across the counter toward her. "I'm sure you'll appreciate that I can't discuss past jobs. But I do maintain a small, very exclusive list of clients, who pay well for quiet solutions to delicate problems. And they would pay extremely well for someone of your particular talents."

Ivy knew *exactly* how much unscrupulous people would pay for what she could do. She'd carry the shame of that until her dying day.

Never again.

She swallowed the acid rising in her throat. Much as she wanted to spit in Gaze's face and tell him where he could stick his offer, she was standing on his territory. Surrounded by his people.

Who were also surrounding Hope.

It took all her control not to look round at her sister. Ivy picked up the champagne glass, taking a sip as cover for her furiously racing thoughts.

Have to play this cool. Make him think he's got me interested.

"I know how much I'm worth," she said. "Why should I let you take a cut?"

"Because I can provide what your previous employer didn't." Gaze leaned back, resting his elbows against the countertop. Ivy was pretty sure he knew exactly how well the posture showed off the hard swells of his biceps. "Protection. I know your previous experiences with this line of work, Ivy. You were, if I may be so blunt, appallingly wasted by Killian Tiernach. You nearly went to prison because of his mistakes."

"Yeah, well," Ivy muttered, the shame of the memory heating her cheeks. "*He* did. I don't want to risk getting into that sort of trouble again."

"I would never ask you to." Gaze's voice dropped to that deep, seductive murmur again. "A unique treasure such as yourself should never be put at risk. *I* would treat you as you deserved."

Which, apparently, is from three feet away, Ivy thought with dark humor. For all his flirtatious manner, Gaze was being very careful to stay out of arm's reach.

Just like everyone did.

Ivy leaned a little closer, as though his attempt to charm her was working. To his credit, Gaze didn't flinch, although his broad shoulders tensed.

"You've got my attention," Ivy said. Under the excuse of turning to gesture at the luxurious apartment, she scanned the party for Hope. "You're clearly doing well for yourself, and I could do with some cash. What sort of—oh, crap."

One of Gaze's hands shot up, touching the frame of his sunglasses. "Something wrong?"

"No. Just my irritating sister picking the worst possible moment to interrupt, as usual." Ivy faked a grimace, putting her champagne down. "She needs me to take her to the bathroom. Where is it?"

Gaze dropped his hand again. "Just down the hall. But I'm sure I could get someone—"

"I'll be right back," Ivy called over her shoulder, already striding away.

Hope was deep in conversation with her fellow teens in the corner, but she broke off at Ivy's approach. "Well?" she demanded eagerly, swiveling round. "Did you like him? Is he—"

"He wants to offer me a job." Ivy took hold of the handlebars of Hope's wheelchair. "We're going to discuss the details after I've taken you to the bathroom."

"What?" Hope said, as Ivy briskly wheeled her through the crowd. "I—"

"Need to go *right now*, I know." Ivy desperately prayed Gaze wasn't one of the sorts of shifters that had supernaturally good hearing. "Come on, let's make this fast. I want to get back to the party."

As Ivy had hoped, *that* finally clued her sister in that something was badly wrong. Miracle of miracles, for once Hope actually shut up.

Under the pretext of opening the door, Ivy bent level with Hope's ear. "How'd you get up here?"

"Elevator," Hope whispered back. "It's that way. What's going on?"

"Tell you once we're out."

Miracle of miracles, the hallway was empty. Ivy jabbed at the elevator call button with a shaking hand. Her venom sweated into her gloves as the machine crawled upward agonizingly slowly.

Come on, come on!

She breathed deeply, trying to calm herself. She had to reduce the concentration of her venom, so that her touch would paralyze rather than kill. There was no way that a crime boss like Gaze would have left all the exits unguarded. If she couldn't rush Hope past whatever thugs he had stationed in the lobby, she'd be forced to fight.

There was one line she'd never crossed. No matter what other terrible things she'd done, what mistakes she'd made…she'd never killed.

She'd sworn she never would.

"It's okay, Ivy," Hope whispered as the elevator *binged* at last, doors sliding open. "Everything's going to be fine. Just breathe."

"Leaving so soon, Ivy Viverna?"

Ivy's hammering heart lurched. Thrusting Hope into the elevator, she spun on her heel. Gaze stood at the end of the corridor, calmly surveying her through his dark lenses. A pair of monstrous dogs padded at his side, their coal-black backs level with his waist. A hot, baleful orange light burned in the dogs' throats, behind their snarling fangs.

Hellhounds!

"Hope, go!" Ivy yelled, jerking off her gloves.

"Not without you!" From the sounds of the doors trying and failing to close, Hope must have been holding the *Door Open* button.

Once, just *once*, Ivy wished that Hope would do as she was told.

She didn't dare take her eyes off Gaze and the hellhounds. She kept her hands raised and ready, deadly venom gleaming on her palms.

"Stay back," she warned, fighting not to show how she was shaking. "Or I'll show you what I can do."

She could only pray that he wouldn't take her up on the offer.

"I would, in fact, very much like to see your skills." Gaze's hand went to his sunglasses, sliding them down his nose. "But first, I'll show you mine."

He looked straight at her.

The force of his eyes took her breath away. They were red, red as blood, from edge to edge. No pupil, no white. Nothing but crimson, filling her vision, swallowing her whole.

Ivy couldn't look away. A strange fire filled her blood, like nothing she'd ever known. In all the world, there was nothing but him, and her.

Holy crap. He really is *my mate!*

Then, as the burning heat in her veins continued to rise, Ivy realized that her one true mate probably shouldn't set her aflame with *pain*.

"I did say we had much in common, Ivy," Gaze murmured. His mouth curved in slight, strangely wistful smile. "Wyverns are nearly as rare as basilisks."

"Hey, asshole!" Hope yelled. "Think fast!"

Something pink and glittery hurtled past Ivy's shoulder. Gaze's eyes flickered, instinctively tracking the motion.

Ivy was never, *ever* going to complain about Hope's terrible taste in handbags again. Her paralysis broke the instant Gaze was distracted. Before the basilisk could capture her again with his stare, she squeezed her own eyes tight shut.

"Hope, *go!*" Ivy shouted, and gave herself up to her wyvern.

It surged up from her soul in an emerald storm of teeth and rage. The corridor would have been too small for a proper dragon to shift, but when her wings were folded, Ivy was only the size of a large horse.

Still keeping her eyes closed, she braced herself on her folded wing-joints, and breathed out a blast of acid. Her wyvern wanted to melt the flesh from her enemy's bones, but she held her full strength in check.

Even a mild dose of her acid was still enough to hurt. Yelps of pain echoed down the corridor. She hoped she'd gotten the basilisk, but she didn't dare open her eyes to check.

To her eternal relief, she heard the elevator doors slide shut behind her. Hope was finally on her way to safety.

Ivy blindly breathed out another covering blast of acid, half-spreading her wings to make sure no one was trying to sneak past. No yells this time, so she guessed Gaze and his shifters must have retreated.

The elevator *binged*, counting down floors as it descended. Ivy frantically tried to remember how tall the apartment building was. It would surely only take a few minutes for the elevator to reach the lobby.

Got to find a window. Fly down to meet Hope, get her to safety—

Something crashed into her, knocking her head over tail backward. She slammed into the wall, her attacker a cold, hard weight on top of her. She was only poisonous to the touch in human form; in wyvern form, her armored scales covered her venomous skin.

Powerful coils wrapped around her body. They squeezed, trying to crush the life out of her. It took all her willpower not to open her eyes.

Spit! Strike! Kill!

Completely disoriented, Ivy unleashed a blast of acid—not the diluted form she'd used before, but her full, steel-melting strength. Her unseen assailant let go of her, slithering away as she blindly whipped her head from side to side.

Walls sizzled, melting under her deadly breath. Sparks showered over her scales as the acid ate through electricity cables. The whole building shook as the power went out. The music still emanating from the party abruptly went dead.

And in the sudden hush, Ivy heard the deep, metallic groan of the elevator cable giving way.

CHAPTER 2

*H*ugh Argent had a splitting headache. As usual.

It was rather ironic, considering that as a paramedic he was carrying an emergency kit full of modern medicine's finest painkillers. But not even morphine could do anything to help the migraine brought on by close proximity to non-virgins.

Being a unicorn shifter was, quite literally, a pain.

"You all right back there, Hugh?" Dai asked from the driver's seat. The red dragon shifter glanced over his shoulder, looking concerned. "I can hear you grinding your teeth from here."

"I'm fine," Hugh snapped, forcing himself to unclench his jaw. "It's just that this bloody overgrown fish is taking up all the space."

Next to him in the rear seat, John Doe obligingly tried to fold himself smaller. This was about as effective as a carp trying to fit into a teacup. No matter how the sea dragon twisted his seven-foot-tall bulk, his legs or elbows jabbed into Hugh.

Just the briefest contact was like brushing against an electric fence. Even the layers of fire-resistant turn out gear Hugh wore couldn't do anything to protect him from the searing jolt of touching someone who wasn't chaste. And unfortunately, since John had found his one true mate last year, he was extremely *unchaste*.

"I am sorry, shield-brother," John rumbled, giving up. Despite his efforts, he'd invaded Hugh's personal space so thoroughly, he'd practically conquered it in the name of the sea dragon Empress. "This vehicle is not built for my kind, I fear. Please tell me if there is anything I can do to alleviate your discomfort."

How about keeping it in your pants for one night? Hugh wanted to say. *Let your mate get some sleep for once. It's a wonder the poor woman isn't walking bow-legged by now.*

But he had to hold his tongue. John and Dai couldn't know the real reason for his grumpiness. They didn't even know what sort of shifter he was.

Fire Commander Ash was the only person Hugh had ever told. He'd had to, in order for the Phoenix to allow him to join the all-shifter Alpha Fire Team.

Hugh could trust Ash's discretion—the reclusive Phoenix was even more tight-lipped than Hugh himself. But sharing his true nature with the entire team...? That would be inviting disaster.

Staying aloof kept him alive. He couldn't tell his colleagues what he was, no matter how much his secretiveness distanced him from them.

Of course, some distance is starting to sound a lot more appealing, these days.

Hugh sighed, rubbing his pounding forehead. With four of his five colleagues now mated, Alpha Team wasn't the peaceful refuge it had once been. Much as he tried to be happy for his friends' happiness, the brutal fact was that he now spent every working moment feeling like they were collectively driving a fire axe through his skull.

He couldn't even hope that their enthusiasm for carnal pursuits might wear off over time. Dai had been joined to *his* mate for over three years now, and Hugh could tell that they still spent practically every night dancing the horizontal tango.

Dai caught his eyes in the rear-view mirror. "What are you glaring at me for?"

"Nothing," Hugh muttered. "Just thinking how nice it would be if your toddler wasn't such a good sleeper. Are we there yet?"

"Actually, yes." The red dragon shifter parked the fire truck outside a towering apartment block. The power seemed to be out—despite the late hour, all of the windows were dark. "This is it, according to Dispatch. Let's go."

Grabbing their gear, they piled out of the truck. The searing agony in Hugh's head diminished to a dull throb as he trailed Dai and John into the building at a discreet distance. He easily ignored the familiar low-level pain, focusing on the job at hand.

"East Sussex Fire and Rescue," Dai called, aiming his flashlight at a small knot of people clustered at one end of the lobby. "Which of you—hey!"

The group had taken one look at the approaching firefighters and scattered like startled rabbits. Hugh jumped back as a group of men barged past him, practically sprinting for the door.

"I don't know who those were, but they were definitely shifters," he said, wrinkling his nose at the unmistakable canine scent still hanging in the air. "And evidently ones with guilty consciences."

"Songs of our deeds have spread wide," John said, sounding rather satisfied about that fact. "Wrong-doers flee rather than face our wrath."

"I suppose we're not exactly hard to recognize," Dai said, glancing wryly up at the towering, indigo-haired sea dragon. "But *someone* here called for the fire department."

"That was me."

As one, they all turned their flashlights in the direction of the voice. A tall teen girl wearing black motorbike leathers flinched under the beams of light, her shoulders hunching defensively. Her eyes flicked in the direction of the exit.

"It's all right," Dai said, his lilting Welsh voice gentle. "You aren't in trouble. We just want to know how we can help."

The girl shifted her weight from foot to foot, looking on the verge of flight. "There was, there was a fight. Up in the penthouse. The elevator broke—please, you have to rescue her!"

"Someone's trapped in the elevator?" Hugh asked.

The girl nodded. "On the tenth floor, I think, but Gaze wouldn't let anyone go look. There was a big crash."

Dai turned his flashlight, scanning the darkness. "Show us the way."

The girl bit her lip, her face creasing in an agony of indecision. "I can't, Gaze told us all to scatter—I gotta go before my pack notices I'm not with them. Please, hurry!"

"Wait-" Dai started, but he was talking to her back. The dragon shifter blew out his breath in exasperation as she bolted out the door. "Well, at least we know why we're here."

Damsels in distress, Hugh's inner unicorn whispered. *Hurry!*

John was looking worried. "This 'elevator'...that is the unnatural box that defies gravity, is it not? Will any be alive to rescue, if it has plummeted from a great height?"

"Don't worry, elevators are packed with safety features," Dai said absently, still searching the lobby for a way up. "We'll just be rescuing whoever's trapped inside from boredom. I bet Hugh won't even have anything to do."

"How refreshing," Hugh said. He picked out a door across the lobby with the beam of his flashlight. "There's the stairs. Let's go to work."

Despite Dai's confidence, a strange sense of urgency twisted Hugh's gut. His unicorn was agitated, the silver glow of its horn bright as the moon in his mind's eye. It was all he could do to hold it back, following Dai and John up the stairs rather than shoving past them and charging ahead at full speed.

"Hold a moment, my brothers." John stopped, his head cocked to one side. "What is that sound?"

In the pause, they all heard it—the low, inhuman groan of metal subject to unbearable stress.

Metal on the verge of breaking.

Dai's eyes met Hugh's. "So much for safety features," the red dragon said grimly. "Come on!"

They took the steps three at a time now, their work boots thumping on the treads. A few mundane humans were milling uncertainly around on the tenth floor, evidently drawn from their apartments by the power cut.

"Oh!" An elderly woman clutched her nightgown closer around her at their sudden appearance. "Is there a fire? Should we evacuate?"

"No, ma'am," Dai said, politely touching the edge of his helmet. "But we need to make sure everyone's safe. Can you tell us where the elevator is?"

"That way." The old lady pointed down the corridor. "Is that what made that awful noise?"

"Shit," Hugh muttered under his breath. He raised his voice, aiming his best glare at the spectators. "All right, back inside, people! We can't do our job with you lot breathing down our necks!"

The gawkers unwillingly retreated into their apartments. With the humans out of the way, Hugh could see the double metal doors of the elevator at the end of the hallway. It was immediately apparent what had made the 'awful noise'—the doors were buckled outward. Hugh guessed that the falling elevator must have somehow hit them and become wedged.

Dai rapped on the distorted metal. "East Sussex Fire and Rescue! Can anyone hear me?"

"Help!"

The trapped girl sounded young. From the way her thin, panicked voice seemed to be coming from near the ceiling, the elevator was evidently stuck somewhere between this floor and the one above.

"Don't worry. We're going to get you out." Dai was already prizing at the doors, without noticeable effect. "John!"

The seven-foot-tall sea dragon braced his feet, fitting his massive fingers into the twisted seam of the doors. The tendons of his neck stood out as he applied his full strength. The doors emitted an ear-splitting squeal, moving the barest fraction of an inch.

"It'll move, but we need more leverage." Dai's broad shoulders bunched as he too threw his full weight against the door, forcing it open a tiny bit more. "Hugh, crowbar!"

Hugh extracted the tool from their gear, tossing it to the dragon shifter. His own hands clenched as he watched the two men strain to open the door. He hated not being able to help, but there wasn't any room for him to add his strength as well.

"I'm going to go up to the next floor," he said abruptly, unable to contain his burning need to do something. "Maybe I'll be able to see something from up above."

Be careful, Dai said telepathically, too out of breath for words. *Just look, and tell us what you see. Don't take any risks.*

Since Hugh's talents were usually best deployed on the back lines, away from the heat of danger, it was understandable that his colleagues were somewhat over-protective of him. Still, it was bloody annoying. He *was* a fully trained firefighter as well as a paramedic.

"I can take care of myself," Hugh snapped, grabbing another crowbar. "Try not to sprain anything in my absence."

He hastened to the next floor. The elevator doors here weren't as damaged as the ones below, though they were still a little bent. Hugh worked the crowbar into the rippled gap, braced himself, and heaved.

He might not have the brute size of a dragon, but he was still a mythic shifter. The doors slid open with a screech of protest.

Hugh angled his flashlight into the dark void of the elevator shaft. The reason for the elevator's bizarre position was clear—all but one of the main cables had snapped. A couple of the loose ends were hanging free, swinging slightly.

"What in the name of all that's holy did *that?*" he muttered, staring at the dangling ends.

They looked dissolved, like acid had eaten through the thick cables. Playing his flashlight beam down the one remaining cable, he could see deep pits in its surface. Whatever had destroyed the other cables had nearly gotten this one too. He had a nasty feeling that it was only a matter of time before it gave way as well.

He panned his flashlight lower—and jumped so badly that he dropped the damn thing.

Bloody hell, was that a face?

The flashlight clanged away down the side of the shaft, but not before the wildly spinning beam of light had flashed across someone crouched on top of the elevator.

"What the hell do you think you're doing?" Hugh yelled, his voice echoing down the narrow shaft.

"I've got to rescue my sister!" From the voice, the figure was a woman, though Hugh couldn't make out anything other than a vague impression of a short, curvy form.

"That's *our* job, you idiot!" Belatedly, Hugh remembered his three rounds of remedial sensitivity training. "I mean, we have the situation fully under control. Please, leave this to us professionals."

The woman didn't look up from whatever she was doing. "Like hell I will!"

So much for trying to do this by the book.

"Don't you dare make me come down there!" he yelled.

"Bite me!"

His inner unicorn stamped a hoof. *She calls to us! We must go!*

Personally, Hugh was not certain that 'bite me' qualified as an appeal for help, but there was no arguing with his unicorn's compulsion to race to the aid of fair maidens. Or, in this case, a cranky and annoying one.

With a growl of irritation, Hugh felt around the inside of the elevator shaft until he found the internal access handholds. Before he could talk himself out of it, he swung himself into the darkness.

"What the hell are *you* doing?" the woman shouted up as he started to climb down.

"My damn job, thank you very much." Hugh groped for the next handhold. It was as black as the devil's own armpit down here. "Which you aren't helping with."

What on earth are you doing? Dai's telepathic voice demanded inside Hugh's head. *What's all that shouting?*

Little busy right now! Hugh sent, and slammed his mental walls up. He couldn't risk getting distracted, and he didn't want to divert Dai and John from the equally important task of getting the elevator door open.

He jarred his foot unexpectedly against the roof of the elevator cage, and bit back a curse. The single, overstrained support cable groaned in answer.

"Watch out!" The woman sounded simultaneously pissed off and frantic. "You'll bring it down!"

"Do I look like an idiot? I'm not going to put my weight on it." Bracing himself on the access ladder, Hugh stuck his other arm out, groping for the woman in the darkness. "Come here. I'll get you to safety."

She scrabbled away from his searching fingertips. "Don't touch me!"

"I'm not trying to feel you up, woman," Hugh snapped in exasperation. "Just take my hand."

"I can't. I lost my gloves." Her voice came from low down, as if she was on her knees. "And I can't get this bastarding access hatch open!"

Despite the swearing, her voice was trembling on the verge of tears. Clenching his jaw against expected pain, Hugh reached out again. The tips of his fingers brushed a denim-clad shoulder.

"Huh," he said in surprise.

How about that. She's a virgin. Practically rarer than I am.

She flinched from his touch. Typical. The first adult in months who hadn't given him a screaming headache on contact, and she was as evasive as a buttered ferret.

He tightened his grasp, not letting her slip away. He could feel her jerky, labored breaths as she fought to contain her sobs.

"I promise, everything will be all right," he said more gently. "My friends are getting your sister out. I can tell that they've nearly got the door open."

She went still under his hand. "Really?"

"I promise." From her scent, she was a shifter, though he couldn't tell what kind. "We're all shifters too. I can sense them telepathically. They'll have her out in just a second."

An ear-splitting screech echoed up the shaft. Hugh steadied the woman as the elevator cage shuddered underneath them.

We have her, shield-brother! John's telepathic voice was a deep, triumphant chord, like a mix of cellos and bassoons. *She is shaken, but unharmed.*

Let me be the judge of that, Hugh sent back. *I'm on my way.*

"Your sister's out of the elevator," he said out loud. "But I want to check her over. I'm a paramedic. My colleagues are excellent firefighters, but considering they tend to view broken bones as minor inconveniences, you really don't want to rely on them for medical advice."

"Hope's safe?" Naked relief was clear in her voice.

"She's safe." Hugh squeezed her shoulder in reassurance. Maybe it was just the fact that he could touch her without pain, but he felt a sudden, deep surge of protectiveness toward her. "Now let me take care of you."

Always, his inner unicorn whispered.

What? Caught off-guard by his animal's unexpected comment, Hugh blinked. He was very aware of the heat of the woman's body, even through her thick clothing.

"I can take care of myself," the woman said, though there was something less certain about her tone, as if she too had felt that peculiar spark of connection. "Move out of the way. You're blocking the ladder."

Hugh cleared his throat. "Yes. Right. Well, at least let me help you up." He struggled to reclaim his usual ironic detachment. "I can't be the only firefighter who doesn't rescue someone. It'll look bad on my mid-year appraisal."

She snorted, shrugging off his hand. "Tough, because I don't need—"

Her words cut off in a scream as the last elevator cable snapped. On pure instinct, Hugh lunged, losing his own foothold in his haste to catch her.

He slammed back against the wall, dangling from the access ladder with one hand, the other clamped around the woman's bare wrist. His arms screamed in protest, nearly wrenched out of their sockets.

"Let go! Let go!" the woman shrieked, which was not the usual response of someone dangling over a ten-floor drop.

"Damn it, woman, are you out of your bloody mind?" She was actually *clawing* at him. "Do you *want* me to drop you?"

"I don't want you to die!"

"Neither do I, thank you very much! So stop thrashing about!"

HUGH! Dai and John's mental shouts blasted his mind, nearly making him lose his grip on the slippery ladder.

"Damn your eyes, are you *all* trying to kill me?" Hugh snarled. His boots scrabbled at the side of the elevator shaft, hunting vainly for a foothold.

We're coming, Dai sent, his telepathic tone frantic. *The ladder's destroyed down here, we have to go up to the next floor. Just hold on!*

"Oh, well, and here I was considering letting go," Hugh said under his breath. "Take your time. I'll just be hanging around."

The woman had finally stilled, much to his relief. "You…you're still alive?"

"You sound," Hugh grunted, finally getting a toe-hold on the ladder with one foot, "surprised."

"You're touching me! You should be dead! I can't control my venom, not in a situation like this!"

The penny dropped. There was only one shifter in all of Brighton —probably in all of Britain—who was *that* deadly.

Hugh had never met her, but he'd certainly heard enough about her. He'd had more than one occasion to curse her name as he frantically battled to save someone from her venom.

"You're that bloody wyvern shifter, aren't you?" he demanded.

A moment of silence.

Then, "Yes," she said, in a very small voice.

Well, that explained the fizzing tingle where his hand gripped her bare skin. As a unicorn, Hugh was able to neutralize any poison on contact.

"My venom really isn't affecting you," the woman said in disbelief. "How is that possible?"

Shit.

Unicorns weren't the only type of shifter who could heal, but they *were* the only type powerful enough to counteract even a wyvern's deadly abilities. He could only hope that the fact that unicorns were meant to be extinct would stop her from guessing what he truly was.

"I'm just very stoic." Hugh gritted his teeth as he hauled her up one-handed. "Actually, I'm in terrible agony. Oh, the pain. Argh."

She clung to the rungs next to him, her curvy body pressed tight against his. He still had hold of her wrist. He could feel the wild beat of her pulse.

She brought her hand up, blindly tracing the line of his jaw in the dark. Hugh's own blood leaped at the tentative brush of her fingertips against his skin.

"No one's ever been able to touch me," she whispered. "Who *are* you?"

Flashlight beams stabbed through the darkness from above, illuminating her face at last. Hugh looked into her wide, emerald eyes…and knew.

"Oh shit," he said. "I'm your mate."

CHAPTER 3

He's my mate.

It was all Ivy could do to keep her hands tucked safely in her armpits. Her palms tingled—not with venom, but with a desperate hunger to reach out and touch him. She couldn't tear her eyes away from the paramedic's elegant profile as he knelt next to Hope, checking her for injuries.

Normally, the sight of someone else near Hope caused her wyvern to fly into a jealous rage. But her beast was quiet, as intent on the paramedic as he was on his patient. Her wyvern didn't mind that he was touching its treasure...because *he* was its treasure too.

And oh, he was *beautiful*.

His white hair gleamed in the dim corridor as if spun from moonlight. His skin was pale too, flawless as fine pearl. His high, sharp cheekbones could have been carved by Michelangelo. A strong jaw and chin balanced the elegant lines of his brow and nose, making his features unmistakably masculine.

For all his unearthly good looks, there was nothing delicate or fragile about him. She'd felt the strength in those swift, long-fingered hands when he'd saved her from falling. Even shrouded in the shapeless, bulky firefighter uniform, his shoulders were broad and powerful.

No one could ever call him merely *pretty*. He was beautiful, like lightning. He looked like an angel—but not the insipid Christmas-card sort. He was an avenging angel, filled with a fierce power so bright it hurt the eye.

And she was meant to be his mate.

No wonder he'd taken one look at her, and said *Oh shit.*

He hadn't so much as glanced at her since. She tried to tell herself that he was just being professional, that he had to concentrate on Hope…but in her gut, she knew better. He was the most breathtaking man she'd ever seen, and she was…her.

Ivy, the wyvern shifter. The freak. Ugly. Unwanted.

Untouchable.

Yet he *had* touched her. The heat of his skin had seared her to her very bones. She felt like she would carry the invisible brand of his fingers around her wrist for the rest of her life.

He'd been in contact with her venomous skin for at least two minutes. And yet he was still alive.

Was it because he was her mate?

Her hands shook. She clamped down on them with her arms, hugging herself. A terrifying new emotion was growing in her heart, battling her wyvern's ever-present rage.

Hope.

She thrust the unwanted feeling back down, trying to lock it away again. The naked dismay in those pale blue eyes had been painfully obvious even in the dimness of the elevator shaft. Even if he *could* touch her, why would he want to? Looking like he did, he could have anyone. He probably *did* have everyone he wanted.

Ours, her wyvern snarled. *No one else's. Our mate! Kill rivals!*

Just the thought of someone else touching those perfect features had her inner wyvern on the verge of murder. Ivy swallowed hard, forcing back the burn of acid in her throat.

He doesn't want you, she reminded herself savagely.

Her life—her *sister's* life—depended on her being tough. She'd spent her entire life fighting the whole world, tooth and claw, in order to keep Hope fed, sheltered, and out of the foster care system. The lessons she'd learned on the streets were burned into her soul.

Never rely on anyone.

Never trust anyone.

And never, ever show a hint of weakness.

If he didn't want her, well, screw him. She wasn't going to beg. Letting someone know that you needed them more than they needed you was like handing them a loaded gun. No way was she giving anyone that much power over her.

"Ma'am?"

With a heroic effort, Ivy managed to tear her eyes off her mate—no, she couldn't keep thinking of him like that. Turning away from *the bastard,* she looked up at the firefighter who'd spoken. It was the red-headed one, with the soft Welsh accent. The other one—a towering, dark-skinned man—had gone down to check that the crashed elevator hadn't started an electrical fire.

"Here," the firefighter said again, holding out a pair of gloves at arms' length. From his wary stance, he knew full well what she was. "I think it would be a good idea if you put these on."

They were clearly his gloves, part of his turn out gear. Ivy accepted them, being careful not to get close to his bare skin. The thick fire-resistant material dwarfed her hands, engulfed her from fingertip to elbow.

The red-headed man's broad shoulders eased down a little once her skin was safely covered. "That's better. I'm Firefighter Daifydd Drake of the East Sussex Fire & Rescue Service."

"I know who you are." Ivy didn't let a hint of fear show on her face, although her heart was pounding. "You're Alpha Team."

There was only one all-shifter group of firefighters in Brighton. Ivy had run into Dai Drake before—though that time, he'd been snarling down at her in red dragon form. She'd met some of the other members of the team before too, under less than pleasant circumstances. Since then, she'd done her level best to avoid their paths crossing again.

Which, apparently, was exceedingly ironic. She forced herself to keep her eyes fixed on Dai rather than glance again at the gorgeous paramedic.

"I remember you too," Dai said, in a tone of voice that made it clear he too didn't relish the memory. "There was a large amount of property destruction involved on that occasion as well. I need to ask you a few questions."

"Back off, Dai," the bastard snapped, before Ivy could respond. He didn't look up from his examination of Hope. "Leave my—patients alone. I'm not having you badgering them while I'm working."

Had he hesitated, just fractionally? What had he nearly said instead?

Bastard, bastard, bastard, she mentally chanted, ruthlessly forcing herself to remember the look on his face when he'd first met her eyes. *He's an arrogant bastard, and don't you forget it.*

Unfortunately, it was kind of hard to focus on how horrible he was when those strong hands were treating her sister with such exquisite gentleness. Ivy had been forced to watch Hope stoically suffer through far too many rough, careless medical examinations in the past. A lot of doctors seemed to think that just because Hope couldn't move her legs, she couldn't feel anything in them either.

But there wasn't even a hint of discomfort in Hope's expression as the bastard carefully tested her limbs and spine. The usual drawn tightness in her face had smoothed out, as if for once she wasn't in any pain at all.

"I don't think you've suffered any spinal injuries," the bastard said. Nonetheless, a slight crease marked his brow, as if something was bothering him.

Even his *voice* was beautiful. He had an unmistakably upper-class English accent, the sort that you only got by being born with a solid silver spoon in your mouth. Every cut-glass syllable just made it even more painfully clear that they were from completely different worlds.

"What the hell?" he muttered, apparently to himself. His long fingers hesitated at the nape of Hope's neck. "What *is* this?"

Ivy's heart skipped a beat with fear. "What's wrong?"

"Apparently everything," he said, still without looking up at her. "But whatever it is, it's not from the fall. Hope, exactly what is your condition?"

"Motor neuron disease," Hope lied, with the smooth ease of long practice. "It's degenerative, and incurable. Don't worry, I couldn't use my legs even before I fell down an elevator."

"Hmm." The bastard sounded less than convinced. "You're very young for motor neuron disease."

"I'm just super-special," Hope said cheerfully. "Can I sit up yet?"

"I'd rather put you on a body board, just to be safe. You should stay at the hospital overnight for observation."

"No hospitals," Hope and Ivy said in unison.

The bastard let out an annoyed breath. "Why does *no one* ever want to go to the hospital?"

"Must be your bedside manner," Dai said, green eyes crinkling with amusement. Then his expression turned more serious. "Miss, you really should go to the hospital. They can take proper care of you there."

"I can take care of her," Ivy said sharply.

"You're going to be needed elsewhere," Dai said, voice hardening. "The police are on their way. They'll take you to the station so you can give a statement."

Ivy took an involuntary step back. "No. I don't have anything to say to them."

Hope struggled up to her elbows, shrugging off the bastard's hands when he tried to get her to lie flat again. "You can't arrest her! It was an accident, that's all!"

"No one's getting arrested," Dai said. "Yet. But we do need to get to the bottom of what happened here."

Cold fear gripped her stomach. Ivy knew that the shifters in the police force were just itching for an excuse to lock her up. There were too many officials who thought a wyvern was far too dangerous to be allowed to run around loose.

"No," she forced out, through her tightening throat. "No police."

Dai's jaw tightened. "Ma'am, I'm afraid I really have to insist."

Behind him, the bastard's eyes flicked to Ivy's. It was only for the briefest moment, but she had an uncanny certainty that in that fraction of an instant, he'd seen straight to the center of her soul.

And in return...

She saw him. Not the glittering surface, all sharp-edged beauty and sharper words. In those ice-blue eyes, she saw an aching loneliness, mirroring her own. She *saw* him.

Just for a split second. He jerked his eyes away from hers, as though whatever he'd seen had burned him.

"No," he said, and for a moment Ivy wasn't sure whether he was talking to her or his colleague. "No, Dai. Both these two have gone through quite enough for one night."

Dai shook his head. "This is a major incident, Hugh. The police will need to carry out a full investigation."

"Then they can start by chasing down the witnesses who apparently decided to leave an innocent girl dangling in a deathtrap!" The bastard rose to his feet in one lithe, powerful movement, squaring off against his taller colleague. "I'm calling a car to take these two to the hospital, or home, or wherever they damn well want to go. If you want to hand them over to the police, you'll do it over my dead body!"

His unexpected words took all the breath out of her. No one had ever, *ever* leaped to her defense like that. Yet there he stood, jaw and fists clenched, ready to fight to protect her.

Mate, her wyvern said softly. *Our mate.*

"Whoa." Dai held up his hands, eyes widening in surprise. "Calm down. If it's your medical judgment that they shouldn't be questioned tonight—"

"It is," her mate snarled. "And if the police don't like it, I shall cordially invite them to kiss my arse."

Dai gave him an odd look, but backed down. "Well, in that case, let's get them out of here as quick as we can. Commander Ash would not be amused by you starting a fistfight with the police over jurisdiction. I'll go make some calls."

Heart hammering, Ivy waited until the red-headed firefighter had disappeared down the stairs. She fidgeted with the too-big gloves, looking down at her hands. She had no idea what to say.

"Thank you," she muttered.

Her mate nodded curtly, busy lifting Hope into the now somewhat battered wheelchair. He seemed to be trying to avoid meeting Ivy's eyes again.

Our mate, her wyvern insisted. *Claim him!*

Ivy squared her shoulders, taking a deep breath. "I think maybe we should talk."

"You heard Dai." He knelt to do up Hope's straps, gaze fixed on his task. "You need to get out of here before the police arrive."

"I mean…later. Some other time." Ivy noticed that Hope was giving her a very strange look, and rushed to add, "Uh, that is, so we can thank you properly. For saving us. Um."

He straightened, his hands on Hope's handlebars. He still didn't quite look at her. "If you want to thank me, then there is something you can do."

A surge of heat flooded through her at the thought of just how she could thank him properly. Her lips on his, those strong hands twining through her hair, running her hands over his naked skin…

"A-anything," Ivy stammered.

He met her eyes at last…but this time, there was no crack in them. His pale blue eyes were cold and hard as ice, impenetrable and unfeeling.

"Never come near me again," he said.

CHAPTER 4

Hugh sat in his usual shadowed corner of the Full Moon pub, and felt like the biggest asshole on the entire planet.

Because you are, his unicorn informed him.

His beast was utterly disgusted with him. Its light was no brighter than a distant star in the depths of his soul. It had withdrawn so far, he probably wasn't capable of curing so much as the common cold at the moment.

He'd hurt his mate.

He wasn't sure whether his unicorn would ever forgive him for that. He wasn't sure whether *he* would ever forgive himself.

But he'd had no choice. He'd looked into those amazing, vibrant green eyes, and recognized the terrible loneliness hidden behind her aggressive manner. If he'd given her even the slightest hint of encouragement, she would have put her heart into his hands.

And sooner or later…he would have destroyed her.

Better for her to hate him. The way she'd carried herself, the squared set of those strong shoulders and the line of her beautiful, stubborn mouth—he could tell that she was ferociously independent. She'd take his betrayal and use it to armor her soul, so that he'd never be able to hurt her again.

He just wished there was some way he could armor *himself* against the memory of her heart-piercing eyes.

"Is there something amiss, shield-brother?" John asked from the other side of the table. All six firefighters of Alpha Team had gathered for their customary Sunday evening drink. "You are unusually quiet tonight."

"Just a headache." Though in truth, at the moment the customary pain was much less than usual.

Normally, sitting in the busy pub gave him a screaming migraine. The Full Moon was the only pub in Brighton which catered exclusively to shifters. The place was always packed with people hoping to encounter their one true mate, or at least a one-night stand.

With his unicorn shunning him, however, the repulsive mix of lust and desire in the air just gave him a dull ache behind his temples. Even the close proximity of his mated colleagues wasn't sparking the usual pounding agony.

"Just a headache?" Griff shot him a sidelong look, eyebrows drawing together a little. "You sure that's all it is?"

Hugh silently cursed himself. It was bloody inconvenient having a colleague who could detect lies. The last thing he needed was to be scrutinized by the griffin shifter's uncannily perceptive stare.

"Well, it was an eventful day," he said, which certainly *was* true. He pushed aside his barely-touched beer. "I'm tired. Think I'll head home early."

"Not so fast." Dai leaned back against the wall, blocking his escape route. "You still haven't explained what all that was about today, with the wyvern. You always said that if you ever met her in person, you'd blister her ears for the trouble she's caused you. What happened? Why did you leap to her defense like that?"

Hugh scowled at the dragon shifter. "I don't want to talk about it."

"Well, I do," Chase said, putting his drink down. There was an angry glint in the pegasus shifter's usually laughing black eyes. "From what Dai and John said, you caught her red-handed. What were you thinking, letting her slip away like that? She should be behind bars, not running around loose."

"Ivy's not a bad person," Griff said. "The poor lass has had a tough life, that's all."

"So have lots of people." Chase's lip curled in disgust. "And yet somehow, most of them manage to survive without resorting to becoming assassins-for-hire."

Dai sighed. "And now I'm sorry I asked. Do you two really have to have this argument yet *again*?"

"Apparently," Griff said. "Since Chase is still being an enormous cock on the subject."

"I'm not the one who keeps insisting we should all make friends with a vicious criminal!" Chase slammed his fist down onto the table, making the pint glasses rattle. "Damn it, Griff, she tried to murder my mate!"

"No, that was *your* cousin." Griff folded his arms across his chest, meeting the pegasus shifter's glare without flinching. "He's the one who stabbed Connie with wyvern venom. Ivy never wanted to harm anyone. She's not responsible for what he did with the poisons he forced her to make."

Normally, this would have been the point where Hugh leaped in with some cutting remark. He'd always been on Chase's side in this argument.

But that had been...before.

"The sword is innocent of the hand that wields it, true," John said in his deep, resonant voice. "But a person is more than a weapon. She should not have allowed herself to be used so."

"She was desperate, John," Griff said. "And Chase's cousin was threatening to hurt her little sister if Ivy didn't comply with his demands. What was Ivy supposed to do?"

John shook his head, his long indigo dreadlocks shifting over his massive shoulders. "Dishonor is dishonor, no matter the circumstances. I admire your compassion, oath-brother, but you debase yourself by associating with such a creature."

"She's not a creature!"

Heads turned at neighboring tables. Hugh realized that he'd half-risen, fists clenched.

"Gentlemen." Fire Commander Ash's voice was as quiet as always, but held an unmistakable note of command. "I will not have you disturbing the peace of Rose's establishment."

Rose, the middle-aged swan shifter who owned the Full Moon, was indeed giving their corner a narrow-eyed look from behind the bar. All the firefighters subsided at once, like guilty schoolchildren who'd just realized the teacher had returned.

No one wanted to get on the wrong side of Rose...mainly because it would also mean attracting Ash's wrath. And the Phoenix was *not* someone you wanted to piss off.

Not for the first time, Hugh wondered just what *was* Ash's connection to Rose. It was clear the pair had some sort of history, but the Phoenix was even more closed-mouthed about his secrets than Hugh himself. For her part, Rose seemed entirely oblivious to the fact that she had the most powerful shifter in Europe wrapped around her little finger.

"Now," Ash said, fixing Hugh with his unnervingly calm, fathomless eyes. "*I* would like an explanation, Hugh. Why did you break protocol by removing the witnesses from the scene?"

"I just..." Hugh's hands clenched on the edge of the table. "I just felt sorry for her, okay?"

Griff's eyebrows shot up. "Who are you, and what have you done with our paramedic?"

"Hugh, you never feel sorry for *anyone*," Dai said. "You once berated me for three solid minutes while I was literally bleeding out on the floor."

"You deserved it," Hugh retorted. "And you were perfectly fine. It takes at least five minutes to bleed to death from the femoral artery."

Ash tapped one finger on the table, drawing their attention again. "Hugh, while I appreciate your professional desire to put the needs of your patients first, the police were not pleased by your actions today. They have submitted a formal complaint to me."

"So?" It wouldn't be the first—or even the fifth—black mark he'd collected. "You going to fire me?"

A hint of exasperation entered Ash's usually impenetrable expression. "You know that your talents are invaluable to the team. Nonetheless, I would appreciate it if you would refrain from putting me in a difficult situation. Again."

Hugh dropped his gaze, feeling a twinge of guilt. The Phoenix had always shielded him from questions, providing a safe space where Hugh could secretly put his power to good use without attracting too much attention. Hugh would forever be grateful to him for that. The Phoenix deserved better from him in return.

"Sorry, Commander," he muttered. "It won't happen again."

"Pity it's not likely to," Chase said, picking up his beer. "But if you do somehow find yourself dangling that damn wyvern over an elevator shaft again in the future, do us all a favor and drop the vicious little bi-"

It wasn't a conscious decision. Before Chase had even finished the sentence, Hugh was vaulting across the table at him, driven by pure, white-hot fury. His fist connected with the pegasus shifter's nose with a very satisfying crunch.

Chase toppled backward in a crash of breaking glass. Griff and Dai shot to their feet, grabbing Hugh's arms to restrain him. The searing pain of their bare hands jolted him back to his senses.

"What the hell, Hugh?" Chase sounded too startled to be angry. He struggled upright, blood streaming down his face. "What in God's name is the matter with you?"

His chest heaved, his own breath sounding loud as a chainsaw in the deathly silence. Every shifter in the pub was staring at him in frozen shock.

"Hugh!" Rose descended on them like a small, plump thundercloud, her dark eyes flashing. "Heaven knows we all want to thump Chase sometimes, but you know there's no brawling in my pub."

"My sincere apologies." Ash's hand closed like a manacle around Hugh's wrist. Hugh's skin prickled with the not-quite-pain of being touched by someone who wasn't a virgin, but who'd been celibate for decades. "Gentlemen, assist Rose in cleaning up this mess. Hugh, outside. *Now.*"

Hugh had no choice but to follow Ash out of the pub. His face burned at the scandalized whispers rising in his wake.

Ash barely waited until the door had closed behind them before rounding on him. The Phoenix's expression was as controlled as ever, but heat radiated from him like a bonfire.

"Explain," Ash said, his voice ice-cold.

Hugh scrubbed both hands over his face, struggling to get a grip. His unicorn was still ablaze with fury, wanting nothing more than to charge back into the pub and skewer Chase. He breathed deep, deliberately drawing in Ash's faint smoke-and-scorched-brass scent. The Phoenix was alpha enough to make even his unicorn grudgingly settle, subdued by the presence of an even greater power.

His first instinct was to invent some lie, claim that he was just stressed and overworked…but he owed Ash the truth.

"Ivy's my mate," he said, reluctantly.

The shimmering heat haze surrounding Ash disappeared, as abruptly as if Hugh had dumped a bucket of water over his head. He regarded Hugh for a long, silent moment, his dark eyes even more unreadable than normal.

"I take it," the Fire Commander said at last, "that this is not cause for celebration."

Hugh let out a hollow bark of laughter. "It's an utter disaster."

"Because of what she is?"

"No." Hugh leaned back against the old stone walls of the pub with a sigh, tension draining out of his shoulders at last. "Because of what I am."

Ash's eyebrows drew down, very slightly. "I do not follow."

Hugh gestured at his own forehead. "You know my…handicap?"

Hugh had been forced to tell Ash the real reason for his migraines, around the time that Griff had met his mate. The Fire Commander had needed to know, since Hugh's issues with the unchaste had started to affect his ability to work as closely with the team.

Ash blinked, which for him was a rare display of extreme surprise. "Your sensitivities extend even to your mate? Her touch would cause you pain?"

Hugh's mouth twisted. "It's worse than that. Let's just say that there's more than one reason why there aren't many of my kind."

Unicorns had been hunted nearly to extinction during medieval times. As far as most shifters knew, they *were* extinct. But even before they'd been targeted for their horns, they'd never been numerous.

A unicorn could mate…but only at a terrible cost.

It would be worth it, his unicorn said softly, in the depths of his soul.

Hugh shook his head free of the ridiculous thought. He absently rubbed his left bicep, tracing the lines of ink hidden under his sleeve.

"I can't have a mate, Ash," he said. "And that's why I don't want the rest of the team to know about her. The damn idiots would never let it go. I wouldn't be able to explain without revealing what I am."

Ash was silent for a moment. "Even if you are unable to…there are other ways of showing love."

"You think I haven't thought of that?" Hugh snapped. "Could *you* be around your true mate, every day, unable to claim her?"

Ash's gaze flicked sideways, to the closed door of the pub. "It is preferable to never seeing her at all."

"No, it's not," Hugh said. "Better to cut her off cleanly, rather than torment us both with something we can never have."

"I thought that too, once," Ash said, very quietly. "But you will find that it is not so easily done."

Hugh looked at him, raising an eyebrow. "You sound like you're speaking from experience."

The hint of human warmth in Ash's face fled, his expression hardening back into its usual impassive lines. "I was merely referring to John and Griff. They too attempted to deny their mates. You know how successful *they* were."

"I'm not them. I'm used to dealing with constant pain." Hugh straightened, setting his shoulders. "And I'll do whatever it takes to protect my mate. Even from me."

CHAPTER 5

"I'm not going." Hope's bottom lip stuck out like a toddler about to throw a tantrum.

Ivy dumped an armload of clothes into the duffel bag lying open on the bed. "Yes you are."

"We can't run away again!" Hope swiveled her wheelchair, blocking Ivy's path as she headed for the dresser again. "Not now, when things are finally looking up! We've got a nice apartment, you've got a job, I'm doing well at school, I've got friends—"

"Yeah, well, you should have thought of all that before you decided to snuggle up to a shifter crime boss, shouldn't you?" Ivy said. "Move out of the way."

"I didn't *know* that's what Gaze was!" Hope didn't budge. "As far as I knew, he was a nice guy. I looked him up on Facebook! He has a charity helping out homeless shifter kids!"

Ivy snorted. "No, he has a tax-deductible scam that supplies him with brainwashed foot soldiers for his little mafia. Obviously. Why can't you ever *think?*"

"Oh, yes, because that's clearly the reasoning process of a well-balanced and healthy mind," Hope snapped back. "Excuse me for not wanting to live my entire life like a paranoid sociopath."

"You're only *alive* because I look out for you!" Ivy kicked Hope's wheelchair out of the way with one booted foot, regardless of her sister's squawk of outrage. "And if we want to stay alive, we have to clear out. Right now. Tonight."

Hope's battered wheelchair jammed as she tried to reverse out of the corner. It hadn't been in great shape even before it had been dropped down an elevator. Now one of the axles was bent, and kept sticking unpredictably.

"Here," Ivy said, feeling a stab of guilt as her sister wrestled with the unwieldy machine. "Let me help."

"I can take care of myself," Hope snarled.

Hope's thin hands tugged futilely at the rims. Ivy could only watch for a few seconds before she couldn't stand it anymore. Without a word, she took hold of the wheelchair handlebars. Hope's shoulders stiffened, but she didn't protest as Ivy dragged the heavy device backward.

"Goddamn piece of crap," Ivy muttered over the groan of protesting metal. "I'm gonna get you a new one, I promise."

"With what?" Hope's lower lip was still stuck out mulishly, but now there was a hint of a tremble about it. "Running away and starting over is going to wipe out every penny of our savings."

Ivy flinched from the uncharacteristic bleakness in Hope's voice. She knew the reason.

After nearly two years of scrimping, they'd almost saved enough for the down payment on a basic electric wheelchair. Hope never complained, but it was painfully obvious that she'd been finding it harder and harder to manage the manual one.

At the rate she's been slowing down, she won't be able to move herself at all in a matter of months.

Her wyvern stirred, and Ivy quickly shoved the grim thought to the bottom of her mind. There wasn't anything either she or her beast could do about her sister's degenerative, fatal condition. But her animal didn't understand that.

Her wyvern would burn down the world, because nothing mattered without Hope.

"I'll figure something out," Ivy said, trying to sound confident enough to convince even herself. "One problem at a time. Let's just concentrate on getting out of here."

"Do we really have to go?" Hope said plaintively, as Ivy started packing again. "You got off last time with the police, with the plea-bargain and giving testimony against that awful pegasus Killian. Couldn't you, I don't know, offer to turn Gaze in?"

"For what? Throwing a Christmas party?" Ivy made a face. "He never flat-out *said* he did anything illegal. Even if he had, it would just have been talk. I'm the one who committed actual property damage."

"It was self-defense. He did attack you first."

"Yeah, and I'm sure any jury is really going to take my word for that. Besides, the police are the least of our worries. *Think*, Hope. I defied an alpha crime boss in front of his own gang, and destroyed half his apartment to boot. You think someone like Gaze is just going to let that slide?"

Hope bit her lip. "We could...we could ask for help."

Ivy let out a bark of disbelieving laughter. "From who? The police?"

"From Alpha Team."

Ivy jumped as if Hope had zapped her with a taser. Underwear cascaded out of her hands, scattering over the bed.

How did she guess? What gave me away?

"No. Definitely not. No way." Ivy scrabbled for the fallen pants, keeping her back turned to hide her expression. "You heard him, he doesn't want anything to do with me."

"What?" Hope sounded baffled. "You mean Hugh? Never mind him, from what I've heard he's rude to everyone. I was talking about Griff. He's always been nice to us."

"His name's Hugh?" The words slipped out before she could catch them.

"Well, I don't think there can be *two* white-haired shifter paramedics in Brighton, so yeah, I'm betting that was Hugh Argent. Griff's told me about him."

Ivy battled herself, but couldn't restrain her raging need to know.

"Did Griff, uh, happen to mention what sort of shifter Hugh is, by any chance?"

"No." Even with her back turned, Ivy could feel Hope's narrowed eyes boring into her neck. "Why are you so interested?"

Ivy's face burned. "Uh, no reason."

"Ivy..." The pitch of Hope's voice rose in a delighted, disbelieving trill. "Do you *liiiiiiiike* him?"

"No!" Ivy whirled, fists clenching in handfuls of underwear. "Of course not."

"You do! You do like him! You never like anyone!" Hope's eyes widened. "Is he your mate?"

Ivy opened her mouth to deny it... but her wyvern rose up, choking the words in her throat.

He was her mate. She couldn't claim otherwise. Not even to herself.

Hope let out a strangled shriek of excitement. "He is! Oh my God, Ivy! Why didn't you tell me straight away? Can he touch you?"

Ivy rubbed absently at her wrist, still feeling the lightning-jolt of those strong fingers closing over her bare skin. "Yeah. He can."

"Ha!" Hope made finger-guns at her. "See? I was right all along. I *knew* that your true mate wouldn't be affected by your venom."

"Yeah, yeah." Ivy tossed a pair of underpants at her sister's smirking face. "You also thought an evil basilisk shifter crime boss might be my one true mate, so don't gloat too much."

"But this is perfect!" Hope plucked the underwear from her head, throwing it back into the half-open dresser. "If Hugh is your mate, then Alpha Team will *definitely* protect us from Gaze. And I bet Fire Commander Ash will be able to sort everything out with the police too. We don't have to run!"

"Yes, we do." Ivy retrieved the pants, stuffing them into the suitcase. "Because they'll be selling snowcones in Hell before I ask *him* for help. You heard him, Hope. He never wants to see me again."

Hope's beaming smile flickered uncertainly. "He can't really have meant that. He has to be a shifter of *some* kind if he's on Alpha Team, so he must know that he's your true mate."

"Yeah, well. He clearly doesn't want to be."

Hope chewed on her lower lip for a moment. "Maybe...maybe he was just in shock. Or—I know! Maybe he was being all snarly because of his overpowering attraction to you. Maybe he had to be rude so that he didn't sweep you up and carry you off to claim you there and then!"

Ivy gave her sister a level look. "Do you ever actually listen to the words coming out of your mouth?"

Hope ignored this, digging into the side pocket of her wheelchair. "Call him. You have to."

Ivy groaned. "Hope. Are you seriously suggesting that I dial emergency in order to make a booty call?"

"No," Hope said, rolling her eyes. She pulled out her cellphone and waved it in Ivy's direction. "I'm suggesting that you call him at home. Or even better, turn up in person. I have his number and address right here."

Ivy stared at her sister. "Why on earth do you have Hugh Argent's home number and address?"

"Griff gave it to me," Hope said absently, scrolling through her contact list. "In case we ever had an emergency."

Ivy's forehead furrowed. "What do you mean, an emergency?"

"You know, with your..." Hope made a vague hand-gesture that encompassed Ivy's entire body. "With your venom."

Ivy shook her head, still baffled. "No paramedic would be able to help if I accidentally touched you."

"Hugh's not just a paramedic. He's got healing powers. Really strong powers. Griff made me promise not to tell anyone, but he said Hugh can heal just about anything."

Ivy froze.

The tingle of his bare skin against hers, the lightning-strike impact of his touch... maybe it *wasn't* because he was her true mate. Had he been counteracting her venom?

And if he was powerful enough to do that...

"Hope." Ivy crouched down so that they were eye-to-eye, her heart hammering against her ribs. "Tell me *exactly* what Griff told you about Hugh."

CHAPTER 6

*H*ugh stared into his tea, and contemplated the void of the rest of his life.

Normally, it was a relief to retreat to his house and shut out the rest of the world on his days off. Now, however, the silence of his soundproofed study seemed oppressive. No matter how he tried to relax with his favorite lapsang souchong and a good mystery novel, his nerves were wound tight. Not even the purring cats on his lap were helping.

He kept finding himself looking up, listening for…something.

Something that wasn't there.

Something missing.

If only we knew what that could be, his unicorn said snippily. *Truly, a mystery for the ages.*

Anyone who thought that unicorns were all sweetness and light had never lived with one in their head. His beast could be a sarcastic sod when its horn was out of joint.

With a growl of frustration, Hugh pushed aside his stone-cold tea. Much to the displeasure of his cats, he rose. Even though he should have been exhausted after his twenty-four-hour work shift the day before, a strange, restless energy filled him.

He raked his hands through his hair, casting around for something to do. He'd already washed up the single plate from his breakfast. Every book on his oak shelves was perfectly sorted into its proper place. Even the oriental rug only had a few cat hairs clinging to it.

Everything in his entire house was arranged exactly to his liking. He'd never invited anyone—not even his fellow firefighters—to enter his home. It was the one place where he could escape the constant, incessant onslaught of other people's lusts and desires and emotions. It was his sanctuary.

Now, it felt empty.

Work, he decided. That was what he needed. A purpose. He needed to get out there and do what he was made to do.

Yes, his unicorn agreed. *So go to her.*

"Oh, shut up," Hugh muttered under his breath as he hunted for his shoes.

He wasn't on call at the moment, but he was a familiar enough sight at the local hospital. A white coat and a confident manner would mean he wouldn't be challenged.

He'd ghost through the critical care wards, touching a shoulder here, pretending to take a pulse there. And there would be five or ten or two dozen people who'd start to feel much better, and never know the true reason why.

And you will still feel the same, his unicorn murmured.

"That doesn't matter," Hugh said out loud to his animal, as he looped his hospital pass over his neck. "I don't have to be happy to help people."

Which was just as well, given that he didn't expect to ever see his mate again.

Hugh opened his front door, and found himself staring down into a pair of blazing emerald eyes.

"Can you heal my sister?" Ivy demanded.

∽

Hugh had treated patients in many difficult circumstances. He'd lost count of the number of times he'd had to perform CPR while things literally exploded around him. On one occasion, he'd even been on fire himself. And of course, there had been the memorable time he'd struggled to heal a gaping chest wound while floating on a magical iceberg above the biggest shark in the entire sea.

None of those occasions compared to now. It took all of Hugh's control to keep his eyes on his patient, when all he wanted to do was gaze at the astonishing sight of Ivy in his house.

Even without looking at her, he could track her every movement as she prowled around his study, wary as a stray cat. The heat of her body warmed the whole room like a log fire on Christmas Day. Her fresh, clean scent was a mix of wild mint and storm air, with an underlying womanly fragrance that had his unicorn pawing the ground.

Focus. Hugh shut his eyes, wishing that he could close his nose as well to that intoxicating scent. He concentrated on his sixth sense instead; the subtle feel of energies running through Hope's body.

Her eyebrows twitched under his palm. "That tickles!"

"Sorry." Hugh moved his hand from her forehead to the nape of her neck. "Just a few moments more."

He frowned as he once again encountered the strange darkness that he'd briefly sensed before. To his senses, the energy running through Hope's nerves seemed to flicker and spark, like faulty wiring. It reminded him a bit of the acid-pitted cables in the elevator shaft. It was like her nervous system was being eaten away by some malign substance.

It wasn't an injury, or a disease. It wasn't congenital, either—her body knew that something was wrong, and was trying to fight it.

"You don't have motor neuron disease," he said, opening his eyes and drawing his hand back again. "In fact, if I was making a diagnosis, I'd say you've been poisoned."

Hope bit her lip, glancing at her sister as if seeking permission. Ivy jerked her chin down once in a slight nod.

"I was," Hope said, turning back to him. "By our mom. In the womb."

Hugh's eyebrows rose. Shifter pregnancies were complicated at the best of times. A mother who was a wyvern shifter, her very blood venomous...that had to make it difficult to carry a pregnancy to term. In fact, he would have placed money on it being impossible for a wyvern shifter to give birth to a normal human.

But there was Hope, right before his eyes.

"Chronic poisoning." Suddenly, her condition made a *lot* more sense. "How the hell did you survive gestation?"

"Our mother can control her venom," Ivy said. She tucked her gloved hands under her armpits, shoulders hunching. "Most wyverns can."

"Once Mom found out she was pregnant, she tamped down her toxicity as much as she could," Hope said. "She didn't shift once, the whole time, even though it made her weak and sick. She wanted to give me a chance to survive if I turned out not to be a wyvern shifter."

"And she wanted to avoid another me," Ivy said in a low voice. "Just in case it turned out Hope *was* a wyvern shifter."

The quiet pain in her tone seared him more than the loudest scream of agony. He clenched his hands at his sides, forcing down the urge to touch her. To hold her and soothe away all her hurts...

"What's that supposed to mean?" He was having to concentrate so hard on holding himself in check, the words came out harsher than he'd intended.

Ivy didn't flinch, but her shoulders stiffened. "Forget it. It's none of your business."

"If it's part of your family medical history, then it *is* my business," he countered. "If I'm to have a chance of healing your sister, then I need to know everything."

Actually, he was pretty sure he already knew as much as he needed...at least when it came to Hope. Ivy was another matter, though. He couldn't ignore that momentary flash of pain. He had to know what had caused it.

Even if he couldn't do anything about it.

Ivy raised her chin, glaring at him icily. "Our mother shifted a lot when she was pregnant with me. She thought that might be why I'm venomous all the time, even in human form. Why I'm broken."

"You're not broken," Hope said staunchly. "No matter what Mom says."

A little wyvern girl with big green eyes, told by her own mother that she was broken. A mother who named her younger daughter *Hope*. It was a good thing he was never likely to meet the woman. It was generally frowned-upon to attempt to turn one's mother-in-law into a shish-kebab.

Not that she was ever going to be his mother-in-law. Hugh forcibly reined in his vengeful unicorn, tamping down its righteous fury. There was a better way that they could serve their mate.

Hugh touched Hope's wrist with two fingers, feeling again the old, malign influence of the venom in her blood. Her immune system was like a weary army, ground down by long years of war, nearly ready to break. The poison was slowly eating away at her nerves, paralyzing her body an inch at a time as her defenses failed.

"So." Ivy's face was set in an uncaring mask, but a desperate hope shone in her eyes. "Can you heal her or not?"

With all his heart, he wanted to shout *Yes, yes!* If he could have restored Hope in a single touch of his horn, he would have shifted then and there, and secrecy be damned. He would have done anything to finally see his mate smile.

"I don't know," he said reluctantly, hating the way his words snuffed out the light in those emerald eyes. "Maybe. I'd need more time."

"How much time?" Ivy demanded.

"I haven't a clue. I've never tried to heal anything like this before. I mostly deal with trauma patients." He spread his hands in Hope's direction. "Something like this, damage done over years…I don't know if I can reverse it."

"What about just stopping it?" Hope asked. "So it doesn't get any worse? I mean, it would be kinda nice to be able to move my legs, but I'm much more interested in not suffocating to death before my twentieth birthday."

Hugh rubbed his fingers together, thinking it over. "I'm pretty sure I could at least stop your condition from getting worse. But it could take weeks to purge all the venom from your body."

Hope's face fell. "Oh. We don't have weeks. We have to go today."

"You're leaving?" Even though he'd fully intended to never see his mate again, his heart still lurched at the thought.

"Not anymore," Ivy said firmly. "If this is even a possibility, we're not going anywhere."

"I thought we had to." Hope looked up at her sister, biting her lip. "What about the police? And Gaze?"

"Don't worry about the police," Hugh said, before Ivy could respond. "The shifter police would still like to talk to you both, but they know the acid spray was an accident. Griff had a word with his friends on the force and explained the situation to them."

"I *told* you he would," Hope said triumphantly to her sister.

Ivy scowled, looking more irritated than pleased at this news. "Great. So now we're even more in his debt."

What sort of life has she led? Hugh wondered. *To be so wary of accepting help...what happened to them?*

"It's not a matter of debt," he said. "He has a soft spot for you two. Who's Gaze?"

"My problem." Ivy squared her shoulders. "And one I'll sort out."

Hope looked worried. "Ivy—"

"I said I'll deal with it. If Hugh can heal you, it's worth any risk to stay." Ivy turned to him. "Well? Are you willing to try?"

He opened his mouth to say *Yes, of course*...and hesitated.

Unbidden, his mind flashed back to his residency. How confidently he'd swept into the hospital, feeling like some all-powerful, benevolent god. Certain that he could save everyone with just one touch of his hand.

And look how well *that* had turned out.

Am I being arrogant now? What if I'm wrong? What if I can't heal Hope?

No matter Ivy's assertion that she'd handle the mysterious 'Gaze,' it was clear the pair were in serious trouble if they'd been planning to skip town today. Was he putting his mate at risk for nothing?

Ivy strode forward, breaking his introspection. Planting herself squarely in front of him, she looked him straight in the eye.

"You do whatever it takes to heal my sister," she said. "And in return, I swear I'll get out of your life. Forever."

"Ivy, no!" Hope exclaimed, looking horrified. "You can't. He's your mate!"

Ivy ignored her sister, focused on him like a laser. "You'll never have to see me again. That's what you want, isn't it? Here's your chance. A one-time deal."

He lifted his own chin, meeting her blazing gaze head-on. "And what if I don't like this deal?"

Ivy ground the heels of her boots into his oriental rug, planting her feet like a boxer squaring off. "Then I'm not moving an inch. As God is my witness, if you don't try to heal my sister, I will haunt your steps like your own damn shadow. I will follow you at work. When you go shopping, I'll be there, staring at you between the aisles. I will break into your house and move all your stuff and sleep in your bed."

His unicorn thought this was an *excellent* idea.

"I will rub my scent on everything you own," Ivy said, apparently warming up to her theme. "Your whole territory will reek of me. I'll be the last thing you smell when you go to sleep, and the first thing you see in the morning."

Also excellent. Hugh was distantly aware that he should probably be interrupting, but he couldn't drag himself away from the captivating vision of waking up to find Ivy in his bed. Naked. Her tousled hair spread over his pillow, her warm curves nestled against him...

"I will hide in your bushes. I will open all your mail and write creepy comments." Ivy appeared to grope for more threats. "I will—I will *sing* to you."

"You really don't want her to do that," Hope interjected. "I've heard her in the shower. She's terrible."

Hugh cleared his throat. It was hard to form words when most of his blood wasn't making it as far as his brain. He was very glad his white coat hid his crotch.

"Well, I certainly don't want you to sing at me," he said. "Or open my mail, for that matter."

All the rest however, she was more than welcome to do, and twice on Sundays. *Damn it*, he had to get control of himself. Fifteen minutes in her presence and he was already reduced to a raging mass of hormones. This was a disaster.

He folded his own arms, mirroring Ivy's belligerent pose. Surreptitiously, he gripped his biceps, reminding himself of what was written there. What was still unwritten. His fingernails dug into his own muscle, the small bite of pain a bitter forewarning of all the pain that he would cause if he weakened.

He took a deep breath, bracing himself for what he had to do. "If I help your sister, you promise you'll leave me alone?"

"I swear it on my sister's life," Ivy said, as Hope stared at him in mute betrayal.

Hugh forced himself to hold out his hand. "Deal."

Ivy looked down at his outstretched hand as if she'd never seen one before. His heart broke for her as he realized that probably she never *had*. Not one held out to her, at least.

Slowly, Ivy clasped his hand in her own gloved one. "Deal."

CHAPTER 7

This was a terrible idea.

The barista behind the slate-and-reclaimed-wood counter was already giving her the hairy eyeball. Ivy's grungy layers of thrift-store denim clearly didn't fit in with the trendy cafe's carefully-cultivated shabby-chic decor. Ivy sipped the overpriced latte that she couldn't afford, making it last as long as possible, and tried not to dwell on how badly wrong this deal could go.

But she had no choice. She'd do anything to buy Hope even the slightest chance of recovery.

The deal she'd struck with Hugh, now *that* had been a good bargain. She'd gotten the one thing she wanted more than anything else—a chance for Hope—and in return all she'd had to give away was something she couldn't keep anyway.

Yes we can, hissed her wyvern. *Our mate! Go back, claim him, now!*

Ivy grimaced, mentally muzzling her beast. Her unruly wyvern was even more agitated than usual, baffled and furious by the agreement she'd made with Hugh. The stupid animal couldn't understand just what a good deal it was.

And now she could only pray that she could strike another one.

"I have to say, Ivy Viverna." Gaze slid into the booth opposite her, eyebrows raised over the rims of his mirrored sunglasses. "That was not a Facebook message I was expecting to receive this morning."

The basilisk shifter *did* fit in with the hipster decor. Dressed in slim jeans, an ironic vest, and a white dress shirt with sleeves carefully pushed up to display his muscled forearms to best advantage, he looked more like a lifestyle blogger than a crime boss. He made a slight gesture at the barista, who simpered and started fixing what was obviously his regular order.

Gaze turned his attention back to Ivy, studying her for a long moment without speaking. Even though his eyes were hidden, his scrutiny still made the hairs rise on the back of her neck. She hadn't forgotten the agonizing burn of being pinned by his unshielded stare.

"I'm curious to hear why you wanted to meet." Gaze accepted an espresso from the barista, and waved her off again. "I thought you'd have had the sense to skip town by now."

"Yeah, well." Ivy leaned back, trying to copy Gaze's relaxed, assured pose. "I have some business that I need to take care of."

Gaze's head tilted slightly. "Business involving Hugh Argent?"

Ivy's coffee cup rattled on its saucer as she twitched. "Are you following me?"

"Oh, come now, Ivy. You're smarter than that." Gaze picked up his own coffee, taking a casual sip. "Of course I'm having you followed. You didn't think that you could just walk away after last night, did you?"

"No." Ivy's tongue was dry in her mouth. "That's why I want to make a deal."

"I distinctly recall that you rejected my very generous offer. In no uncertain terms."

"I've...things are different. My sister's starting some new medical treatment which means we have to stick around Brighton for a bit longer." Ivy folded her hands on the table to hide how they were shaking. "And that means I don't want to be on your bad side. I know I can't protect my sister from you, not on your home ground. So. What will it take to get you off my back?"

She already knew the answer. He was going to want her venom.

Deadly poisons, powerful acids, addictive hallucinogens…a wyvern shifter could make all kinds of useful things for a man like Gaze.

Once again, she was putting herself under the thumb of a dangerous, amoral criminal. Only this time, she was going into it with her eyes wide open. She knew exactly what she was doing.

To save Hope, she'd sacrifice her very soul.

Gaze contemplated her for a long, agonizing minute. It was impossible to tell what was going on behind those mirrored sunglasses.

When he spoke, however, his words were the last thing Ivy had expected. "Tell me more about this medical treatment."

Ivy was so wrong-footed, she could only blink stupidly at him. "Huh?"

"Hope told me she has motor neuron disease." Gaze leaned his elbows on the table, his posture oddly intent. "That's incurable, as far as I'm aware."

"Yeah, uh…we just found out about this new thing. It's kinda experimental. Never been tried."

Gaze tipped his head forward, his sunglasses sliding down his nose just far enough to expose his glowing, blood-red eyes. Before Ivy could look away, she'd once again been caught by that burning stare.

"You have been only two places since the incident last night," Gaze said softly, as buzzing pain vibrated through her paralyzed body. "Your home, and that of Hugh Argent. Your sister is still there with him now. Tell me the truth, Ivy. Your sister has not been miraculously offered some new experimental treatment. Hugh is healing her. And I want you to tell me everything—*everything*—you know about him."

He pushed his sunglasses back up to cover his eyes again, freeing her. Ivy had to breathe deeply for a moment, every nerve in her body still quivering as if she'd stuck her fingers in an electric socket.

"Go to hell," she croaked.

Hugh was an asshole, but he was still *her* asshole. Ivy hadn't a clue why Gaze was so interested in him, but she sure as hell wasn't going to throw her mate to the basilisk.

Gaze raised his hands, and she couldn't help flinching—but he just steepled his fingers, regarding her calmly through his shades. "You seem interestingly loyal to the paramedic, considering that you'd never, as far as I'm aware, met before yesterday. And I have never known Hugh Argent to let *anyone* into his house—and believe me, I have had my best professionals fail to secure an invite, no matter how they attempted to seduce him. So why you and your sister?"

"Guess he's got a soft spot for hard-luck cases," Ivy said, while her wyvern snarled at the idea of other women throwing themselves at Hugh. "It's called compassion, asshole. Look it up in the dictionary some time."

Gaze chuckled under his breath. "Oh dear, Ivy. It seems I know Hugh considerably better than you do. From what I have heard, he would never do anything merely out of pity. For a medical professional, he is remarkably acidic."

"Maybe that's why he likes me," Ivy said, trying to ignore the part of her that wished that was true. "We've got something in common. Why do you care, anyway?"

"There are rumors about the paramedic. Rumors that interest me. And if he truly can heal your sister—and oh yes, Ivy, I know full well that she does not really have motor neuron disease—then I am *very* interested indeed. So interested that I am prepared to offer you a deal."

"What kind of deal?" Ivy asked warily.

Gaze leaned back in his seat. "Find out what sort of shifter Hugh Argent is. In return, I will leave you alone. You *and* your sister."

"That's it?" Ivy squinted at him, suspecting some sort of trick. "You just want to know his animal? Why don't you just have your goons follow him and wait until he shifts?"

"Because he never does. Believe me, I have spent considerable time and effort trying to unravel the mystery that is Hugh Argent. If you can do that, then you would have my gratitude. Which is something that you sorely need."

Ivy chewed on her lip, every instinct screaming that this was too good to be true. She'd been fully prepared to give Gaze whatever he wanted…and what he wanted turned out to be such a tiny, trivial thing. There had to be some sort of catch.

"Are you trying to find out if he's something defenseless?" she asked, eyes narrowing. "Because if you're thinking of kidnapping him and forcing him to work for you, let me remind you that he's already got a boss. I can tell you that Fire Commander Ash does *not* appreciate anyone messing with his people."

Gaze's mouth tightened. "Oh, I am fully aware that the paramedic is under the protection of the Phoenix. That inconvenient fact is all that is stopping me from making rather more direct inquiries, shall we say. I have been forced to take more subtle approaches. But you, it seems, may be the key to unlock his secrets at last."

"You're wrong," Ivy said, unable to keep the bitterness out of her voice. "Even if I wanted to, I can't find out squat for you. He hates me. He told me to my face that he never wants to see me again."

Gaze's eyebrows rose. "I find that difficult to believe. Seeing as not only is he helping you with your sister, apparently he is on his way to this very location even as we speak."

Ivy stared at him. "What?" she said blankly.

"With, and I quote," Gaze's head tilted to one side, as if he was communicating telepathically with someone, "'a face like a pissing thunderstorm,' according to the somewhat crude man I have on his tail. For someone who you claim has no interest in you, Ivy, the paramedic seems remarkably protective."

Ivy was still chewing *that* one over when Gaze pushed aside his espresso, rising. Chairs scraped as four other people—ranging from a hulking skinhead to a teen girl in black motorbike leathers—stood as well. Ivy tensed, readying herself to pull off her gloves, but they merely fell into position behind their boss, like bodyguards around a celebrity.

"The time is not yet right for Hugh Argent and myself to cross paths," the basilisk shifter said, adjusting his sunglasses. "So I must take my leave. I look forward to your report with *great* anticipation. Oh, and Ivy?"

This time, Ivy was prepared. She jerked her eyes away, fixing them on Gaze's shiny shoes to avoid his stare…but she couldn't block out his voice.

"If you do not give me Hugh Argent's secrets, then I *will* come after your sister." All of Gaze's fake friendliness fell away, his tone dropping to a cold, poisonous whisper. "No matter how far you run, how well you hide, I will find you. And then, I will turn you both into living statues. Unmoving, unbreathing, undying...but suffering. Trapped in agony. Forever."

Gaze straightened. "A pleasure doing business with you," he said, in a totally normal voice. "I expect results soon, Ivy. *Very* soon."

Ivy sat frozen, as motionless as if he'd already carried out his threat, as Gaze waved his people to follow him out. Her wyvern screamed to be released, wanting nothing more than to obliterate Gaze, all his henchmen, and the entire building. She gripped the edge of the table hard, venom sweating into her gloves as she fought to control her furious animal.

The tall girl in the black leathers hesitated as she passed Ivy's seat. Through the mist of her wyvern's rage, Ivy dimly recognized her as one of the teens Hope had been chatting with at Gaze's party.

The girl's eyes flicked from Ivy to the other gang members' retreating forms, and back again. "Is Hope okay?" she mumbled.

Ivy very nearly spat acid straight into her face. Swallowing hard, she got a grip on herself. "Piss off."

The girl flinched, but didn't back down. "She's not answering my messages. I just need...I just want to know if she's all right. Please?"

"Jezebeth!" the tattooed skinhead snapped from the doorway. "Heel!"

The girl jumped. "So, uh, yeah!" she said loudly, baring her teeth in a snarl that was wildly incongruous with her pleading eyes. "Do what the boss says, or you'll regret it!"

Ivy counted under her breath, both to focus herself and to make certain Gaze's gang would have moved off. When she reached five hundred, she slid out from the café booth herself. Tugging her gloves up, she headed for the door—and nearly ran smack into the muscular chest of Hugh Argent.

"What are you doing here?" he snarled.

His ice-blue eyes were narrowed with anger, blazing in his handsome face. His short, spiky white hair bristled like the fur of an enraged wolf. He looked even more pissed off than he had after rescuing her from the elevator shaft.

"What are *you* doing here?" Ivy snapped back, bristling herself.

"Hope told me more about Gaze after you left." Hugh's jaw clenched. "I shouldn't have let you go out alone."

"*Excuse* me?" Ivy glared at him. "I'm not your damn property. And why do you care, anyway?"

Hugh made a low, frustrated growl under his breath. "Because—because—oh, sod this. Come on."

He reached for her arm, and she reflexively jerked back out of reach before remembering that he was immune to her venom. They circled each other like a pair of fighting cats, glaring. There was a brief tussle as they both attempted to open the door for the other, which Hugh won. Ivy had to settle for walking past with icy dignity, spine straight, trying to ignore his delicious, masculine scent.

"How did you find me anyway?" she asked as they set off down the street. Then she groaned. "No, wait, stupid question. Ponyboy."

She knew full well that he was friends with Chase. The pegasus shifter had the irritating ability to home in on people, even from several miles away. Ivy had run afoul of Chase's special skills before.

To her surprise, Hugh shook his head. "I'm not foolish enough to mention you to Chase. No, you can blame your sister. Turns out she knows all your Internet passwords. She found the messages you exchanged with Gaze."

"I am going to email links to her fanfics to her entire school," Ivy muttered. "The whole world will know of her secret passion for Twilight Sparkle."

Hugh raised an eyebrow.

"Don't ask," Ivy advised.

"I have a suspicion that in this case, ignorance is bliss." Hugh's taut shoulders had eased down a little, though he was still stalking along as though the entire world personally offended him. "In any case, once your sister realized what idiocy you were planning, she enlisted my help in stopping it. Too late, I fear."

"Good thing you didn't get here faster, or you'd have ruined everything." Ivy glared up at that annoyingly perfect profile. "And you were supposed to be watching over Hope! She's got the common sense of a bar of soap, and you just left her alone?"

"No, actually, because unlike certain people *I* make plans that include contingencies. I took her to Griff's place before I came to find you. I didn't want her unguarded, not when you've apparently managed to offend the entire criminal population of Brighton."

Ivy didn't like being even more in debt to Griff, but at least she knew he could keep her sister safe. Even her wyvern had to admit that the griffin shifter was a powerful protector.

"Anyway." Hugh glowered down at her. "You've still got all your limbs, which is more than I was expecting, but I'm betting you didn't escape from that meeting without giving up something. What did he want?"

Ivy couldn't meet his eyes. She looked down at her boots, shoving her hands deep in her pockets.

"I said I'd take care of Gaze, and I did," she said. "That's all you need to know."

Despite her words, her gut twisted. There *was* more that Hugh needed to know. Was he even aware that Gaze was targeting him?

"Have, uh, you ever run across Gaze before?" she asked, trying to keep her tone casual.

"Never heard of him. But from what Hope's told me, I don't trust him as far as I can kick him. No matter what arrangement you think you've made, you're still in danger. So you're both staying with me until this is over."

Surprise jerked her head up again. "What?"

He lengthened his stride, taking the lead. "I hope you like cats."

Dumbfounded, Ivy stared at his broad back. "But—you hate me."

"I'm a paramedic and a firefighter," he said without turning round. "It's my job to rescue people, even when they're bloody idiots. Now keep up."

It was clear the conversation was over. Ivy could only trail at his heels, struggling to keep up with his longer legs. Inside, she was a turmoil of emotion. Confusion, hope, anger, delight…and underneath it all, a terrible, bone-gnawing guilt.

She'd made a deal with Gaze to find out Hugh's secrets.

If it came down to protecting her sister or her mate…who would she choose?

CHAPTER 8

*H*ugh had been angry enough before. Now, having seen Ivy's apartment when they'd made a brief stop to pick up her things, he was *bloody furious*.

"Did you know how they were living, Griff?" he demanded into his phone—quietly, since Ivy was in his guest room overhead and he didn't want her to overhear. "There were *holes* in the *floor*. I thought you said you'd helped them get an apartment! That wasn't an apartment, it was a fire-trap waiting for its chance to star in a tragic local news story!"

"It was the best I could do." Griff's rich Scottish voice sounded rather less patient than normal. "Rory, no! For the last time, don't do that with your peas! Ross, use your own spoon, not Danny's—and there go the peas again. Hugh, do you *really* need to talk now?"

Hugh held the phone away from his ear as a deafening clatter crackled out of the speaker. It sounded like someone had just thrown an entire cutlery drawer on the floor. Quite possibly someone had. Hugh was beginning to suspect that one—or both of—Griff's year-old twins might possess the power of telekinesis.

"Look at it this way," he said, when the din had abated marginally. "I'm giving you an excuse to skip out on feeding time at the zoo."

"Hayley, my love, could you take over here? Sorry, Hugh says it's important." The background noise faded away, thankfully. "Right. What were you yelling at me about again?"

"Ivy and Hope's apartment. Or rather, hovel. That decrepit pile of bricks should have been demolished thirty years ago. Couldn't you have found them anything better?"

"I offered to help cover the cost of a decent place, but they wouldn't accept a single penny from me." Griff sighed. "All they would let me do was negotiate with the landlord for them, so that they could afford *anything* on Ivy's wages."

"And that's another thing! She told me what she does for a living." Hugh clenched his free fist, his temper rising again. "A whip-smart woman like Ivy, and she spends her days scrubbing toilets?"

"Says the Eton and Oxford-educated man who spends most days elbow-deep in bodily fluids himself," Griff said dryly. "You do realize that you could have been angry about this for two entire years, right? At least *I've* been trying to help them."

Hugh winced, his friend's words slicing through him like a scalpel. Griff had been the only member of Alpha Team—probably the only shifter in Brighton—who'd been willing to even talk to Ivy after what had happened with Chase's mate. In the past, Hugh had thought it foolish, not to mention a betrayal of Chase. Now he could only be thankful for the griffin shifter's kind heart. How much worse could things have been for Ivy and Hope if Griff hadn't stepped in?

How much better could things have been for them if we had? his unicorn said, with its usual knack for spearing him straight in the guilt.

"Well, I'm...I'm helping now," he said, rather lamely.

"I'm glad you are," Griff said. "Even if I'm astonished that Ivy's accepting it. She's suspicious of any sort of assistance, poor lass. I told her that they could always come to me if they needed anything, but she's only ever done that once. And unfortunately, on that occasion, I couldn't help."

"What did she want?"

Griff blew out his breath. "For me to persuade Ash to burn out her wyvern."

Hugh let out a startled curse word. "Seriously?"

"Oh yes." The griffin shifter's tone was grim. "Thankfully he refused."

The Phoenix's most feared power was his ability to permanently destroy a shifter's inner animal. Hugh had only seen Ash do it on a handful of occasions, as a last resort to neutralize dangerous criminals. He hoped never to have to witness it again.

It did more than just remove a shifter's abilities. It burned away part of their soul, fundamentally changing their core nature. The thought of Ivy's fierce, stubborn personality going up in smoke, leaving behind a vacant-eyed, smiling husk...just the mental image made his unicorn flatten its ears in distress.

"I can't believe Ivy even asked," Hugh said. "Didn't you tell her she was basically volunteering for a lobotomy?"

"I tried. But she was desperate. She'd gladly sacrifice half her mind and soul if it meant she'd be able to touch her sister. But Ash wouldn't even contemplate it. You know how he feels about using his power that way."

Hugh made a mental note to buy Ash a beer at the next pub night. Of course, the Phoenix would only stare at it in polite bafflement—Hugh had never seen him drink anything stronger than water—but it was the thought that counted.

"Let's all be grateful for his restraint," he said. "Pass me over to Hope, will you? I need to talk to her about a change of plan."

"Hugh!" Hope's high-pitched squeal blasted his eardrums, nearly making him drop the phone. "Is everything okay? Did you get to her in time?"

"Yes, and no. I'll tell you the full details later, but suffice it to say that I'm not having you two running around loose. We stopped by your place to get your clothes and things. You're both staying here until all this is settled."

"Here...with Griff?" Hope said dubiously. "Um. It's kind of crowded, you know. I mean, I love little Danny, and the twins are beyond adorable, but I'm not sure that—"

"No, I meant stay here with me. I've got plenty of space."

There was a long pause from the other end of the line.

"Me *and* Ivy?" Hope sounded like he'd just proposed they book a suite at the International Space Station. "In your actual house?"

"Well, I'm not going to store you with the potting forks in the shed," Hugh said in exasperation. "Yes, in my house."

"Aaaaaand...let me get this straight. Ivy is in your house right now. With you. Alone."

"What, you think we're having a party without you? Of course we're alone. Tell Griff I'll be picking you up after dinner."

"Okay." Hope's voice raised, going distant as if she was holding the phone at arm's length. "Hey, Griff! Hugh says I need to stay with you tonight!"

"What?" Hugh spluttered. "No! I said—"

"Griff says that's no problem," Hope said sweetly. "Pick me up in the morning, okay? Have a nice evening!"

"No, wait, what?" He was talking to a dead line. "What the hell? Hope!"

"Something wrong?" Ivy had come into the kitchen, carrying a large, lidded plastic box in her arms.

Hugh stared at his phone, completely baffled. "Apparently, your sister would rather stay in a house full of screaming children than come here."

"What? Why would—" Ivy stopped mid-sentence, apparent enlightenment dawning. She let out a low, heartfelt groan. "Why that little—I swear, I am going to kill her with my bare hands."

"Why? What's she up to?"

Ivy circled past him, keeping her box between them like a shield. "It's not important. Let's just say that I'm pretty sure her latest dumb scheme is doomed to failure. Just forget it."

Hugh redialed, but the call went straight to voicemail. Hope must have switched Griff's phone off. He tried contacting Griff telepathically, but the griffin shifter was clearly preoccupied, probably with attempting to force nutritious vegetables into the protesting mouths of his three children.

"I could go get her anyway," he said to Ivy.

"Don't bother." Ivy was busy unpacking her box on the worktop. "You'd only have to prize her off the doorframe while she yells her head off. Hope has never been shy about making a scene to get what she wants."

Hugh opened his mouth to argue further, but was distracted by Ivy pulling a pan and a packet of ramen out of her box. "What on earth are you doing?"

"Making myself some dinner," she said, flashing him a look as though *he* was being the weird one. "Is it okay if I use your stove?"

Hugh looked pointedly at the pan already simmering away there. "You mean the stove that I am currently using to cook dinner?"

"Yeah, well, obviously I'll wait until you're done."

"You don't honestly think I'm intending to eat all this myself, do you?" Hugh lifted the lid, releasing a fragrant waft of steam redolent with saffron and paprika.

"I dunno. Some—some types of shifter need to pack away a lot of protein." For some reason, Ivy stumbled over the last sentence, her cheeks flushing. "I thought you might be a polar bear. Or just really hungry."

"Neither. And this is to share. So put your terrible cardboard noodles away and get a plate."

Ivy hesitated for a second, then took a scuffed tin plate out of her box. It was the sort of thing sold at army surplus stores. There was a big red X scrawled in enamel paint across the bottom.

"Something wrong with *my* plates?" Hugh asked as he ladled paella onto it.

"Contamination."

Hugh stared at her. "What in God's name do you think I have? Cooties?"

Ivy snorted. "Not you, dumbass. Me."

She turned away, digging one-handed in her box until she extracted a knife and fork. Like the plate, both were marked with an uneven slash of red paint.

"Don't touch anything marked in red," she said, waving them at them as she sat down at the table. "They're the ones I use. You shouldn't handle anything that's been in my mouth, just in—"

She stopped, a strange expression creeping over her face.

"And you've just remembered I'm immune to your venom," Hugh said, taking his place opposite her. "Feel free to take off your gloves, by the way."

"I shouldn't." Nonetheless she toyed with the fingertips, clearly tempted. Then she shook her head, picking up her fork decisively. "No. I can't risk falling into bad habits, even when Hope isn't around."

"Is she the reason for all that?" Hugh asked, tilting his head to indicate the box of red-banded cooking utensils and tableware.

"Mmhm. She's horribly sensitive to my venom, thanks to her condition." Ivy poked suspiciously at her paella, as if she was trying to defuse it. "Even the tiniest trace of my spit could send her into anaphylactic shock. What is this?"

"It's not a bomb, so you can stop looking at it like it's about to go off in your face. It's vegetarian paella. Fennel, broad beans, artichokes, a few Kalamata olives. Nothing elaborate."

She shot him a look. "We have very different definitions of the word elaborate."

With a slightly dubious expression, Ivy tried a forkful. Her eyes widened, and then drifted closed. The sheer bliss on her face made an electric jolt shoot straight to his groin.

"Oh my God," she moaned, her eyelids fluttering open. "That's *amazing*."

Hugh's own fork hung frozen in mid-air as she dove in with unabashed enthusiasm. Every one of her tiny, breathy sounds of pleasure made his blood surge. The flash of her pink tongue licking away a stray grain of rice; the way her glistening, generous lips closed softly over the fork, sliding lusciously down the gleaming tines—

We're not really thinking about forks here, are we? his unicorn commented dryly.

Ivy caught him staring, and flushed deep red. "What?" she snapped. "Something wrong with my table manners?"

"N-no," he croaked. Under the table, he was harder than he'd ever been in his entire life. "Just pleased you're enjoying it."

He grabbed his ice water as an excuse to avoid further conversation, downing half of it in a single swallow. It was genuinely tempting to tip the rest of it into his lap, but then he'd have to stand up. As it was, he was going to have to find an excuse to leave before dessert. He didn't think he could watch Ivy enjoying tiramisu without serious risk of coming in his pants.

Ivy was now self-consciously picking at her food, pushing the rice around her plate. "So...vegetarian, huh? That's unusual for a shifter."

"We're not all apex predators, you know." Hugh cast around for a change of topic, and was saved by Mr. Mittens trotting into the kitchen with a hopeful expression. "But you *are* an obligate carnivore, you walking waste disposal. Go on, there's nothing here for you."

"Who are—" Ivy looked down as Mr. Mittens wound around the table legs. "Oh shit, you weren't kidding about the cat!"

"You don't like cats?" Hugh said in dismay, as Ivy scrambled up onto her chair like a '30s film starlet who'd seen a mouse.

"I love cats," Ivy said, shrinking back as Mr. Mittens stood on his hind legs to bat at her shoelaces. "That's the problem. Don't let him touch me, I don't want to hurt him!"

"Oh, right. I see the issue." Hugh captured Mr. Mittens and deposited him on the table, where he promptly attempted to make a beeline for Ivy. "No, you suicidal fuzzball, stay over here. Have an olive. Have *all* the olives. Ivy, we may have a problem here."

Ivy lowered her feet back down again, though she was still watching Mr. Mittens as though he might suddenly spring for her face. From the enraptured way the old tomcat was gazing at her as he gummed his olives, it was probably a valid concern.

"Sorry, I honestly thought you were joking about having a cat," she said. "You didn't strike me as a pet person. And it's unusual for a single guy to have a cat."

Hugh wrestled Mr. Mittens back again. "I don't have a cat."

Ivy raised her eyebrows. "In which case, I have some very bad news to tell you about your dog."

"I have six cats," Hugh said. "And it's their feeding time."

Ivy scrambled up onto the table as a tidal wave of fur poured into the kitchen. "Shit! Hugh, do something!"

Hugh hastily put his half-eaten dinner on the floor, instantly attracting all feline attention. His cats crowded around, Ivy forgotten as they investigated the irresistible lure of people food.

"Sorry about this," Hugh said, heading for the cupboard to get the cat bowls. "Don't worry, I'll shut them all in the kitchen overnight. And even if one does accidentally brush against your skin, I can always heal them, you know."

"Yeah, but I'd still have hurt them." Ivy crouched on top of the dining table, every muscle poised and ready, her eyes fixed on the purring horde. "Why *do* you have so many cats?"

Hugh didn't say anything for a moment. He occupied himself with the can opener, cats winding around his feet. His first instinct was to say something flippant, like that he was saving them up until he had enough for a coat...but it felt oddly like a betrayal. He couldn't pretend that his pets weren't important to him.

"I rescue them," he said at last. "From the local shelter. I take the ones that no one else wants, the shy or sick or angry ones. I give them a home, and they give me...contact. I don't like being around people. But cats are different."

"I get it." Ivy's voice turned wistful. "I wish I could have a cat. They look so soft."

Mr. Mittens rubbed against his ankles, meowing for attention. The black-and-white cat was clearly too stuffed full of paella to be interested in mere kibble. Hugh picked him up, stroking his long, glossy fur. Mr. Mittens purred, arching into the touch.

He had his cats. But Ivy didn't have anything at all. She couldn't touch anyone, not even her own sister.

She'd never stroked a cat.

"Ivy," he said, going over to the table. "Take off your gloves."

She looked from him to the cat and back again. "Are you out of your mind?"

"You won't hurt him." Hugh shifted Mr. Mittens to one arm, freeing his other hand. "Just take off your gloves."

She started to protest, but the words died in her throat as he caught her wrist.

"Trust me," he said softly.

Holding her wide green eyes steadily with his own, he peeled off her glove. Her fingers trembled under his own.

Concentrating, he quested out with his healing power. Ivy caught her breath, trying to jerk back. He closed his fingers firmly around her hand, holding her still.

"What are you doing?" she whispered.

"Neutralizing your venom," he said, guiding her hand to Mr. Mitten's soft fur. "You *can't* hurt him, Ivy. Not while I'm in contact with you both."

"Oh," Ivy gasped, as the purring Mr. Mittens rubbed against her fingers. Tears brimmed in her eyes, making them as luminous as jewels. "*Oh.*"

Hugh kept his hand on the back of hers as she stroked the cat, concentrating on channeling his power through her. His unicorn's approval glowed in his soul, soft and pure as the light from its horn.

Ivy's green-streaked hair shadowed her face. He couldn't see her expression, but he could feel the soft drip of tears on the back of his hand.

"I thought you were an asshole," she said quietly.

He let out a huff of laughter. "I am."

Ivy shook her head, her glossy, chin-length hair swinging. "You're a paramedic, and a firefighter. You save people. And stray cats. And, and, you're helping Hope. And you came to find me when you thought I was in danger. You're a good man, Hugh."

She raised her chin, meeting his eyes at last. Her mouth trembled, but her gaze was steady.

"I'm not a good person," she said. "And you're going to hate me even more. But I need to tell you something."

Hugh listened with mounting concern as Ivy explained exactly what had happened during her meeting with Gaze. When she got to the bargain she'd made, he started, accidentally squeezing Mr. Mittens. The old cat yowled, retaliating by sinking all four sets of claws into his arm. Hugh barely noticed, cold with shock.

"Me?" he said, as the cat jumped down. "He wants you to find out my animal?"

Ivy crossed her arms, her shoulders hunching. She'd drawn away during her confession, though she was still perched on the table. She avoided his eyes, instead watching Mr. Mittens stalk away with his tail held haughtily high.

"I'm not going to tell him anything," she said. "Not now. But I...I considered it." She took a deep breath. "Please, *please*, don't take it out on Hope. She's innocent of all of this, and her condition is terminal. If you don't heal her-"

"Of course I'm still going to heal Hope," Hugh said, cutting her off. He raked a hand through his hair, pulling on it. "Stupid, stupid, stupid!"

Ivy flinched. "I—"

"Not you, me," he snapped. He paced a few steps, agitation burning in his muscles. "I was stupid. Arrogant. Even my father warned me— God, I should have been more careful!"

He'd thought he'd been so clever. That he'd found a way to use his talents without betraying his secret. He'd grown cocky, careless, healing people more and more openly. He'd told himself that it was fine, that even if other shifters grew curious about his powers, they'd never have a chance of guessing the truth.

Now, it seemed, someone had.

We are hunted, his unicorn said uneasily. *And in the hunt, there are only two choices. Do we run...or do we fight?*

"Fight," Hugh answered his inner beast out loud. "I'll be damned if I run. This is my home. I'm not letting some jumped-up snake drive me away."

Ivy slid off the table, intercepting his path. "Don't underestimate

Gaze, Hugh. He's dangerous. But if you're planning to confront him…I'll help."

"You most certainly will not," he snapped.

Gaze had clearly worked out that Ivy was his mate. If the basilisk shifter had decided to use her as a hostage rather than a spy…Hugh's blood turned to ice at the thought of what could have happened. There was no way he wanted Ivy anywhere near Gaze again.

"We made a deal," he said harshly. "I heal your sister, you vanish. I'm changing the terms. You vanish. I'll still heal Hope, but I want you gone."

NO! His unicorn reared in his mind, horn blazing. *This is wrong, WRONG!*

Ivy squeezed her eyes shut for a moment. When she opened them, moisture was caught in her long, dark lashes.

"Okay," she said, her voice quiet and defeated. "I'll go now."

"Not literally right now, you imbecile!" Hugh grabbed her shoulder, spinning her back to face him. "You can't just walk out into the streets with no resources and no plan."

"What do you care?" Ivy's voice raised, her tears turning to anger. "I don't get you at all, Hugh! If you're going to hate me, can't you at least be consistent about it?"

"You're my bloody mate, woman!" Hugh had never wanted to shake someone so much in his life. "Of course I don't hate you!"

"Well, you've got a weird way of showing it!" Ivy yelled straight back. "Most of the time you act like you can't stand the sight of me!"

"I can't stand the sight of you because when you're around all I can think about is kissing you!"

The words hung in the air.

"Really?" Ivy said blankly.

"Well, no." Hugh let go of her, scrubbing both hands over his face. "I was being polite. My thoughts don't just involve kissing."

Ivy swallowed hard. "So…why don't you?"

"Because I don't think I'd be able to stop."

"I wouldn't want you to," she said softly.

She was close, so close. He could feel the heat radiating from her, trembling in the air between them. He couldn't look away from her full, soft lips, half-parted in invitation. A single step forward, and he could claim them...

He turned on his heel, before he could fall headlong into disaster. He braced his arms on the kitchen counter, chest tight, struggling to master himself.

"You should go." The words felt rough in his throat. They were the precise opposite of what he wanted to say. "Before we do something we'll both regret."

"I wouldn't regret it." He heard her draw a deep breath, as if she was bracing herself for a fight. "Hugh. I know you don't want me as a mate."

Oh, but he did, he did. He clenched his jaw, his chest hurting with the effort of staying silent.

"And I get it, I really do." The bleak resignation in her voice tore his heart. "I don't fit in your world, I have way too much baggage, I'm —I know that it could never work. I'm not asking for that."

She'd sidled up alongside him as she spoke. Hugh stared down at the granite countertop, not daring to look at her.

Hesitantly, she put her bare hand on top of his. Hugh closed his eyes, the sweetness of the simple contact singing through every inch of his body.

"All I want is to be touched," she whispered. "Just once. Please."

He knew that he should pull his hand out from under hers. He knew that if he did, she would never ask again.

And the thing trembling in the air between them would be broken forever. She'd made herself utterly vulnerable, though it went against every harsh lesson life had taught her. If he pulled away now, she would never, ever trust him again.

He turned his hand palm up, lacing his fingers through hers. Gripped tight. Felt her strength in return, her hand squeezing as desperately as if once again he was the only thing stopping her from falling.

And he knew what he had to do.

"Ivy," he said. "I need to show you my animal."

CHAPTER 9

"You don't have to do this," Ivy protested, as Hugh drew her down the corridor. "You *shouldn't* do this, Hugh. If I don't know, then I can't betray you."

"I'm not worried about that." He kept a firm hold of her hand, unlocking a door with the other. "And you need to know."

The door swung open, revealing a set of plain wooden steps leading down into darkness. Hugh descended without hesitation, pulling her after him. Ivy clung to his hand, his fingers strong and reassuring around her own.

Her boot unexpectedly sank into something soft and springy rather than echoing from another wooden step. Ivy stumbled, only Hugh's grip saving her from falling flat on her face. She put out a hand to catch herself, but her fingers encountered rustling leaves instead of a wall.

"What the—?" Ivy reached out again, tentatively, and felt something that she could have sworn was the rough bark of a tree. "What is this?"

A click, and the room filled with a soft blue light. It was dim and diffuse, but seemed dazzling after the pitch blackness. It illuminated the sharp planes of Hugh's face like moonlight, silvering his cheekbones and tracing the curve of his lips. There was something vulnerable about his eyes that she'd never seen before.

"This is where I shift," he said.

Ivy stared around. Her first impression was that they stood, impossibly, in a forest glade. A full moon glimmered through the branches overhead, riding high in a pitch-black sky speckled with distant stars. Soft spring grass rustled under her feet.

But...it was all fake.

The air was dry and sterile rather than filled with the lush green scent of growing plants. The grass underfoot was plastic. The tree trunks were real, but only fabric leaves hung motionless from their branches. The moon was just a light bulb in a paper globe shade; the stars, glowing paint.

"You shift here?" She revolved on the spot, taking in all the carefully-detailed fakery. "Why?"

"I can't risk being seen. I can hide myself from human eyes, but other shifters would still be able to see me. So I built this. So I could pretend." Hugh smiled his edged, bitter smile. "Pathetic, I know."

She'd never stood in a room so permeated with sadness. The thought of him down here all alone, trying to pretend that fake grass was real and that the ceiling was full of stars...her throat closed up.

"Why?" she whispered again.

He released her hand at last. He walked to the center of the room —it only took two steps—and turned to face her.

"Because this is what I am," he said.

He shimmered...and the sad glow of the light bulb moon washed away, replaced by a truer, softer light.

Her legs folded like wet noodles. She sank to her knees on the plastic grass, never taking her eyes off that brilliantly white form.

He took a step forward. Where his silver hoof touched the fake turf, the scent of rain-washed earth rose up, impossibly. Fabric leaves seemed to unfurl like butterfly wings, yearning toward his glimmering light. The air hung still, yet she could have sworn she felt a whisper of a spring breeze on her skin, warm and scented with blooming lilacs.

She put out a hand, her fingers trembling. His great, graceful head dipped, the silken mane falling like a waterfall over the powerful arch of his neck. His velvet-soft, pure white muzzle touched her palm.

"Hugh," she whispered.

His fragrant breath sighed against her skin. As gracefully and easily as the setting moon, he knelt down, his long, strong limbs folding underneath him.

He lay his head in her lap.

A slight, strangled noise escaped her, half-sob, half-laugh. She was Ivy Viverna, the wyvern. The monster.

And a unicorn was resting his head in her lap.

Barely daring to touch him, she traced the sweeping lines of his head. His sapphire eyes drifted closed as she stroked his nose, his cheek, the elegant points of his ears. His fur was softer even than the cat's had been. His mane flowed like fog through her fingers.

He sighed a little, leaning into her. His pearlescent horn nudged against her shoulder. It was at least three feet long, spiraled like a seashell, glimmering with a secret light. Holding her breath, she hesitantly ran her fingers up the hard length. The glow brightened, silver sparks swirling like miniature fireflies in the wake of her touch.

Tears streaked her cheeks. When had she started crying?

She bent her own head, hiding her face in his white mane. Her arms hugged his neck. She pressed herself against his warm hide, breathing in his scent of lilac and rain. She felt like she'd finally stopped after a lifetime of running; finally put down a burden she hadn't even known she'd been carrying. In the peace that settled over her like a blanket, she heard the soft sound of wind in leaves.

She didn't know how long they knelt there, while the fake forest grew and whispered around them. It could have been a minute, or a century. She would have been content not to move for the rest of her life. But all too soon he stirred, his ears lowering a little in resignation. He drew back, and she had to let him go.

The unicorn stood—not with a horse's ungainly scramble, but as smoothly as a falcon taking flight. He dipped his head again, that sweeping horn descending on her like a sword blade. She caught her breath—but the needle-sharp tip just settled lightly on her own forehead.

Light flared, so bright that she had to squeeze her eyes shut against it. When she opened them again, Hugh stood before her, head bowed.

"So," he said. "Now you know."

The grass was just plastic again, rough under her palm. The fabric leaves hung limp from dead branches. But she could still feel his light glowing inside her, in some secret center of her heart. She knew that it would be there until the day she died.

"Y-you," she croaked. She licked her lips, and tried again. "You're a unicorn. Literally, a unicorn."

He raised his head a little, though his eyes were still in shadow. "You probably have some questions."

"Yes! Like, how can you even exist?" Ivy scrambled to her feet, the strange spell finally breaking. "You can't be a unicorn! That's not a real thing!"

Hugh's mouth quirked. "Says the wyvern."

"That's different. We're just rare. Not *fairy tales!*"

"I'm a mythic shifter, same as you. Just a little more mythic than most. Unicorns have always been real, Ivy. But we've been in hiding for the past seven hundred years or so."

"Even from other shifters? Why?"

He tapped the center of his forehead, one eyebrow raising ironically. "Give you one guess."

Ivy hugged herself, struggling to contain her churning emotions as her mind raced. "That's why Gaze wants you, isn't it? For your horn."

"A live unicorn can cure a lot of things. Wounds, poison, critical injuries...but even we have our limits. We can't restore a lost limb, or lost youth. We can't fix congenital problems, where the body doesn't know that anything's wrong." His eyes went bleak. "I can't cure cancer."

She wanted to hold him again, and stroke away the old anguish shadowing his face. But something about the way that he stood, straight-backed and rigid, kept her hands at her sides. She'd just been closer to him than she ever had been to anyone in her life, but now he seemed as remote and untouchable as the moon.

Hugh shook himself a little, his usual ironic mask sliding back into place. "But a *dead* unicorn…now that's more powerful. I'm a walking jackpot, as far as Gaze is concerned. If you were old and dying and rich, what would *you* give to be restored back to the prime of life?"

Ivy's heart contracted at the thought of his shining beauty being snuffed out. But Gaze was a monster. If anyone would kill a unicorn, he would.

"I'll never tell," she vowed. "But you shouldn't have trusted me with this, Hugh. It's too big. I wish you hadn't—"

The words died on her tongue. No matter what, she couldn't regret that perfect moment. She couldn't regret seeing his true self.

Hugh put his hands in his pockets, his shoulders hunching a little. He still didn't quite look at her.

"I didn't show you in order to explain why Gaze wants me." There was a rough catch in his voice. "I showed you so that you'll understand why I can't…Ivy, you must know the big thing about unicorns. What all the legends and myths say."

For a moment, she thought he was still talking about his horn. Then it struck her. The *other* thing about unicorns.

The reason why he'd put his head in her lap.

"You like virgins," she said, and immediately wished the fake grass would swallow her up. "Um. That came out wrong."

"It's not so much a matter of *liking* virgins." A faint flush stained his sharp cheekbones. "But being around anyone who isn't chaste gives me a screaming headache. Even people who have been celibate for decades still make me flinch a little. Virgins are the only people I can touch without pain."

She digested this for a moment. "You can touch Hope, right?"

"And this is really not where I was expecting this conversation to go," he muttered. "Yes, Ivy. Your little sister is definitely still a virgin. Anyone else whose sex life you'd like to enquire about?"

"Um." She was certain she was red as a brick. "Yours. If you…how do you…?"

"I don't."

All that masculine beauty, and he was just as untouched as she was?

"*Ever?*" Ivy said in disbelief.

"Ever." He met her eyes at last, and the raw, desperate hunger in them stole the breath from her lungs. "I want you, Ivy. So badly that it's all I can do not to take you up against a wall here and now. But I *can't*. I'd lose my unicorn."

She blinked. "Is that supposed to be a metaphor?"

"No. If I—if I made love to you, it would kill my unicorn. Literally."

She stared at him.

He let out a harsh bark of laughter, raking both hands through his hair. "And my bloody suicidal beast just said, *It would be worth it.*"

"Let me get this straight," Ivy said slowly. "If we have sex, you'd never be able to shift again?"

"Worse than that," he said in a low voice. "I'd lose my powers. Lose my ability to heal. Hell, I might even lose the connection to you. I don't know. But I do know I wouldn't be a shifter anymore."

"Wait. Wait." Ivy held up her hands, her mind reeling. "I need a minute."

She paced from fake tree to fake tree, struggling to wrap her head around everything that he'd told her. What he was, what he'd risked to show her, what he still risked just by being near her…

"Okay," she said, turning back to Hugh with her hands on her hips. "So what about anal?"

CHAPTER 10

He'd heard her wrong.

"Sorry," Hugh said. "Would you repeat that?"

"Anal." Ivy had gone bright red from throat to forehead, but she enunciated the word with exaggerated care. "Could we have anal sex?"

He hadn't heard her wrong.

"I mean, I'm just trying to work out all the rules here," Ivy continued, when he failed to respond. "Does anal count as sex as far as your unicorn is concerned?"

"Yes," he said, in a somewhat strangled tone. "Yes, that…that would definitely count."

"Okay. What about oral?"

He couldn't help his gaze dropping to her full lips, moist and pink. How would she look, splayed out before him, her secret folds equally swollen and inviting…

He cleared his throat. "Y-Yes. That would count too."

"I guess it's still, um, penetration." Ivy tapped her lips, her eyebrows drawing down. "What about—"

He held up a hand, stopping her before she could start describing any more intimate acts. His trousers were already getting uncomfortably tight.

"Ivy, it's not a matter of whether any Tab A has been inserted into a particular Slot B," he said. "How can I put this delicately...lesbian couples give me headaches. And I've met a few married women who *didn't* set off my unicorn. Married women with children. And, I can only assume, extremely incompetent—not to mention inconsiderate—husbands."

From her blank look, she wasn't following.

Oh God. He was far too English to be having this conversation.

Prude, his unicorn commented, with a distinct undercurrent of amusement.

He sighed. "Orgasms," he said bluntly. "It's orgasms."

"Oh shit, so *I* give you headaches!" Ivy exclaimed...and went an even darker shade of red.

"Ah, solo activities *don't* count," he said, his own face heating. "Otherwise, let's face it, there wouldn't be any unicorn shifters past the age of puberty."

His unicorn was now openly snickering at his discomfort. He turned away from Ivy, partly to hide his embarrassment, but more because her curves made it very difficult to keep a discussion of sex purely on a clinical level.

"It's got nothing to do with any old-fashioned notions of purity or innocence." It was easier to talk with his back to her, though he was still sharply aware of her presence. "I'm sensitive to the ebbs and flows of energy in a human body, it's how I'm able to heal. And sharing pleasure with another person creates an energy so strong, it's overwhelming to my senses. My unicorn can't handle it."

"I think I get it," she said. "It's like you're a microphone tuned to pick up the slightest whisper. And then suddenly someone yells into you at the top of their lungs."

He nodded. "And if I felt that sort of energy myself, it would burn me out entirely. Like too much current through a fuse."

She was silent for a long moment. Then he heard her boots crunch on the fake grass, coming up behind him. Her arms slid around his waist.

"It's just a hug," she whispered. She rested her forehead against his back, keeping her own torso at a chaste distance. "That's all. Because I think you've needed one for a long, long time, Hugh."

He closed his eyes, encircled by her gentle embrace. There was nothing sexual in it. Just the wordless comfort of human closeness, freely offered, asking nothing in return.

Of course she'd known how desperately he needed that simple contact. She knew even better than him what it was to go without touch.

Heal her. His unicorn looked at him from the depths of his soul, compassion and sorrow mingling in its sapphire gaze. *As she heals you.*

He let out his breath in a long sigh. He turned in her arms, putting his own around her. He felt her breath catch as he pulled her close against his side. He buried his face in her dark hair, as she'd hidden hers in his mane earlier.

"Ivy," he whispered.

She clung to him, holding on as fiercely as he did to her. Her warmth pressed against him, the curves of her breasts against his chest sending fire through his blood. He couldn't help digging his fingers into her generous hips, pulling them harder against his own.

"Hugh," Ivy gasped into his shoulder, as the exquisite softness of her belly pressed against his rigid length. "I'm pretty sure this is no longer just a hug."

"I can't stop myself around you." Hugh drew his head back a little, far enough to see her face. "But you can. Stop me, Ivy."

She drew in a breath, parting her lips—but he pressed one finger against them, forestalling her words.

"But not yet," he said.

He gently drew his finger down over her bottom lip, her breath hitching as he followed that lush, pillowy curve. Her eyes were all pupil, wide and dazed with desire. His fingertips skimmed the line of her jaw, cupping her face.

"Hugh," she breathed, as he bent down to her.

"Not yet," he repeated, and closed his mouth over hers.

Soft, so soft, softer than he could ever have imagined. But there was strength there too, in the way she pressed up against him, giving him back as much as he gave her. She opened to him but claimed him in return, her tongue wonderfully bold against his.

Her hands came up to tangle in his hair. The light scratch of her nails made him groan into her mouth, his hips jerking helplessly with every crook of her fingers. He pressed harder against her, near-blind with the need to be closer to her. Closer, deeper, claiming every inch.

Her back hit a wall. He growled in satisfaction, trapping her body against his, her mouth under his own. He was drunk on the sweet taste of her, on the needy little noises she made deep in her throat. He wanted to hear her make more of them. He wanted to make her scream out her pleasure, wanted to hear her say-

"Stop," she gasped against his mouth.

That single word was a choke chain around his neck, dragging him back from the brink. He broke off the kiss, though every part of him cried out in protest. Chest heaving for breath, he leaned his forehead against hers.

She released his hair, her hands drifting down to rest on his shoulders. He could feel her body trembling with barely restrained desire, as much as his own was. Gradually, their racing hearts slowed.

Ivy sighed. "I hope you have a very, *very* cold shower."

"Frigid," he murmured. "I'm not even sure it *can* go hot."

She let out a brief, shaky laugh. "I call first dibs."

She pushed at his chest. He drew away, but only far enough to look into her face. Gently, he traced her flushed, swollen lips.

"Thank you," he whispered.

She smiled at him, but it didn't reach her eyes. "For stopping?"

Dipping his head, he brushed her mouth with his own. Lightly. Tenderly. Just once.

"No," he said, releasing her at last. "For starting."

CHAPTER 11

After the world's longest ice-cold shower, some deep breathing, and a lot of yelling at her inner wyvern, Ivy was finally ready to face Hugh again.

And mate him, her wyvern agreed.

Ivy groaned out loud, wishing that she could shake her animal. *NO. We've been over this five times. He can't. We're not going to make it any harder for him.*

Don't need to. Her animal's eyes gleamed wickedly. *He felt hard enough already.*

Ivy shook her head, squashing the dirty beast back down to the bottom of her mind. It was a good thing Hugh and she hadn't attempted telepathic communication, she decided. His unicorn would probably vaporize on the spot if exposed to her wyvern.

She finished buttoning up her epically unsexy flannel pajamas, which she'd settled on as the least enticing items of clothing she owned. Just to be safe, she threw her ratty, shapeless old dressing gown over the top, and pulled on her thickest pair of work gloves.

She examined herself carefully in the mirror. Excellent. She looked like a homeless person inexplicably prepared for a spot of arc welding. Nothing about her even hinted at sex.

Well, apart from her mouth, which still looked thoroughly ravaged. And the heightened color in her cheeks. And her fever-bright, half-stunned eyes, the eyes of someone who had just been kissed near-senseless...

She gave her arm a sharp pinch through her layers of clothing, hauling herself back from that dangerously intoxicating memory. She had to have more self-control. It couldn't happen again.

One kiss is more than you ever thought you'd have, she reminded herself as she slipped out of the guest room. *And he risked everything to give it to you. Remember that.*

She headed down the corridor to Hugh's room. The door was half-open, and she couldn't hear running water. He must have finished his own shower.

"Hugh?" she said, knocking on the door frame as she entered. "I think we need to—"

And what she thought they needed to do radically altered in her mind, because he was wearing a towel.

He'd clearly *just* finished his shower. His white hair stuck up in tousled spikes, while his bare torso gleamed with moisture. The towel wrapped around his waist barely came midway down his lean, muscled thighs.

He'd frozen, his hand white-knuckled on his towel. He stared at her as if she'd entered wearing a lacy negligee rather than mismatched tartan flannel.

She should turn and run. She should apologize. She should at least close her eyes.

Instead she blurted out, stupidly, "You've got tattoos."

Hugh's throat worked convulsively. "Yes."

Ivy took a step forward, fascinated despite herself. It was the last thing she would ever have expected, from his upper-class accent and sophisticated manner. But he was inked from chest to elbow like a dockhand.

An intricate black snake twisted around a staff in the center of his chest. Twining vines spread out across his pecs and looped over his shoulders. They curled down his arms in elegant spirals, emphasizing the hard swells of his biceps.

The design was beautiful, but oddly unbalanced. His left arm was a riot of springtime foliage, each tiny leaf exquisitely detailed. But on his right arm, the vines were mostly bare. Only a few dry, dead leaves clung to them, as if a winter wind had swept the rest away.

Hugh turned away, revealing more vines and leaves inked across his shoulder blades. Ivy knew that she shouldn't stare, but she couldn't tear herself away. He was a living piece of art, even more breathtaking than she could ever have imagined.

He opened his wardrobe, the leaves twining around his left arm seeming to stir as his muscles flexed. "Don't tell anyone."

"Why?" They must have taken hours upon hours of agony—it was difficult to permanently tattoo shifters, what with their rapid healing. She couldn't imagine going through all that, only to keep the end result secret.

He turned back a little to give her one of his sharp, humorless smiles. "Because people would ask what they mean."

Her fingertips longed to trace the inked lines. To follow the curving black paths over his gleaming skin, spiraling tantalizingly close to his taut nipples before sweeping up toward his collarbones, over his muscled shoulders, around and down…

As he pulled a pair of trousers out of the wardrobe, Ivy abruptly became aware of just how long she'd been staring at him. Face heating, she turned on her heel, staring fixedly at the wall as cloth rustled behind her.

Our mate is naked now, her wyvern pointed out helpfully.

Ivy squeezed her eyes shut. "So, uh, guess I shouldn't ask what they mean, huh?"

He was silent for a long moment, so long that she very nearly turned around to look at him. Then, "Come here," he said.

She turned, and sucked in a startled breath. He'd pulled on a pair of soft jogging pants, but his torso was still bare. He met her eyes steadily, his own dark and still. She couldn't interpret his expression.

"Come here," he repeated, holding out his hand. "Lie down with me, and I'll tell you about my tattoos."

She knew she shouldn't, but she couldn't help going to him. Gently, he drew her down onto the bed, tucking her under his arm.

"Is this a good idea?" she murmured, as her head settled onto his bare shoulder

He stroked her hair back from her neck. "How many layers of clothing are you wearing?"

She had to stop and think about that one. "Six. Including two pairs of underwear."

His chuckle vibrated through her chest. "Then I think we're safe."

His arousal was obvious, but his arms were gentle, holding her without asking for more. The sweetness of the embrace brought strange tears to the corners of her eyes. She blinked them away, ignoring the longing pooling between her own thighs.

"Tell me about your tattoos," she whispered.

He tapped the center of his chest. "I got the Staff of Asclepius during my final year of medical school. A cliché, I know. In my defense, I was blind drunk at the time."

She traced the twisting snake with a gloved finger. "I thought the symbol for a doctor had two snakes. And wings."

"That's a caduceus, the Rod of Hermes. It's the symbol used by U.S. Army medics, but it doesn't actually have any traditional association with medicine." He snorted. "If you come back with one of those tattooed on your body at Oxford, be prepared for excessive mockery from your more well-educated colleagues. I was drunk, but not *that* drunk."

She giggled, and then stopped abruptly as what he'd just said percolated through her brain. "Wait. You studied medicine at Oxford University? And you're a *paramedic?*"

His shoulder tensed under her cheek. "I never finished my training. I got the degree, but I quit six weeks into my hospital residency."

"Really? Why?"

"My headaches," he said in a low voice. "University was bad enough, being surrounded by hordes of horny students, but the hospital was even worse. So many people, in such a small space…I could barely function. I tried to work despite the migraines, but even when I forced myself to touch patients, there were too many I couldn't heal. I'm best with things like wounds and burns, life-threatening injuries. In hospital, there were too many people I couldn't help."

I can't cure cancer, he'd said before.

Ivy caught his hand in her own, drawing it up to her mouth. Softly, she kissed his knuckles, and the joints of his strong, clever fingers.

"Tell me more about your tattoos," she said, releasing him again. "You can't have got them all when you were drunk."

He let out a soft huff of laugher. "No. Though I *was* badly hungover when I got these put on." He indicated the intricate vines curling along his collarbones. "It was a few months after I'd dropped out. I was something of a mess. Living at home, searching for a purpose. After the third time my father hid a hooker under my bed—"

"What?"

"It's a long story. Suffice it to say that he's a terrible human being. Anyway, I stormed out, drove randomly half the night, and ended up here in in Brighton. Spent two days getting shit-faced at the Full Moon pub and generally feeling sorry for myself. Then on the third day Rose marched over to me, said that there was someone I needed to meet, and introduced me to Fire Commander Ash. While, let me add, I was still completely plastered. Worst job interview ever."

Ivy smirked at the mental image of Hugh being grilled by the Phoenix while three sheets to the wind. "Can't have gone too badly, since he hired you."

"Well, I told him what I could do, and why. Which I would never have done while sober, so I can thank two bottles of vodka for my job." His flippant tone turned more serious. "In any event, Ash gave me back a purpose. And the first thing the next morning I went out and got the vines, to make sure I never forgot it again. To help me stay focused."

Ivy touched one of the dry, dead leaves on his right pectoral. "Stay focused on what?"

He was silent for a moment. Then he took her hand, drawing it across his chest so that her forefinger rested on one of the budding leaves on the other side.

"John Doe," he said. "Sword through the heart."

Ivy drew in a sharp breath, but he was already was moving on. Following the curl of the vine, he guided her fingertip to a triple spray of leaves springing from a single stem.

"Griff. Three times. I hope he's bored with endangering himself, because I'm running out of skin there." Another leaf. "This was a woman in a traffic incident. Never knew her name, but she would have bled out before the ambulance arrived. Anyway. You get the picture."

She lifted her head to stare at him, speechless. He avoided her eyes, looking down at his left arm as if it belonged to someone else.

"A leaf per life. Terribly melodramatic, I know." His tone was light, but there was a forced edged to his self-mockery. "But once I'd started, it seemed churlish to stop. Would be rude to decide that someone wasn't worth recording, after all."

She flattened her hand over his bicep. Her fingers covered at least a dozen leaves just there. And the curling vines covered his shoulder, down his arm, round over his back…

"This part's empty," she said, following the vines down to his elbow.

"Just waiting to be filled in." He shrugged. "I wanted the unfinished design to be there, staring at me accusingly, if I was ever tempted to stop."

"Stop getting tattoos?"

"Stop healing," he said softly. "Give up my unicorn. Like I said, the tattoos help keep me focused."

Her eyes went from the half-filled vines on his left arm to the nearly empty ones on his right. Only a handful of dry, curled leaves clung there…

"Hugh." She touched one of the autumn leaves, and he flinched. "If the growing leaves are people you've saved, what are these?"

He was silent for a long, long moment.

"The people I didn't," he said at last. "And I pray to God that side *is* finished."

He kept score on his skin. Lives saved versus lives lost, measuring his worth by the slow creep of ink down his arms.

She'd thought his tattoos beautiful, until she'd learned their meaning.

She sat up, spreading both of her gloved hands across his shoulders. Her hands were too small to blot out more than a small fraction of the design. She wished that she could scrub the black marks off his skin, take away the terrible guilt and pressure he carried with him wherever he went.

"You're more than just what you can do, Hugh," she said fiercely. "You don't have to keep score. I wish you wouldn't."

He smiled a little, sadly. "I'm not, and I do. But thank you for the sentiment."

Oh, how she wanted to show him how much she treasured him. To hold him close and wordlessly tell him over and over that he was loved for himself, not for his talent. She longed to caress every inch of his unblemished skin, until he knew bone-deep that his value wasn't just marked in black ink.

As if sensing her thoughts, he drew her back down again, tucked her head under his chin. She stretched her arms, hugging him tight. She closed her eyes, feeling the warmth of his bare skin against her cheek, the rapid beat of his heart in her ear.

"I told you about my tattoos because I want you to understand why I can't mate you, no matter how much I want it," he murmured.

"You think I'd want you to give up your unicorn?" she said, taken aback that he could even have thought such a thing. "I'd never ask that!"

"Ivy, being a unicorn means shifting in secrecy and endless headaches. God, if that was *all* it meant, I'd make love to you here and now, and bless you for finally ridding me of the wretched beast. But that's not all it means. I could give up the unicorn, but I can't turn my back on the people who need me. The people who will need me in future."

She ran her thumb over his left shoulder. So many lives owed to his powers. So many more that could be saved.

"I understand," she said, meaning it with her whole breaking heart. "But Hugh, I don't know if I'm strong enough for this."

He laughed a little, his warm breath stirring her hair. "Have you seen yourself, woman? All the crap the world throws at you, and you stride through it all like a damn queen. You're the strongest person I've ever met. Why do you think I trusted you tonight, when I didn't trust myself to stop?"

She took a deep breath, bracing herself to reveal her deepest, darkest secret. "Hugh, I touched Hope once."

He stilled underneath her. "I'm not following."

"Our mother was always so careful not to leave us alone. Mom thought I was jealous, she was scared I wanted to hurt the baby…but I didn't. I just wanted to hug my sister. Just once. And one night when I was ten and Hope was two, Mom forgot to lock my door. So I snuck into Hope's room, and I put my bare hands through the bars of her cot, and I touched her."

His hand came up to gently stroke her tense back. "That's understandable. You were a child, Ivy. You didn't know-"

"I *did*, Hugh. Mom told me over and over every single day how dangerous it was, how I mustn't ever go near the baby. I did it anyway. Hope spent eight weeks in intensive care, and when she came out she couldn't use her legs anymore. She'd been a late developer, but she'd been pulling up, she'd been starting to toddle…and I destroyed all that. She's never walked because of me, Hugh. Because I had one moment of weakness."

"Oh, God," he muttered, his tone bitter with self-loathing. "Ivy, I'm so sorry. I never meant—it's not fair for me to put such pressure on you. I promise, I won't put you in that position again."

She was *not* going to cry. He'd called her the strong one. She was going to be strong for him now, no matter how badly her heart was hurting.

She forced out the words she had to say. "So you still want me to leave?"

"No!" His hands tightened convulsively on her back. "God no. I never *wanted* you to leave, Ivy. In case you hadn't worked it out by now, your mate can be a damn idiot sometimes. I was scared to tell you my secret, so I pushed you away instead."

"Well, you can't," she said. "I *can't* go, Hugh, not when you're in danger from Gaze. No matter how hard it's going to be, I need to be here to protect you."

His chest muscles stiffened underneath her. "I can take care of myself. A unicorn is fifteen hundred pounds of muscle behind a five-foot spear, not a sparkly pony."

"All right, Stabby McStabface, don't get your horn in a twist," Ivy poked him in the side. "I'm talking about *me*, not you. I may be just a wyvern, but I'm still a dragon at heart. I can't leave my treasure unguarded. I'd lose my mind."

"I'm your treasure?" His voice was softer than she'd ever heard.

"You're my mate," she said, simply. "You'll always be my mate. No matter what."

Neither of them said anything for a while, holding each other in silence.

"I think it was easier," Hugh said at last, "when you thought I despised you, and I hoped that you hated me."

Ivy couldn't disagree.

CHAPTER 12

Hope knew the second she rolled through the door that her plan had worked.

I am the greatest sister in the world, she thought smugly, and waited for Ivy and Hugh to tell her their good news.

To her surprise, however, the happy announcement didn't come. For some reason, Hugh and her sister seemed hell-bent on pretending that they *weren't* now mated.

They still maintained a constant, careful distance, sidling round each other as though terrified they might spontaneously combust if they so much as bumped shoulders. They exchanged only the minimum of words, their voices polite and strained like two strangers stuck in an elevator together.

But though they were still determinedly keeping their hands to themselves, their eyes were all over each other. Hope could have toasted marshmallows in their heated gazes. They were basically walking heart emojis.

Hope guessed that Ivy's pride was holding her back from admitting what had clearly happened. After all, Ivy owed all of her newfound happiness to Hope's awesome matchmaking skills. Now she'd have to finally accept that her little sister was actually smarter than her when it came to some things.

Hope would, she'd already decided, not make a big thing of it. She would accept Ivy's grudging apology gracefully, like the mature adult she was. She wouldn't rub her sister's nose in it.

Well, not *much*.

For now, though, Hope played along. She obediently lay back on the couch and held still under Hugh's tingly-tickly healing hands, and secretly laughed her head off over the way that Ivy was clearly checking out his butt whenever he bent over.

Not that Hope could blame Ivy for that, she had to admit. Hugh was easy on the eyes, if you were into the whole angst-and-muscles thing. And dudes, of course. Ivy could have done a whole lot worse, when it came to a mate.

He'd be good for Ivy, Hope decided. Whatever his inner animal might be, he was clearly no pushover. He could handle her sister. And maybe, in his magic hands, Ivy would finally chill out a little. Let Hope live her own life at last.

So Hope held her tongue, even though it just about killed her to pretend that she hadn't noticed the way they were drooling all over each other. She knew her sister well enough to know that it was better to let Ivy come clean in her own time, when she was ready.

After all, she'd have to admit the truth soon. It wasn't like any shifter could actually keep their hands off their fated mate for long. It was kind of hilariously tragic, watching the pair of them try.

At least, it was funny at first.

As the morning wore on and they *still* didn't admit their secret, it started to get old.

By the afternoon, it was downright irritating.

When Hugh went off after lunch to take a nap—apparently healing wore him out, although Hope herself felt as refreshed as if she'd been floating in a hot tub all morning—she couldn't hold her silence any longer.

"Well?" she demanded of her sister, once they were finally alone.

Ivy didn't look round from washing up her tin plate and cutlery from lunch. "Well what?"

"Are you going to tell me about Hugh or not?"

Ivy's fork and knife clattered against each other as she twitched. "I don't know his animal. And don't you dare bug him about it, either. It's rude to pry."

The tense line of Ivy's back, the too-quick answer to a question Hope hadn't actually asked…Hope knew when her sister was lying.

But why? she wondered. If Hugh had shown Ivy his shift form last night—and Hope would now have bet her busted wheelchair on that—what reason could she possibly have for lying about it? Especially to her own sister?

She set the mystery aside for later consideration. "That wasn't what I meant. Come *on*, Ivy. Tell me what's up with you and Hugh. You know you have to eventually."

Ivy's shoulders stiffened, but she didn't turn around. She seemed focused on her task, dumping each cleaned item back into the Box o' Death, as they called the red-banded plastic container where Ivy stored everything she'd handled with bare hands.

"Ivy. Ivyyy." When her sister still didn't respond, Hope scaled her voice up to her most annoying whine. "Ivyyyyyy. You know I can keep this up all day. Ivyyyyyyyyyyy."

Steel clanged on steel as Ivy threw a fork into the Box o' Death with a rather excessive amount of force. "I am *so* not discussing my private life with you."

"I knew it!" Hope cackled with delight. "You totally did it! You banged Hugh and now you're mated!"

Ivy wheeled on her, face red with embarrassment. "Will you shut up? He's only upstairs, he'll hear you! And no, we did not and we are not and this is none of your business anyway!"

Hope lifted her eyebrows at her sister. "Excuse me, but it definitely is my business. Or are you going to tell me that we're still going to be moving out of Brighton once this is all over?"

Ivy's eyes slid away. She fiddled with the cuff of her glove.

"Well…no," she admitted. "I mean, we haven't worked out all the details yet-"

"Because you were too busy banging," Hope interjected smugly.

Ivy shot her a death glare. "Because it's *complicated*. It's…really complicated."

Something about the way Ivy's voice fell on the last few words made Hope pause. She looked at her sister. Really *looked* at her.

Ivy had been lit up like a neon sign when Hugh had been around, but now that secret glow had guttered out. There were dark smudged circles under her eyes, as if she hadn't slept at all. Hope had assumed that Ivy *had* been up all night…but for reasons that should have left her satisfied and smug, not pale and drawn.

"Ivy," she said in concern, rolling a little closer. "What's wrong?"

Her sister turned away, bracing her hands on the edge of the sink as if it was the only thing keeping her upright. She stared out the window, but Hope was pretty sure she wasn't seeing anything but visions of a certain hot paramedic.

"It's really complicated," she said again, quietly. "I can't say much more than that, Hope. I promised Hugh I wouldn't tell his secrets to anyone. Not even you."

"But you are mated, right?"

Ivy let out a long sigh. "We're mates. But we're not mated. That's all I can—what's she doing here?"

"What?" Hope craned her neck, but her wheelchair was too low down for her to be able to see anything out the window other than sky. "Who?"

"It's one of Gaze's thugs." Ivy had ducked out of sight herself, as if taking cover from a sniper. "She's across the street, staring at the house."

"How do you know she's one of Gaze's people?"

"I recognize her from the party, and she was at the cafe with him yesterday, too. Actually, she asked after you. Tall black girl, cornrows, wears motorbike leathers?"

Hope's heart skipped a beat. *"Betty?"*

Ivy raised an eyebrow at her. "You know her?"

"Betty? Oh w-well, kind of, I guess," Hope stammered. "I mean, yeah, I know her a bit. She goes to my school. We're in some of the same classes. She's my partner. In biology. At school, I mean."

Both of Ivy's eyebrows had now risen. "You're lab partners with a juvenile delinquent?"

"Betty's not a delinquent," Hope said defensively. "She's smart. Really, really smart. And funny and brave and loyal and—" She noticed that Ivy's eyes had narrowed suspiciously, and hastily changed tack. "Um, and just a really good partner. Biology partner. At school. Like I said. Yep."

Was she babbling? Oh God, she was babbling.

"We're more casual acquaintances, really," she finished lamely. She tried to stop there, but couldn't help herself. "Uh, so, you said she asked about me?"

"Yeah." Ivy had gone back to peering suspiciously out the window.

Hope waited, but Ivy didn't say anything further. "Well?" she prompted. "What did she ask? How did she look? Did she seem angry, or worried, or, or—look, just tell me *exactly* what she said and how she said it, okay?"

"If Hugh hadn't vouched for your innocence, I would definitely be worrying about now," Ivy muttered.

"What?"

"Nothing." Ivy let out a long-suffering sigh. "Hope, about this crush—"

"I don't have a crush on Betty!" Hope yelped. "Who said anything about crushes? I just like her for her brain. Because she's so smart. Did I mention she was smart?"

"Yeah, you did. Several times." Ivy rubbed the bridge of her nose as if she had a headache. "Hope, don't you get it? She works for Gaze. No doubt he ordered her to cozy up to you in order to get to me. She was using you."

Hope flinched from the stark statement. It was exactly the fear that had been gnawing at her ever since the disastrous party. The worry that had kept her from responding to any of Betty's increasingly frequent messages.

"Betty wouldn't do that," she said, trying to convince herself. "I'm sure she's not part of anything bad. She's only knows Gaze because his charity runs her shifter orphanage."

Ivy rolled her eyes. "So she's one of his little street minions. Wonderful. And now he has her spying on us."

Hope caught her breath as the truth dawned on her, chasing away her deepening clouds of misery. "No she isn't! She can't be working for Gaze!"

"She is *right there*, Hope. I can see her."

"Exactly! If she was *really* spying on us, you wouldn't! She's a hellhound, she can do their invisibility thing. If she's letting us see her, it's because she wants us to know that she's there."

Ivy stared at her, clearly having only heard one word of this explanation. "Your so-called lab partner is a *what*?"

"Hellhounds aren't all bad, you know," Hope said defensively.

"The clue is in the name! There's a reason they aren't called heavenhounds!"

"Oh, like *you* can talk, wyvern? At least Betty doesn't literally spit acid!"

"What's going on?" Hugh had appeared in the kitchen doorway. He rubbed his eyes, his hair sleep-tousled. "What's all the yelling about?"

"We're being watched," Ivy reported tersely.

The bleariness vanished instantly from Hugh's face, his muscular shoulders tensing. "Gaze?" he asked, striding to join Ivy at the window.

Ivy moved over to give him room, though her right hand twitched as though she'd nearly reached out to touch him. "One of his minions."

"She's *not*—" Hope started, but neither of them was listening to her anymore. They both stared out the window with inhuman, predatory focus.

"*Shifters*," Hope said under her breath, like a swearword. She waved her hands futilely, trying to attract their attention. "Come on, guys. Snap out of it. I'm not going to let you eat Betty."

"I know that girl." Hugh's ice-blue eyes didn't warm at all. "She's the one who called the fire department the other night. She told us that Hope was trapped in the elevator."

"There, see?" Hope said triumphantly. She started to swivel her wheelchair round. "I told you Betty was good. I'm sure she's just here to check that I'm okay. Let me go out and talk to her."

Ivy grabbed onto her handlebars, hauling her back. "You aren't going anywhere. I'll handle this."

Hugh's hand shot out, gripping Ivy's shoulder before she had taken more than a step. To Hope's infinite satisfaction, he held *her* in place.

"I'm not letting you risk yourself," he said. "It could be a trap to lure you out."

"It could be a trap to lure *you* out," Ivy countered, glaring at her mate with the protective possessiveness that Hope knew so well. "You're not going out there alone either."

"Oh, good." Hope folded her arms in exasperation. "So I guess we're all just going to sit here until we run out of food and are reduced to eating cat kibble."

"No." Hugh's jaw tightened. He looked like a soldier steeling himself for a deadly battle. "It's time to call in reinforcements."

CHAPTER 13

"They're here," Rose announced, coming back into the Full Moon's private meeting room. There was a small crease of worry between her eyebrows. "Do you want me to show them up?"

"I'll go down," Hugh said, rising from his seat. "It's best if I prepare them."

"I'll get some drinks then." Rose headed off, shaking her head. "I think we're going to need them."

"I still think it would be better if I wasn't here," Ivy muttered, her face pale above her black scarf. "Hugh, are you really sure about this?"

He squeezed her shoulder, as best he could through the many layers of clothing she was wearing. "It'll be fine. They'll love you, once they get over the shock."

Despite his confident words, his apprehension rose as he descended the stairs. He paused in the corridor behind the bar, squaring his shoulders. Then he pushed open the door.

"Hugh! The man of mystery!" Chase sprang up from a bar stool, his black eyes alight. "What's this all about?"

Hugh winced as the pegasus shifter's electric aura stabbed his senses. Chase's energy was turned up to eleven even at the best of times, and he had clearly spent a *very* enjoyable time with his mate recently.

"Where's Connie?" Hugh asked, glancing around for Chase's wife.

Chase's exuberant grin flickered. "Sorry. She wasn't feeling up to it. She found out all the other mates were going to be here, and, well… you know. It's hard on Connie."

At the other end of the bar, Dai and his mate Virginia were laughing as their eighteen-month-old daughter Morwenna cajoled Fire Commander Ash into a game of peek-a-boo. John stood smiling a little way off, one arm round his own mate, Neridia. The sea dragon knight leaned down to whisper something in his Empress's ear, his other hand gently stroking the proud curve of her pregnant belly.

Hugh winced again, this time out of guilt. Chase and Connie had been trying for a baby for two years now. It had been getting harder and harder for the couple to watch their friends effortlessly spawn.

Hugh had tried to sense what might be going wrong, but the only thing he'd gained had been a splitting migraine. The energies involved in reproductive issues were far too powerful for him to even focus on, let alone handle.

"Sorry," he said to Chase. "For not thinking. And for not being able to do anything."

"You can't fix everything, my friend." Chase clapped his hands, his customary cocky grin springing back again, though there was something a little forced about it. "But enough of that. I normally have to drag you kicking and screaming to the pub, so I'm agog to find out why you've called us all here. What's so urgent? Why did you want us all to bring our mates too? Speak, oh enigmatic one! I breathlessly await your words!"

"Clearly, since you aren't letting him get one in edgeways," Dai said dryly, coming over. "Is Griff joining us too, Hugh? Are we waiting for him?"

Hugh shook his head. "He's busy doing something else. And he already knows what I want to talk to you all about."

Hugh hadn't actually had to do very much explaining, when they'd dropped Hope off again at Griff's house for safekeeping. Griff's eagle eyes had deduced what was going on the instant he saw Hugh and Ivy together.

In fact, from the rather restrained, cautious way that Griff had congratulated them both, Hugh had an uncomfortable suspicion that Griff knew *exactly* what was going on. Still, if the uncannily perceptive griffin shifter *had* worked out why Hugh finding his mate might not be a cause for celebration, he was at least holding his tongue about it.

"Huw! Huw!" Little Morwenna abandoned Ash, toddling over to clutch Hugh's knees. "Up!"

"Morwenna!" Curvy Virginia hurried after her daughter. "You can't just grab Uncle Hugh, he doesn't like it."

"I don't mind her." Hugh picked the child up, putting her on his shoulders. "Want a ride, dragonet?"

She giggled, fisting both hands gleefully into his hair. Despite the tugging, she was actually soothing some of his headache. Her innocent warmth was a tiny oasis of peace amidst the boiling energies of all the adults present.

Hugh took a deep breath, drawing comfort from Morwenna's baby-soft aura. It was time.

"Thank you all for coming at short notice," he said, looking around at them all. "I don't quite know how to say this, but…there's someone upstairs I want you all to meet."

At the back of the group, Ash looked at him sharply, opening his mouth. Chase, however, beat him to it.

"Someone? A *special* someone?" Hugh flinched as Chase slapped him on the shoulder. "You sly dog! Come on, what are we waiting for?"

Before Hugh could stop him, Chase barged past, heading for the stairs. With a lurch of fear, Hugh realized that the pegasus shifter was about to crash in on Ivy without any preparation whatsoever.

"Chase, wait!" Hugh sprinted after him, ducking to avoid hitting Morwenna's head on the low oak beams of the old building. The toddler shrieked with laughter, clutching his face and nearly making Hugh miss his footing. "Stop!"

Too late. Chase had already flung open the door to the private room.

"Welcome!" Chase announced—and stopped dead.

Only the child on his shoulders stopped Hugh from swearing a blue streak. Heedless of the pain, he grabbed Chase's arm, hauling him round. Ivy had flattened herself into the corner, bare hands raised defensively. She must have reflexively yanked off her gloves when Chase had burst into the room.

Hugh interposed his own body in between the two. "Listen, Chase. For once in your life, just listen."

Chase's grin had frozen on his face. "No."

Hugh held onto Chase even though the pain of prolonged contact was near-blinding. "I know this will be hard for you, but—"

"No," Chase said again, flatly. He jerked his arm away, anger glittering in his eyes. "It's not hard, Hugh. It's impossible. That creature hurt my mate."

"*That creature* is *my* mate!"

"Shield-brother, sword-brother, what is amiss?" John had caught up with them, stooping to fit his seven-foot-tall bulk through the door. "If shield-brother Hugh has found his true mate, surely that is—"

He saw Ivy, and froze just as Chase had. "*You.*"

"What is it? Why've you all stopped?" Tall as Neridia was, even she couldn't see over John's shoulder. "John? What's going on?"

John caught his mate as she tried to duck past him. His expression had settled into grim lines. Hugh had a nasty suspicion that if the sea dragon had been carrying his sword, it would have been in his hand by now.

"Stay back, my heart," John said to Neridia, keeping his body between her and Ivy just as Hugh was protecting his own mate from Chase. "That is the wyvern shifter who poisoned Chase's mate. The merest brush of her skin brings death. She taints the very air she breathes."

Hugh's fists clenched. Even though Ivy was behind him, he could sense her shame and misery.

"She's my *mate*," he snarled, hating them all for the way they were staring. "And she needs our help."

"I won't ask you to choose between a friend and your mate, Hugh." Chase turned on his heel, pushing past the others. "Don't ask me to."

"Wait," Ivy called after him, stepping forward. "You don't understand, *Hugh* needs your—"

Hugh caught her hand, squeezing it in warning. They'd agreed—though Ivy had argued against it—that they weren't going to tell the team that Gaze was after him too. It would lead to too many questions about why.

"Let him go, Ivy," he said in defeat. "It's for the best."

"I am sorry, shield-brother," John said, still holding Neridia back. His deep blue eyes were filled with regret. "I owe you my life, and I will gladly assist you in any way that I can. But at the moment my duties to my own mate and Empress take precedence. We too must depart."

"John!" Neridia exclaimed, pushing futilely at his arm. "You're being abominably rude. If this is Hugh's mate, then of course we're going to help her. More than that. We'll welcome her as a new friend, like everyone welcomed me."

"My Empress," John said, turning to her. "You carry our child and the future of the whole sea under your heart. As your Champion and mate, I will not have you in the same room as someone as dangerous as her. We are leaving. Now."

Neridia could only fling a helpless, apologetic look over her shoulder as John steered her out. "I'm so sorry, Hugh, Ivy. I'll try and talk some sense into him."

"In this, you cannot command me, my Empress," John said. He cast a glance at Hugh. "But you still have my sword, shield-brother. Once my Empress is safe under other guard, I will return."

"Don't bother," Hugh spat, incandescent with fury. "If you can't be civil to Ivy, then I have nothing further to say to you."

John bowed his head, his eyes shadowed. "I understand, shield-brother. But you too must understand. No shifter could stand to expose his mate to such danger. I am sorry, but you cannot ask this of us."

Ivy's hand was trembling in his. Hugh gripped her harder, pulling her closer against his side.

"Well?" he said, glaring across the room at Dai, Virginia, and Ash. "Anyone else?"

"Pretty," Morwenna announced from his shoulders. Leaning over, she stretched both chubby fists toward Ivy's green-streaked hair. "Want."

Ivy flung herself out of the toddler's reach, even as Dai lunged. The dragon shifter collided with Hugh, knocking all the breath out of him.

Morwenna wailed in protest as Dai snatched her away. "Noooo! Wenna want!"

Dai's green eyes were ablaze with dragonfire. A hint of red scales rippled over his bare forearms with the instinct to shift to protect his daughter.

"Virginia," he growled, thrusting Morwenna at his mate. "Go back downstairs."

Eyes wide with alarm, Virginia clutched her struggling daughter tight to her chest. "Dai—"

"NOW!" Dai's hands crooked into claws.

"Noooooo!" Morwenna howled, stretching her arms over her mother's shoulder as she was carried away. "Dadda, dadda, daddaaaa!"

"I should go." Ivy's voice shook. "I should never have come."

She took a step toward the door, but stopped dead as a vicious snarl ripped through Dai's throat. His eyes were still a luminous green-gold, his shoulders heaving as he fought to control his dragon.

"Sorry," he gasped, backing away. "Instinct. We'll talk later, Hugh. But John's right. Don't ever bring her near my family again."

That left Ash, and Rose, who'd just reappeared with a tray of drinks. She took one look at the three of them and sighed.

"Well, clearly that went well," she said, putting the tray down on the table. "I've brought you a double Scotch, Hugh. Two, in fact. Sit down, have a drink, and give everyone a little while to cool off. They'll come round eventually. They're your friends, after all."

Hugh took the proffered drink, tossing it back in one swallow. The burn of the whiskey did nothing to soothe the bitter anger tightening his throat.

"I thought they were," he said.

Ivy fumbled for her gloves, pulling them back onto her hands. "I've ruined everything. This isn't going to work, Hugh. Every shifter in the city is going to shun you, just like they do me."

"Oh, sweetheart. Not every shifter." Rose advanced on Ivy with open arms, her soft eyes filled with compassion. "Those silly lads can't help being over-protective idiots when it comes to their mates, but *I'm* not afraid of—"

Ash's hand slammed into the wall. Hugh hadn't even seen him move. One second he'd been standing silently by the door; the next, he was between Ivy and Rose, his arm barring her way.

"No," he said.

"Ash!" Rose shoved hard at his chest, with absolutely no effect. "What do you think you're doing?"

Ash didn't answer her. Wisps of smoke spiraled up from where his bare palm made contact with the wood paneling. He looked over his shoulder, at the white-faced Ivy.

"Leave," he said to her.

"*Ash!*" Rose kicked the most powerful shifter in Europe in the ankle. "You're not my mate, so don't you dare start acting all possessive. This is my house, and I say who is welcome in it!"

Ash continued to ignore the furious swan shifter, his burning gaze fixed only on Ivy. He took his hand off the wall, leaving behind a blackened handprint scorched deep into the wood.

"I will help you if I can," he said, his voice perfectly level. "But you will not come here again."

Hugh reached for Ivy, grasping her gloved hand. With his other, he fumbled in his pocket, for the identification he always carried.

"Don't worry." He flung his firefighter badge at Ash's feet as he pulled Ivy out the door. "We won't."

CHAPTER 14

Six unhappy cats trapped in carriers and crammed into the back of a small car were not shy about making their displeasure known. Ivy was grateful for the cacophony of feline complaints. It made conversation impossible during the long, uncomfortable journey.

Hugh drove with single-minded focus, his eyes fixed on the road ahead and his jaw tight with anger. He'd barely said a word since he'd tossed a grenade and walked away from the smoking ruins of his life. He hadn't so much as glanced back as Brighton had disappeared behind them.

I destroy everything I touch. Ivy stared unseeing out the side window. She couldn't look at Hugh's grim, set profile without guilt churning in her gut. *This is all my fault. I shouldn't let him do this.*

Why not? In contrast to her own black mood, her wyvern was positively jubilant. *Good mate. Good plan. Old territory too dangerous. Find a new lair, where our treasures will be safe.*

Her wyvern did have a point. They had to be safer out here in the middle of nowhere than they were in the heart of Gaze's territory. Surely even his influence couldn't stretch across half of England.

They were hundreds of miles from Brighton by now, in the ridiculously pretty hills and forests of the Wye Valley. It felt like they'd travelled back about four hundred years in time, too. The meandering road was the only sign of the modern world. Even the few villages that they passed through were just teeny thatched cottages clustered around crumbling medieval churches. Ivy, who had spent all her life in big cities, couldn't shake an impression that the entire landscape had been Photoshopped.

"At the risk of sounding like a cliché," Hope said from the back seat. "Are we there yet?"

"Nearly." Hugh turned down an even narrower country lane. "My parents' place is just over the next rise."

"Are you really sure this is a good idea?" Ivy couldn't help asking. "I mean, just the fact that we've run is going to tip Gaze off that…uh, you know. Confirm his suspicion."

"His suspicion about what?" Hope asked.

"Nothing," Ivy said quickly.

She hadn't told her sister Hugh's secret, and she didn't intend to. Hope would only start spamming Instagram with unicorn pictures or something equally dumb.

Hope glared at her in the rear-view mirror. "I can tell when you're not telling me something important, you know. I'm not a little kid. You can trust me with whatever's really going on."

"Says the girl who made friends with a basilisk crime lord," Ivy muttered.

"I heard that!"

"You were meant to." Ivy turned back to Hugh. "Anyway, if Gaze does chase us, I don't want to bring trouble to your parents' door. Won't your family be the first place he'd look? Maybe we should keep driving. Pick a random destination."

Hugh shook his head with a tight, curt motion. "I want to take you somewhere secure. My parents' house is…protected, shall we say. Generations of my family have lived on that land. There's a strong bond between us and the soil."

Hope perked up. "Ooooh. Are they farmers? Are we going to a farm?"

Hugh hesitated. "It's like a farm. Anyway, the land itself is an ally. Shifters can't even cross the property boundary without permission from the family. In the unlikely event that Gaze does track us down, he won't be able to get in. But I don't think he will be able to locate us. It's not easy to find out who my parents are."

"I hate to break it to you," Ivy said, "but there's this thing called Google."

Hugh's mouth quirked. "Which will tell you that Hugh Argent is a deeply private individual with no apparent digital footprint. Mainly because he's fictional. Argent isn't my real last name."

She blinked at him. "What?"

"I didn't want people to be able to easily trace me back to my family. Just in case."

"Just in case of what?" Hope asked.

Just in case anyone worked out he's a unicorn, Ivy realized. If Hugh's secret ever was discovered, it would be open hunting season on his family too.

"Wait," Ivy said as a thought suddenly struck her. "Are there more, uh, people like you in your family?"

"More people like *what?*" Hope was sounding increasingly suspicious. "You mean healers?"

"I'm the only medical professional at the moment," Hugh said, which Ivy interpreted to mean that he was the only unicorn. "But my father was, ah, in the same business. He's not anymore, of course."

"Of course," Ivy echoed.

Naturally, Hugh's father couldn't be a unicorn shifter anymore. Hugh was the living proof of that. Though she supposed he *could* have been a test tube baby. He'd said that solo activities didn't count.

She flattened her gloved hand over her stomach, catching her breath at a sudden vision of a beautiful baby with unicorn-white hair and wyvern-green eyes...but that was just a fantasy. Even if Hugh could donate his side of the necessary materials, she could never carry his child. Her body was as useful as a vat of cyanide when it came to growing a baby.

And anyway, I'd make a terrible mother, she thought bleakly. It wasn't like she'd grown up with a good role model, after all.

Hugh slowed the car as they turned into a graveled road lined with ancient oaks. "We're nearly there," he said. "And this is probably the point that I should mention something."

Ivy looked at the trees, which were planted way too evenly to be natural. The rolling fields and scattered copses beyond them were also much too artfully photogenic. The whole landscape looked suspiciously designed.

"Hugh," she said. "When you said your parents had a farm, I was picturing something a lot muddier."

Hugh cleared his throat. "I said it was *like* a farm. Well, actually, it's quite a few farms. More of an estate, technically. And that's my parents' house up ahead now."

Ivy followed the line of his pointing finger…and her jaw dropped.

A vast building rose in stately splendor amidst intricate formal knot gardens. The flowerbeds were bare and frost-touched at this time of year, but the low hedges were still immaculately pruned into eye-waveringly complex mazes. The setting sun glittered from dozens upon dozens of tall, elegant windows, and gilded the warm yellow stones of the ancient manor house.

If it was a manor house. Quite possibly it was technically a castle. It had honest-to-God *turrets*.

Speechless, Ivy stared from the towering building to Hugh. He looked moderately embarrassed, as if he'd just been forced to reveal that he had foot fungus.

"My real name is Hugh Montgomery Fitzroy Silver," he said as they passed under an ornate archway with huge, open iron gates topped with a heraldic crest. "And my father is the fourteenth Earl of Hereford."

CHAPTER 15

We should have told her, Hugh's unicorn murmured reproachfully.

You think I don't know that? Hugh retorted in annoyance as he helped Ivy carry Hope's wheelchair up the steep front steps and into the manor house.

He'd been fretting for the past fifty miles about how to break the news. *Oh, by the way, when you meet my parents you should technically address them as Lord and Lady Hereford* wasn't exactly an easy thing to drop into casual conversation. Especially not when he'd been trying to avoid thinking about what going back home was going to mean. In the end, his mounting dread had kept him tongue-tied until the absolute last minute.

He watched anxiously as Hope and Ivy stared around the cavernous entrance hall, trying to gauge their expressions. Hope looked frankly shell-shocked. Ivy maintained a better poker face, but she had a death-grip on the handlebars of Hope's wheelchair, as if she was having to lean on it for support.

"Now *that* is a Christmas tree," Hope said faintly, staring up at the twenty-foot gold-decked monstrosity that took pride of place between the two sweeping curves of the double staircase.

"It's too early," Ivy muttered. "By Christmas Day, that sucker's going to be bare twigs and a mountain of needles."

"Oh, my dear, this one is just for show," said a familiar voice. "We always replace it with another one for Christmas itself."

"Mother," Hugh said warmly, stepping forward to take her outstretched hands.

Her familiar lilac perfume enfolded him as she kissed his cheek. "Welcome home, my son."

As always, the touch of her long, elegant fingers sent an odd vibration through his own. It wasn't uncomfortable, precisely; just a disconcerting awareness of deeply-buried but still powerful energies, something like walking over a cold, dormant volcano.

It was probably odd to be disappointed by the fact that one's own mother was still celibate.

Not that he *wanted* her to give him a migraine, but he did want her to be happy—whether it was with his father or not. Preferably not, in fact.

But judging by his mother's touch and aura, she was still living like a nun. With a slight sigh, Hugh released her hands with a parting squeeze.

"Thank you for accommodating us at such short notice," he said.

"This is your house as much as ours, Hugh. You're the future fifteenth Earl, after all." She looked past him at Ivy and Hope. "Won't you introduce me to your…friends?"

Hugh noticed the slight hesitation, and the small crease that appeared between her eyebrows as she looked Ivy in particular up and down. He'd never brought anyone back to the estate before, let alone an undeniably beautiful young woman. Even though he hadn't told his mother what Ivy truly meant to him, she was fully capable of reading between the lines.

His unicorn stamped a hoof in irritation. *Our dam should not have to infer the truth. We should not be trying to hide our mate. She is our mate! We should proclaim that to the whole world with pride!*

Oh, shut up, he snapped back. *I'm not ashamed of Ivy. It's just…private.*

It would only worry his mother if he told her that he'd found his mate. She knew all too well what it meant.

Plus, it might lead to a discussion of *feelings*, and that was just too mortifying to contemplate.

"This is Hope, the girl that I'm treating," he said. "And this is her sister and caretaker, Ivy."

Damn. Despite his best efforts, his voice had softened on Ivy's name. His mother cast him a sharp sideways glance, her eyebrows drawing down still further. Her forehead smoothed out as she turned back to her guests, though, her perfect hostess smile sliding back into place.

"Hugh mentioned that you were, shall we say, in something of a predicament," his mother said to Ivy and Hope. "You are of course very welcome to stay here for as long as you like. Though," she added, her gaze flicking down over Hope's wheelchair, "I am afraid that this house is not the most accessible of buildings. I do hope you will not be too inconvenienced. Is there anything I can do to make your visit more comfortable, Hope?"

Hope stared up at his mother in tongue-tied awe. She looked as though the Queen herself had inquired after her well-being. Her wide eyes flicked to him, silently begging for rescue.

"I'm sure we'll be fine," Ivy said, before he could say anything. Hugh's heart swelled with pride at the way she lifted her chin, refusing to be intimidated by either his aristocratic mother or the grandeur all around. "Thank you very much for your hospitality, uh…your…"

"Technically it's Lady Hereford." His mother waved a hand, brushing the title away like a fly. "But simply Margaret is fine."

"We'll stick with Lady Hereford, thanks," Ivy said firmly. She hesitated. "Uh, just for future reference, what are we supposed to call your husband? The, um, Earl?"

"Hopefully, nothing," Hugh said. "But if you do happen to cross paths, feel free to use any obscenity that happens to spring to mind."

"Hugh," his mother said, a shade reproachfully.

"Sorry." *Not sorry.* "I take it he's at home, then."

"I'm afraid so. I didn't know you'd be coming, or I would have encouraged…alternative arrangements." She waved a hand round at the lavish swags of holly and glittering baubles adorning every pillar and beam of the entrance hall. "But as you can see, he's needed here at the main house this week."

"I did think the decorations were a bit much, even for us," he said, wrinkling his nose at the appalling tree. "I take it the Christmas Ball is imminent?"

Hope's eyes widened even further. "Shut *up*. An actual ball? For real?"

"For charity, in fact," his mother said, smiling. "My husband and I hold it every year, and it's always one of our most successful fundraisers. Even in this day and age, there are still people will pay quite handsomely for the chance to meet an Earl."

"More fool them," Hugh muttered.

"As you may have realized, my son has a very low opinion of his elevated position," his mother said to Ivy and Hope, rather dryly. "In any event, you would both be very welcome to attend the festivities, of course."

Hope looked like all her Christmases had come at once, but Ivy's expression betrayed her dismay.

"Didn't Hugh tell you about me?" she said. "I can't be around crowds."

"I understand that you share my son's need for personal space, albeit for slightly different reasons," his mother said delicately. She cast a significant glance at the discretely unobtrusive butler busy ferrying cases and cat carriers in from the car behind them. "I have informed the staff of your special requirements. You may rest assured that everyone here will respect your privacy."

The butler had disappeared outside again, but Hugh lowered his voice anyway. "They don't know about us. No shifters on the estate. And don't worry about the ball. I'm not going either."

His mother pursed her lips, looking slightly pained. "You know I would never ask you to put yourself in an uncomfortable situation,

Hugh. But it would mean a great deal to your father if you would at least put in a token appearance."

He cocked an ironic eyebrow at her. "You do realize that's an excellent reason not to, as far as I'm concerned?"

"Hugh, I'm pretty sure we need to talk," Ivy muttered under her breath.

"I too am beginning to feel that there is much my son has neglected to tell you," his mother said, shooting him a somewhat sardonic glance. "Hope, dear, let's go and get you settled into your rooms. Hugh, I think perhaps the Chinese Bedroom would suit Ivy."

The Chinese Bedroom was, he noted with dark amusement, the furthest it was possible to be from his own suite without actually being in the stables. His mother *had* picked up on the vibe between the two of them.

He drew his mother aside under the pretext of sorting out the suitcases. "You don't have to guard my virtue," he murmured into her ear. "I do have *some* willpower, you know."

Her gaze flicked to Ivy. "Does she?"

"More than you can possibly imagine." He touched his mother's stiff shoulder, wishing with all his heart that his powers could soothe her anguish. "You don't have to fret, Mother. I'm not going to turn into my father."

"I'm not worried about that." Her expression was as controlled as ever, but her blue eyes betrayed her hidden sadness. "I'm worried that she might turn into me."

CHAPTER 16

The bed had damask hangings.

At least, that's what Ivy suspected the richly-embroidered gold curtain-thingies were. The only place she had previously encountered carved four-poster beds was in fairy tales, where they had inevitably been described as having 'damask hangings.' She had a sudden mad urge to search for a pea underneath the two-foot-thick mattress.

Hugh put her battered suitcase down on the oriental rug, where it immediately lowered the tone of the entire room. Closing the door, he leaned against it as though barricading out the whole world.

"I'm sorry," he said.

"For all this?" Ivy gestured round at the preposterous surroundings. Excluding her suitcase, she was fairly certain she was the youngest thing in the room by several centuries. "You know, I don't know why I'm surprised. You're a unicorn. Of course you come from a castle."

He let out a long sigh, raking a hand back through his hair. "I still should have warned you. I was just terrified that if I told you the truth about my family, you'd refuse to come."

"Well, I probably would have done," she had to admit. "Hugh, your mother is much more gracious about the whole thing than I could have hoped. But I can't possibly stay here."

"Why not?" He took a step forward, a hopeful, entreating light in his eyes. "It's private. Secluded. The estate boundaries are secure, and we carefully vet everyone allowed into our territory. There aren't any shifters apart from ourselves. You'd be free to be yourself, without having to worry about endangering anyone."

She knew that what he said made sense. A dangerous freak like her *should* be locked away in a remote castle, where she couldn't hurt anyone. But to narrow her world down to one house, and a bare handful of people…something deep in her soul recoiled in horror from the thought. A cage was still a cage, no matter how beautiful the bars were.

Hugh would be here, she tried to reason with herself. *It wouldn't be so bad.*

And maybe it wouldn't be…if they could touch.

"What about you?" she asked. "Could *you* be happy here? I got the impression you don't come home very often."

His shoulders tensed a little. He went to the window, brushing back the brocade curtains in order to stare out into the dusk. On this side of the house, the trees crept close to the walls, their tangled branches black and bare. There were no signs of other human habitation, or artificial lights. They might have been the only two people in the world, surrounded by forest older than time.

"I ran away from all this," he said quietly. "I told myself that I was going out into the world to use my talents, that it was my duty…but in some ways, I was just running away from my other duties. Maybe it's time for me to work out a way to balance them both."

He turned back to her, a forced smile stretching his face. "My mother's renowned for her charity work. I'm sure she could find a role for me in one of her projects which would give me an excuse to visit the local hospitals. I could still go out and heal people. I'd just be working undercover. On my own."

She thought of the tight camaraderie of Alpha Team—before she'd ruined it all—and her heart broke for him. But he was standing so straight and tall, so determinedly putting a brave face on things, that she couldn't bring herself to argue with him.

He was willing to sacrifice everything for her. How could she tell him that she didn't want him to?

"Okay," she forced out, through her tightening throat. She matched his smile, attempting to make a joke of it. "But I honestly have no idea what I'm going to do here. Unless your parents could use another maid."

"We do have a lot of toilets," he agreed solemnly. "If you're truly missing your old job, I'm sure I could find you some bleach."

She threatened him with one of the tasseled pillows. He raised his hands in surrender, his smile finally reaching his eyes.

"More seriously," she said, tossing the pillow back on the bed. "If I *am* going to stay here, there's clearly a few secrets you still need to tell me. Like just what's up between you and your father."

"Ah." He dropped down into a richly-upholstered armchair, wincing. "Yes. Though that's not so much a secret as just dirty laundry. Not something the family airs in public."

"I'm not public." She perched on the bed opposite him. "And believe me, your family can't possibly be more dysfunctional than mine."

He raised a wry eyebrow at her. "Want to bet?"

"My mom's in shifter jail for murder," she said simply.

He stared at her, his mouth half-open.

"Right," he said, after a beat. "You win. Good Lord. Who did she murder?"

"Hope's dad." The words came easily, the plain facts worn smooth by time. She'd long ago abandoned any anger or sadness about this part of their past. "We don't have the same biological father. Our mom always just shacked up with a guy for a few months and then moved on. She did it for their own good—she could control her venom pretty well, but she was worried about small doses building up over time."

"I can only imagine that prolonged intimate contact with a wyvern shifter isn't good for one's health," Hugh said. "Present company excepted, of course."

"Anyway, she didn't exactly have good taste in men. Mostly they were just deadbeats, but Hope's dad was different. Dangerous. A viper shifter, and a crime boss, kinda like Gaze. He'd use visitation rights to Hope as an excuse to try to pressure Mom into making him poisons and stuff. Sometimes she'd do it, sometimes she wouldn't. Then, one day when Hope was ten, our mother said no to him once too often. There was a fight." Ivy shrugged. "And she killed him."

"In self-defense, though, one assumes," Hugh said, looking rather wide-eyed by this tale. "Yet she was still jailed for it?"

"Oh, she deserved it," Ivy said, shrugging again. "She could have just paralyzed him if she'd wanted to. But she always had better control over her venom than her temper. Anyway, it was just lucky that I was eighteen and a legal adult by then. It took some fighting, but I got custody of Hope. It's been just us ever since."

Hugh stared up at the ceiling for a long moment. "Suddenly my family dramas seem rather pathetic."

"Well, I told you mine, so now you have to tell me yours." She lifted her eyebrows at him expectantly. "So come on. Why do you hate your father so much?"

He blew out his breath. "You may have noticed that my mother doesn't give me a headache."

Now that she thought about it, it *was* a bit weird how casually he'd accepted his mother's embrace. She'd seen enough of him by now to know that he was nearly as jumpy about touching people as she was.

"I'm assuming you weren't a miraculous virgin birth," she said. "So I'm guessing that just means that your mother, uh, isn't that into certain activities at her time of life."

"She hasn't given me a headache since I was a very small child." The corner of his mouth twisted. "Being in the same room as my father, on the other hand, gives me a splitting migraine."

She blinked at him for a second, not getting it. Then the penny dropped.

"Oh," she said. "*Oh.*"

"Precisely." His mouth tightened into a tense line, an old anger shadowing his eyes. "She's chaste. He isn't."

"Ouch. They aren't true mates then."

"One can only assume not. But that doesn't mean that she doesn't love him, though God only knows why." His lip curled. "I suppose I should be grateful that he at least has the decency to be discreet about his infidelities. If it wasn't for my sensitivities, I doubt I'd know about them. My parents have always led mostly separate existences. Mother and me up here in the main house, Father off on the other side of the estate in the Dowager House. His absence spared me from constant headache…but not my mother from constant heartache. I will never forgive him for that. *Never.*"

The ragged catch in his voice tugged at her own heart. More than anything, she wanted to go over to him, hold him tight and kiss away the pain of the past. But she didn't dare. She was all too aware that they were alone together in a bedroom, just one temptation away from disaster.

From the heat kindling in Hugh's eyes as his gaze swept over her, he was having much the same realization. He adjusted his position, abruptly stiff and awkward.

"Anyway." His practiced, ironic smile flashed like a knife, killing the intimacy trembling between them. "That's why I avoid my father. At least the feeling is mutual. He can't stand to look at me either. But don't worry. He'll *love* you."

She couldn't tell from his bitter tone whether he was being sarcastic or not. "That would be a first. Why?"

"Because you're his big chance. This is the man who took me to a brothel the day I turned eighteen, Ivy. He's tried a thousand ways to pressure me into losing my unicorn. He claims that it's a matter of necessity, that it's my duty to sire an heir to ensure that the family line will continued unbroken. But I think he's just jealous."

"Because you're a unicorn shifter?"

"I have what he lost, and it must eat him alive that I won't give it up." He grimaced. "To be honest, there have been times in my life when I only clung onto my unicorn out of sheer spite. I wanted to keep on hurting him, the way that he keeps on hurting my mother."

"Hugh, this is bad," she said, real fear gripping her stomach. She knew how to face down criminals and lowlifes, but an Earl? Under his own roof? "He's going to work out what we are to each other eventually. What am I supposed to do if he starts pressuring *me*?"

"I won't let him do that," he said with fierce intensity, all his black, barbed humor dropping away. "Don't worry about it."

"But—"

In a single swift movement, he crossed the room. His hands cradled her face, and her half-formed words fell away, burned into ash by the heat of his touch.

"Don't worry about it," he said again. "I can handle my father. He won't bother you."

He was so close that she could feel his breath on her lips. She had to close her eyes, fisting her hands in the coverlet to stop herself from reaching out to him.

He released her again, though she could feel the effort it cost him. "Trust me, you won't even have to meet him. It's perfectly possible to avoid someone for years in this place." His tone was light, but his eyes were still dark with desire. "It's rather a big house."

She let out a shaky laugh, sliding off the bed. "That's the understatement of the century. Come on. Your mother will think we got lost."

"Don't joke. It's a genuine hazard." Hugh held the door open for her. "Once when I was seven, I took a wrong turn in the attic and went missing for two days. They eventually found me trying to make a fire out of an eighteenth century escritoire and a vintage Chanel ballgown. My mother was livid about the ballgown."

She hesitated as she passed, looking up into his face. Despite his light-hearted manner, a cold sense of unease still lurked in the pit of her own stomach. Her wyvern arched its barbed tail, ready to strike.

Defend, her beast snarled. *Protect our own. Kill any threat.*

"It's all right, Ivy," Hugh said softly. Leaning down, he brushed the lightest, gentlest of kisses on her forehead. "You're safe here. I promise."

Far away in Brighton, a dot blinked on a satellite map, marking a location deep in the Wye Valley. Gaze leaned back in his office chair, regarding his laptop thoughtfully.

"Well now," he murmured to himself. "Isn't that interesting."

A few clicks confirmed that the GPS tracker he'd had planted in Hugh Argent's car hadn't moved for several hours. A few more clicks revealed further information about their final destination. Some very interesting information.

He idly turned his mirrored sunglasses over in his hands, thinking. A slow smile spread over his face.

Picking up his cellphone, he dialed his personal assistant, the one that he used for his legitimate work under a squeaky clean fake identity. He'd talk to his *other* assistants later.

But first…he needed tickets to a ball.

CHAPTER 17

The problem with being whisked away to a life of luxury in a fabulous ancient mansion was, Ivy had decided, the bathrooms. Namely, how long they took to reach. Even with Hugh showing her the way, the nearest one to her bedroom was a good five minute hike.

On her own, in the middle of the night, it was a lot longer than that. And now she'd taken a wrong turn on the way back, and had been wandering in increasingly confused circles for what felt like hours. She was pretty sure she'd somehow ended up in an entirely different wing of the house, and possibly on a different floor too.

"Crud," she muttered to herself, swinging her cellphone flashlight around. She'd definitely already walked through this portrait gallery before. Generations of disapproving unicorns glowered down at her from the oak-paneled walls.

Next time I'm bringing a ball of string. Or possibly a trail of breadcrumbs.

Picking what was hopefully a new direction, she set off again. The house was silent around her, her every breath echoing in her own ears. She half-expected a headless ghost to come drifting down the corridor any second.

I wish one would. Then I could ask it for directions.

She turned a corner, and her heart lifted at the sight of a faint yellow glow, shining like a lighthouse beacon from a half-open door. Despite the late hour, someone was still up.

"Uh, hello?" she called as she approached. "Sorry, I'm a guest. I got lost. Could you tell me-"

She froze in the doorway, the words dying in her throat.

A man sat reading in a wingback armchair, his hair gleaming pure silver in the warm light of the single lamp. She knew those pale blue eyes, those finely-modeled features, those cheekbones sharp enough to cut. For a breathtaking second, it was like she looked through time, and saw Hugh as he would be decades from now.

But then the man turned his head, meeting her eyes, and he was nothing like Hugh at all.

It was like the difference between a living animal and one stuffed and mounted behind glass. The same general shape, the same colors, but stiff and frozen in a parody of itself. The coldness that she'd occasionally seen in Hugh's eyes was nothing compared to the glacier-thick ice in this man's gaze.

"You are the wyvern," said Hugh's father, the Earl of Hereford.

Venom slicked her palms, seeping into her gloves. Her inner beast was snarling, recoiling in fear and revulsion, every spine bristling. Every instinct screamed at her that this man was wrong, wrong, a black void where a person should be.

Caught between fight and flight reflexes, Ivy could only freeze as Hugh's father rose. His empty stare swept over her, examining her from head to toe. His expression never changed, but he nodded slightly, as if he'd come to a decision.

"I will pay you ten thousand pounds to sleep with my son," the Earl said.

Sheer outrage broke her paralysis. "You think I'd betray Hugh for *money?*"

"Land, then. Or position." The Earl turned away as if bored, absently running a long finger over the leather-bound books lining the wall. "What is it that you want?"

"I'll tell you what I want." Ivy took a step toward him, clenching her gloved fists. "I want you to back off and leave Hugh alone. He's told me about you. I'm not some pawn you can use against him, you jealous bastard. Mess with him again and you'll be messing with *me*. And I'm not nearly as good a person as he is."

"Ah." The Earl's thin lips curved slightly in a humorless smile. "So you love him."

"Yeah, I do," Ivy spat. "And I won't ever let you hurt him."

The Earl's shoulders rose and fell in a long sigh. "I am not trying to hurt him. I am trying to save him."

"Well, you sure have a funny way of going about it."

The Earl picked up a book, turning it in his elegant hands. "I am the only person who understands him. Who knows precisely what he faces, every day. Tell me, wyvern. Do you know what it is to live with constant pain?"

Ivy hesitated, Hope's thin face flashing across her mind. "Not personally. But my sister does. I know what she endures."

"No," the Earl said flatly. "You do not. Until you have lived in pain, until it has been your faithful companion, close to you as your own bones, then you do not know. I do. And I will do everything in my power to save my son from that torment. If you truly care for him, so will you."

"He doesn't *want* to be saved, asshole."

"I know he does not." The Earl put the book back, toying with the next one instead. "I did not either. I fought my own father for years, certain that I was right. Certain that nothing was worth giving up my unicorn. Swearing that I was never going to turn into *him*."

He took a few steps away, brushing a hand over the back of his armchair, lean and restless as a caged wolf. He didn't seem to be able to stay still for very long. There were deep, bruised shadows under his eyes. Ivy wondered if he was always awake at this time of night, and how much he slept.

"I held out until my mid twenties," the Earl said, not looking at her. "Longer than most of us. Nearly as long as Hugh, in fact. But then my father died, and I inherited the estate. I became responsible for a precious treasure, this land that all my forebears loved before me. It was my responsibility to provide an heir. Even if it meant losing my unicorn. And when I did...I finally learned what it was to live without pain."

He lifted his head, turning to meet her gaze straight-on. There was not a shadow of regret or uncertainty in his clear blue eyes.

"It was worth it," he said.

"Yeah, apparently it was so great that you've been enthusiastically losing your unicorn ever since," Ivy said in disgust. "Don't try and make yourself out to be some hero. Hugh *knows*. He can't help but know. He told me that you're unfaithful to your wife. Is that some ancient noble tradition you have to uphold too?"

His hand tightened on the back of the chair, knuckles whitening.

"I should be grateful," he murmured softly, as if to himself, "that he still hasn't worked out the truth."

"What truth?" she asked suspiciously, suspecting some sort of trap.

He didn't reply for a moment, for once standing perfectly still. Then he let out a long, low sigh.

"I will tell you, because I would not see anyone hurt the same way that I have hurt my wife," he said. "But you must promise that you will not tell this to Hugh."

"No deal," Ivy said promptly. "There's no secrets between us."

His mouth quirked a little, just like Hugh's did when something struck his dark sense of humor. "Knowing my son, I very much doubt that." He gazed at her in consideration for a moment longer. "But I will tell you anyway. Because I think that you truly do love him. And you will realize that this secret would only hurt him."

"Now I'm not sure *I* want to hear whatever it is," she muttered. "But go ahead. Tell me your so-noble reason why you can't keep it in your pants."

"Because none of us can. When the unicorn...departs, it leaves a hole." He fisted one of his hands, right over his heart. "There is only one thing that can fill that aching absence. Even then, the warmth only lasts a short time. A unicorn cannot stand human touch. An ex-unicorn, however, cannot live without it."

Ivy folded her arms, unimpressed. "So touch your wife, jackass."

The Earl's expression shifted only a fraction, but suddenly she could see the old, deep sadness behind that frozen mask. Her wyvern fell silent, wings half-spread, tail lowering uncertainly.

"I would," he said. "But then she could not touch Hugh."

...*Oh.*

"I see that you understand," the Earl said quietly. "Hugh's unicorn is very powerful. For most of us, the sensitivity does not develop until six or seven, but he was flinching away from the unchaste even as an infant. Can you imagine a baby wailing and struggling in his own mother's arms, unable to bear her touch? It near broke my wife's heart when I revealed the reason. I had not told her of the family curse before then. She didn't even know about shifters."

"You didn't tell her what you were?" To hide something so fundamental from your partner felt wrong to Ivy. "You let her take your unicorn without any explanation at all?"

He shook his head. "She was not the one to take my unicorn. I did not want to lay that burden on anyone I cared for, let alone loved. By the time I met my wife, I had been a normal man for several years. I had hoped that I would never have to tell her that I had ever been otherwise. Sometimes, the curse skips a generation. But not this time."

He turned away, going back to his restless pacing. "I could not ask her to choose me over our son. I did not *want* her to do so. I attempted to be abstinent as well, for Hugh's sake, but it nearly drove me mad. My wife proposed a solution. I did not want to accept...but I had no choice."

No one knew better than Ivy what it was like to be trapped in an impossible situation, with no good options. Nonetheless, her shoulders drew up around her ears. It was a shifter thing. Infidelity disgusted her on a visceral level.

The Earl cast her a rather sardonic look. "And now you are thinking that *you* would prefer madness or death to betraying your own life-partner. I know that Hugh shares your opinion. He has never been shy about letting me know just how much I revolt him. He is right to despise me. But not for the reason he thinks. I am not unfaithful to my wife, Ivy. I have never been unfaithful."

The blatant falsehood put her hackles up again. She'd come so close to dropping her guard, even to sympathizing with him. Now she suspected it had all been an act.

"According to Hugh, you give him migraines," she said. "And your wife doesn't. You aren't going to be able to persuade me he's lying, so how do you explain *that?*"

He remained unruffled by her accusing tone. "Did Hugh also tell you what triggers the pain?"

"Yeah." Damn it, she was certain she was blushing. "Orgasms."

"Precisely." The Earl didn't look at her, focusing instead on his fidgeting hands. "I trigger extreme pain in Hugh because I do one of the most selfish, perverted acts imaginable. I take, and give nothing in return. The energy that should flow between myself and my wife, freely and joyously, instead concentrates in me like stagnant water. My wife sees to my needs, Ivy. But I do nothing for hers."

She flinched again, but this time her revulsion wasn't directed at the Earl himself. She hadn't thought that there could be anything worse than not being able to be touched at all, but now she wasn't so sure. To turn what should be the deepest expression of love into some grim, mechanical act, where your partner took no joy in it herself... the Earl was right. It *was* a perversion.

Hugh wouldn't want this for either of his parents. Ivy knew that, down to her bones. But what would it do to him if she told him the real reason his parents were estranged? That it wasn't because of any infidelity, but rather due to Hugh's very existence?

She let out her breath, slowly. "You're right," she said. "I won't tell him this secret. It *would* only hurt him. But he's not a little kid now, you know. He's lived out in the world, surrounded by the unchaste, and managed to survive. Neither you nor your wife have to make this sacrifice anymore."

He cast her one of those razor-sharp, bitter smiles. "The thought has occurred to me. But my wife has spent her life sacrificing herself for the good of others. She would never put her own pleasure above the well-being of her child, no matter that he is a grown man. And she and Hugh have such a close relationship...how can I even think of asking her to consider jeopardizing that? How can I demand that she inflict pain upon our son, just because it pains me to be unable to please her fully?"

"I'm sorry for you both," Ivy said, meaning it. "But I'm still not going to do what you want. I believe that you really think that it would be best if Hugh lost his unicorn. But it *wouldn't*."

The Earl's expression frosted over, that brief glimpse of anguish hidden once more behind thick walls of ice. "For him, or for you, wyvern?"

"What?"

"My wife told me of your nature." He gestured at her gloved hands. "I know that Hugh is immune to your uncontrollable venom. And I do not doubt that you have realized that if he did lose his unicorn, he would no longer be able to touch you at all."

That dark thought *had* occurred to Ivy, during that one precious, shining hour when she'd lain in Hugh's arms, tracing his tattoos. A treacherous little whisper in her mind: *I can do this. I can be strong.*

Because if I give in, I'll lose everything too.

"I-yes, that's true," she stammered, her face heating with shame. "But that's not why—"

"Then prove it," the Earl demanded, a strange intensity burning in his eyes. "Prove you truly love my son. Take his unicorn, and then leave him, for both your sakes. Free him from his suffering. You may not think it now, but your own curse is a blessing in disguise. It will save you from a lifetime pouring out your heart into an emptiness you will never be able to fill. You have no future with my son, Ivy. Whether you sleep with him or not, you will never be enough for him."

"I am!" Ivy shot back, her own anger rising again. "I'm his mate!"

The Earl froze. "Is this true?"

"Yeah." She planted her hands on her hips, facing him head-on. "So you're stuck with me, like it or not. I'm his true mate, and he's mine."

The light in his eyes disappeared, snuffed out like a candle. "Then you are no use to me whatsoever."

She opened her mouth to retort—but paused, as something about his tone struck her. He didn't sound accusing, or angry. Just resigned.

"Why?" she asked.

The Earl didn't answer for a moment. He rubbed his hands over his face, hiding his expression.

"I am less noble than I thought," he said, his tone heavy. "I never told Hugh, because I didn't want him to waste his life on a wild goose chase. And now I find myself tempted not to tell you."

"Tell me *what?*" Ivy demanded.

He dropped his hands with a sigh. He looked suddenly hollow, as if she'd scooped out whatever hope remained in his heart.

"Even if you sleep with my son, you won't break his curse," he said. "You're his true mate. You *can't* take his unicorn."

CHAPTER 18

"He's lying," Hugh said flatly.

He hadn't thought he could hate his father any more. He'd been wrong.

To brutally raise Ivy's hopes like this, all in the hope of tricking her into taking his unicorn...even for his father, it was beyond cruel.

"I don't think he is, Hugh." Ivy twisted her gloved hands together, her face pale.

She'd been evasive and on edge all day, but he'd put that down to apprehension about the ball this evening. He knew how much she feared crowds. But now it was clear that something else had been on her mind. Something much worse.

"Your father showed me some documents from your family archives this afternoon, while you were busy working on Hope," Ivy continued. "Stuff from the time of the third Earl. Private love letters, calling his wife *my mate*. And one single letter from a friend, thanking him for healing a relative. Written three years *after* the Earl married. Your father has evidence that supports his theory."

"He has lies!" His fists clenched, as though he could physically fight the false hope rising, treacherously, in his own mind. "It's a trick.

Forgeries. It isn't true. It can't be true. He just wants an heir for his precious estate. He'd say anything to dupe me into providing one."

"Hugh, he..." Ivy stopped, as if she'd thought better of whatever she'd been about to say. "Never mind. Look, forget about your dad for a minute. What does your unicorn say?"

He didn't want to turn his attention inward, for fear of what he might find. Taking a deep breath, he made himself do it anyway.

Well? he said to his inner animal.

Its sapphire eyes were as steady as always. *She is our mate. We are her mate.*

"You bastard beast, that's not an answer!" He realized that he'd roared the words out loud, and forced himself to moderate his voice. "Are we torturing ourselves for nothing? Is it true that you wouldn't be destroyed if we mated? That I'd still be able to heal?"

The great head bowed. The light from its horn dimmed a little, like a cloud passing over the moon.

I do not know, his unicorn said softly. *All I know is that she is our mate. Nothing else matters.*

"It *does!*" Unable to restrain his frustration, he slammed a fist into the wall, caving a hole into a decorative plasterwork panel. "Damn you!"

"I take it that wasn't a productive conversation," Ivy said.

He shook out his hand, his knuckles stinging. "My mother is going to be bloody furious about that molding," he muttered. "Workmen who can repair eighteenth century plasterwork are rare as unicorns."

With a sigh, he sat down on the bed next to her, before he damaged any more irreplaceable architecture. "My animal's no damn use whatsoever. As usual. What does your wyvern say?"

She went still, her green gaze focusing inward. Her lips moved soundlessly for a moment.

"That we will never hurt you. Because you're our mate." She pulled a face, wrinkling her nose. "But this is the animal who wants to breathe acid over people who cut in front of me at the bus stop, so I wouldn't count on it for good advice."

"So we're right back where we started. We only have my father's word for it. And I can tell you how much *that* is worth." He pressed the heels of his hands hard against his temples, trying to control the turmoil in his mind. "I can't risk it, Ivy. I just can't. If he's wrong—if he's lying—I'd lose everything. We'd lose everything."

"I know." She stared down at her knees. "I wasn't sure if I should even tell you. But I didn't want there to be secrets between us. I'm sorry."

His anger leeched away at the stricken remorse in her expression. He put an arm around her tense, hunched shoulders, drawing her to him.

"No, I'm sorry," he said. "You were right to tell me. I don't want there to be any more secrets between us either. Not ever again."

She leaned against his side, face turned into the hollow of his shoulder. Her arms wrapped around his waist, clinging onto him with desperate ferocity. He buried his own face in her hair. As always, her storm-rain scent spiked longing through his blood.

How easy it would be to pull her into his lap. To feel her sweet heat straddling him, soft thighs wrapped over his hips. To nip and nuzzle lower, following the beckoning curve of her neck. To unbutton her top and lose himself in the intoxicating curves of her lush breasts, pulling wordless sounds of pleasure from her mouth with every lick and suck...

With a sound that was half-sigh, half-sob, Ivy pulled away from him. Her flushed face betrayed that she too had been having much the same line of thought.

"Sorry," she said, abruptly getting off the bed. "I can't—it's not safe for me to be so close to you. I'm not in control tonight. I know you're right, we can't risk it, but I can't help thinking about it."

He knew what she meant. His own head was a raging maelstrom of emotion. Anger and desire, fear and bitter rage, and winding through it all was still a stupid, *stupid* thread of hope. Even now, as he looked at her, some treacherous corner of his mind was still whispering *what if, what if...*

Ivy twitched her shoulders, as if physically shaking herself free of some unwanted thought. "I think I need to get some fresh air and cool off. It's been a while since I shifted, and that always puts me on edge. Is it okay if I go out for a bit?"

"That's a good idea." He attempted a smile. "I might go for a run myself."

"Um." Ivy hesitated at the window. "Not to sound paranoid, but would you mind waiting until I get back? My dumb wyvern gets anxious when Hope's left unguarded, and there'll be a lot of strangers in the house tonight. I think I need to really stretch my wings to clear my head, and I can't do that if my beast is constantly trying to tug me back here."

She looked so small and brave and lonely, silhouetted against the darkening twilight. More than anything, he wanted to go over to her and enfold her in his arms. To show her that she wasn't alone. That she didn't need to be brave. That he would take care of her, in every way that she needed.

But he couldn't.

"Of course I'll watch over Hope," he said. "But she really is safe here, you know. The wards around the grounds are like invisible walls. Not even a flying shifter can enter the property without the permission of someone in the family."

A worried wrinkle appeared between her brows. "Uh, I've got your permission to go in and out, right?"

"You don't need it," he said. "You *are* family."

∼

Ivy soared on emerald wings over the winter-bare woods. Things always seemed simpler when she was wrapped in scales, alone and free in the sky. The cold wind swept the cobwebs of human thoughts from her mind, leaving only the bright, sharp desires of the wyvern.

She swooped low over the forest, her sharp eyes picking out the faint marks of deer-tracks through the leafless canopy. Her talons flexed, acid saliva flooding her mouth in anticipation. Having lived her entire life in cities, she'd never had the opportunity to indulge her predatory instincts.

No. The small still-human part of her tugged at her awareness, like a rider pulling on reins. *Not that way. I'm not going to let you poach the Earl's deer.*

She snarled in irritation, but allowed herself to be pulled off-course. The sweeping lawns in front of their lair offered easier hunting than the tangled woods, after all.

And indeed, there was a whole herd of creatures approaching, foolishly following each other nose-to-tail along the gravel track. Their bright, staring eyes made them easy targets. They didn't smell of meat, but their roaring was annoying, and they were on her territory. Throat swelling, she gathered herself to swoop and rain death upon the intruders.

NO. Once again, that irritating part of her forced her away. *For pity's sake, those are guests arriving for the ball! You can't eat them either!*

She fought, but her other-self was too strong. She was forced to soar upward, aborting her dive. Hissing in anger, she spiraled above the grounds, watching the honking beasts crawl up to the front of the lair, disgorging small two-legged shapes from their innards.

Humans. Strange humans.

You could not trust humans. Even the ones who were supposed to care for you could turn mean and cold between one breath and another. You had to be always on guard, always ready to defend what was yours.

Every instinct screamed at her to destroy the strangers. They were too close to her treasures.

Hugh's there, her human part reminded her. *He'll watch over Hope.*

Her bristling spines settled a little. Her mate was powerful. Even the beasts with the burning eyes would be no match for his incandescent wrath. Yes, she could trust him to defend the lair in her absence.

Satisfied, she swept her wings down, her sleek form cleaving the air. She would hunt. She would return with plump prey, and feed choice morsels to her mate.

Hugh's a vegetarian, her other-self muttered at the bottom of her mind. *What are you going to do, slay a salad?*

But at least her other half wasn't clipping her wings anymore. She soared onward, enjoying the icy bite of the night air. The winds in this new territory were challenging, made unpredictable by the rolling hills below. They sported with her, tugging playfully at her lean form. Far more interesting than the thick, flat air above human cities.

She caught sight of the high stone wall that marked the boundary of the estate, and angled her wings to follow it. Best to stay within her mate's territory, until she could learn who controlled the lands beyond.

Though, she mused, not even the strongest dragon could stand against the combined power of herself and her mate. Together they would expand this great territory even further. They would claim enough hunting grounds to support generations of their offspring—

A strange light caught her attention, interrupting her daydream. She hovered on the wind, narrowing her eyes.

She wasn't the only creature pacing the boundary tonight. A pack of hulking black shapes ran along the outside edge of the wall, occasionally stopping to sniff and paw at it. Though they were four-legged, they were not fat deer or juicy boar.

They were predators.

The flickering light that had caught her attention shone from their open jaws, backlighting vicious fangs. Their red eyes gleamed bright as flames in the dark.

Hellhounds!

Her human half was suddenly alert, once again taking control of their shared body. Her own instincts called her to swoop down and put an end to the much smaller predators, but her other-self kept them high in the sky, invisible against the scattered clouds.

The pack below didn't seem to have noticed the doom hovering above their heads. They kept following the wall, yelping to each other. They seemed to be testing the boundary, searching for a crack in the defense.

What are they doing here? Her human's agitation made their tail curve, their deadliest venom gathering in the stinger at its tip. *Are they Gaze's people?*

One of the hellhounds hesitated, nose tilting upward. She tensed—

but the hound didn't erupt into full-throated howls of alarm, as it surely would have done had it caught her scent. Instead, it barked, attracting the attention of its pack mates. Breaking off from running the boundary, they milled and yipped for a few moments, as though conferring with each other.

Then, as one, they turned tail. The pack headed away from the territory, disappearing into the woods.

None of them looked up, though. And she could still track the lights of their eyes moving through the leafless canopy.

She started to follow, but her other-self jerked her back like a collar around her neck. She struggled and snapped in mid-air, fighting herself. Part of her wanted to fly back to the lair, to warn her mate what she had seen. The other part wanted to hunt down the intruders and punish them for daring to challenge her territory.

Something half-remembered tickled the back of her mind, like a stray feather. Something her sister, her treasure, had said once about hellhounds. About them only letting themselves be seen if they wanted to be seen...

But the ones below were not invisible. Why would they hide themselves, when they didn't even know they were being hunted? Perhaps they had simply tired, and were returning to their own lair. Or perhaps they had been summoned back by their red-eyed alpha.

If she followed them now, they might lead her straight to him.

That thought resolved her divided mind. She extended her wings, catching an air current so that she could silently follow the fleeing pack without so much as a flap to betray her presence.

Mate! she called out in her mind, hoping to reach his. *Mate, enemies are near! Be wary, be on guard!*

She had no sense that he heard. He was too far away, and the bond between them was too weak.

She clamped her jaws shut on a snarl of annoyance. Why hadn't they mated yet? If they were fully joined, she would have been able to reach him as easily as if he flew at her wingtip.

No time for regrets now. All her cunning and focus was needed for the hunt.

Silent and deadly, she shadowed the pack...and never wondered if she was being lured away.

∼

The laughter rising from the ballroom stabbed through his head like knives. His unicorn flattened its ears, shying away from the knots of excited, chattering guests cluttering the corridors. Their vital auras were viciously sharp to his sixth sense.

Hugh clenched his teeth, unable to keep even a semblance of a polite smile on his face as he edged through the crowds. Despite his uninviting expression, he was still aware of heads turning to follow him as he passed. The lustful gazes raked across his skin like steel blades.

Normally he would never have subjected himself to the torment of a party. A dense mass of people dressed in revealing finery, inhibitions loosened by alcohol, intent on flirting and dancing...it was his own personal hell.

But he'd promised Ivy that he'd watch over Hope. And under the throbbing agony in his head was a strange, deeper unease. A nagging sense of wrongness, like a splinter in his mind.

Be on guard, his unicorn whispered again. *There is danger here.*

The whirling energies of the crowd buffeted his animal like a sandstorm, but it set its hooves, enduring the assault. The firefly glimmer of its horn urged him on.

Skirting round a pair of women in low-cut silk ballgowns—and flinching as their appreciative stares stung his shoulders—he finally reached the long gallery that ran along the edge of the ballroom. He peered down over the balcony, scanning the crowds below. The dancing had not yet started, and most people were milling around the edges of the vast room. His eyes skipped from head to head.

Where is she?

His searching gaze snagged on one particular figure. Not a small, thin form seated in a wheelchair, but a broad-shouldered man dressed in a perfectly-tailored tuxedo. His slender white stick and opaque glasses marked him as visually impaired, yet his face turned upward. For a second, Hugh could have sworn that the man's hidden eyes stared straight at him.

"Hugh?"

He stiffened, turning toward the familiar, unwelcome voice. In the general sea of pain, he'd missed the usual stab of his father's approach.

His father stopped a careful five feet away, not coming too close. There was something strange in his expression that Hugh couldn't quite place; a crack in the patrician dignity. If he didn't know better, he would have said that his father looked hopeful.

"You came," his father said, a slight hesitancy in his measured tones. "I take it this means Ivy spoke with you."

"She did," Hugh growled. "But don't worry. I'm not going to punch you in the face in front of a crowd of guests. Must keep up family appearances, after all."

Something flickered across his father's eyes. Relief? Disappointment? It was gone too fast for Hugh to identify, his father's face freezing back into its usual icy mask.

"So she kept her word," his father murmured. "Why *are* you here then?"

"I'm looking for Hope," Hugh said curtly. "Have you seen her?"

"The charming young lady in the wheelchair? Only briefly." His father tilted his head, a small frown curling his mouth. "She seemed happy enough, but broke off our conversation abruptly. She said that she'd thought she'd spotted someone she knew, but she needed to get a closer look to be sure."

Disquiet prickled down Hugh's spine. "Was it—wait, where did he go?"

"Who?" his father asked, but Hugh was already pushing past, heading for the staircase down to the ballroom.

There! His unicorn lowered its head, pointing out a door across the room. It should have been firmly closed and locked...yet now it stood fractionally ajar.

Hugh hurried through the crowd, regardless of the white-hot shock as he brushed past people. The door creaked as he pushed through it, into the shadowed corridor beyond. He was just in time to catch a flicker of movement, the edge of a black jacket whisking round the corner ahead.

"Hey!" he shouted, breaking into a run. "You! Stop!"

EYES! His unicorn reared, horn blazing. *Beware his eyes!*

Swearing under his breath, Hugh squeezed his own tight shut. If the basilisk shifter *had* brazenly strolled straight through his front door, he couldn't risk meeting his stare.

He sped up, trusting in scent and hearing and his unicorn's sense of the man's vital energies to guide him. Even blind, he was faster than the intruder. He'd grown up in this house. He knew every inch of these corridors—

An unexpected obstacle caught his ankle, sending him sprawling. On pure reflex, his eyes flew open...and the world dissolved into crimson.

CHAPTER 19

He came back to pain. Red pain. Pounding through every part of him. His blood had been replaced by liquid agony. He would have screamed, but he couldn't even feel his mouth. Just pain.

"Feeling returns first," said a light, amused voice. "Then hearing. Hello, Hugh Argent. Or should I say Hugh Silver?"

The voice was an anchor in the sea of pain. He clung onto it, letting it pull him back into his body.

Slowly, he became aware of other sensations. The low snarl of a car engine. The coldness of metal around his wrists. The shallow, jerky rasp of his own breath in his throat.

"This will be rather a one-sided conversation for a while longer yet, I am afraid," the voice continued. "Though your sight should be coming back right about…now."

His eyes felt like stones in his head. With great effort, he blinked, and the black-red haze across his vision thinned.

The 'blind' man from the party had replaced his dark glasses with mirrored shades. His tuxedo jacket hung open, tie loosened casually. He lounged opposite Hugh with an ankle crossed over one knee, a whiskey glass in his hand. He looked for all the world like he was on the way home after a particularly extravagant stag night.

"I'd offer you something from the minibar, but you'd only choke on it." The man took a sip of his own drink. "Or spit it in my face. You know who I am, of course."

The crimson agony was slowly ebbing away, but he still couldn't move more than his eyes. He swiveled them, trying to take in more of his surroundings. Dim blue lighting. Wide leather seats. A smoked glass privacy screen behind Gaze, separating them from the driver. He was in a...limousine?

Well, at least I'm being abducted in style.

More importantly, he didn't see Ivy. Nor did he have any sense of her being hurt. Even though they weren't fully mated, he was certain that he would have been able to feel if anything had happened to her.

He let out a ragged breath, relief overwhelming him despite his own predicament. Ivy was okay. He had a vague sense of distant fear and rage, but Gaze clearly hadn't managed to capture her as well.

"Something funny?" Gaze asked.

His smile widened. "You," he managed to croak.

One of Gaze's eyebrows rose above his mirrored sunglasses. "Oh? Please, enlighten me."

"You haven't thought this through." His tongue was still stiff and heavy, making his words thick. "You think that you've captured some great prize. But you've got nothing."

"Come now, unicorn. Pretense cannot save you now. I know exactly what you are."

"Oh?" Even though it hurt to move his face, Hugh copied Gaze's raised eyebrow, mockingly. "Well, I hope you wanted a paramedic. Because that's what you've got. That's *all* you've got. As long as I don't shift, I win."

"You do realize I could simply kill you," Gaze observed, as though commenting on the weather.

"Then you'd have a dead paramedic." Like most shifters, unicorns reverted to human form when they died. "Good luck finding a buyer."

Gaze tapped the rim of his sunglasses meaningfully. "There are ways of encouraging you to shift."

Hugh let out a short, painful rasp of laughter. "Go ahead, basilisk. Knock yourself out. You really don't know anything about me, if you think that torture is going to work."

Gaze leaned forward, still smiling. He pressed a button on the central console.

"Oh," Gaze said, as the smoked privacy glass behind him sank silently down, "I wasn't planning on torturing *you*."

Bound and gagged in the front passenger seat, Hope's panicked eyes met his.

CHAPTER 20

It was a nightmare. Her worst nightmare. Ivy felt like she was underwater, lead weights hanging from every limb. Every sound seemed muffled, apart from the terrified pounding of her heart.

"The police are on their way." The Earl's face was grim and cadaverous. Behind him, security floodlights bathed the entire front grounds in stark, brilliant white. "The staff are still searching the property, but I don't expect they'll find anything."

Ivy was shaking so hard, she could barely get words out. "Did the security cameras catch which car they left in?"

"Vehicles were going in and out of the front gates freely, dropping off late arrivals." The Earl clenched his fist, looking as if he too was having to fight down the instinct to simply run blindly into the night in search of his son. "I have my people scrutinizing the footage and cross-referencing against the guest list, but it's slow work."

Lady Hereford hurried up, her high heels unsteady on the graveled drive. "I've told the guests that there's a bomb scare, and that they need to stay put. They're all locked in the ballroom."

"What about the injured?" the Earl asked his wife. "The ones that monster caught on his way out?"

"The paralysis is wearing off. They're confused and distressed, but don't seem to be hurt." Lady Hereford's pale face crumpled suddenly, like tissue paper. "Edward, I let him in—he had an invitation. This is my fault."

The Earl wrapped his wife in his arms, holding her firmly as she clung to him. "His false identity was rock-solid. You couldn't have known."

"I did know," Ivy said numbly. Every part of her felt cold as ice. "I sensed it when Gaze attacked. But I was too far away to get back in time."

There was no one who could hold *her* and tell her that it wasn't her fault.

Because it was.

The Earl looked at Ivy over the top of his wife's head. "You're his true mate. Can you track him?"

"We aren't fully mated. All I can tell is that he's alive. He's hurting," *oh God*, "but he's alive. So's Hope. But I know someone who *can* track them. You need to call the Phoenix. Fire Commander Ash, of the East Sussex Fire and Rescue Service. He's got a pegasus shifter named Chase Tiernach in his team. We have to get him out here."

It was a slim hope—she knew from experience that Chase's pegasus senses could only track people over about five miles. But she clung onto it anyway. If Gaze was taking his captives back to his home base in Brighton, Chase might intercept him on route. Or the pegasus shifter might be able to fly a search pattern and pick up the trail that way.

And if that didn't work…her mind shied away from even contemplating that.

"If you know these shifters, wouldn't it be better for you to call them?" the Earl asked, his brow furrowing.

"They won't talk to me. But they'll come for Hugh. They're his friends." Ivy turned away. "And anyway, I'm going to be busy."

She rippled into scales, letting the strength and rage of the wyvern fill her. In a single leap, she was airborne. A few of the staff searching through the parked cars nearby turned their heads, blinking in the wind from her wings, but their eyes passed over her unseeingly. Mythic shifters were invisible to ordinary humans, although she noticed that the Earl's gaze *did* follow her emerald form as she spiraled into the sky.

Her wyvern wanted to head in the direction of the main road. *Spit, kill. Destroy everything, until we find our treasures.*

Ivy kept control over their shared body, reining in the beast's murderous instincts. Tearing apart random cars wouldn't help to find Hugh and Hope. Instead, she arrowed toward the boundary of the estate.

We hunt, she told her wyvern, picturing the black backs of the hellhounds.

It was clear now that the pack had been deliberately drawing her away from the house while Gaze infiltrated the ball. But she might be able to turn the tables on them, if she moved fast. Her sense of smell was keen as a snake's, and hellhounds had a very distinctive sulfur-and-wet-dog reek.

Which, she suddenly realized, she could smell *right now*.

A large canine shape sat in plain sight, right outside the front gates to the estate. It was howling like a wounded wolf, over and over, flames showing in the back of its throat.

She practically fell out of the sky in her haste to land. The hellhound sprang back stiff-legged as she crashed next to it in a spray of gravel. The next instant, she had it by the throat, her jaws pinning it down and her tail poised to strike.

WHERE ARE THEY? Ivy snarled telepathically.

The hellhound stared up at her, fiery eyes wide in non-comprehension. Cursing herself, Ivy realized that it hadn't heard her. Hellhounds were a type of faerie creature, just different enough from mythic shifters that they couldn't easily communicate mind-to-mind.

Ivy released the hellhound from her jaws, though she kept her stinger arced and ready. The other shifter made no attempt to escape. It just rolled onto its back, whining and showing its belly in an obvious display of submission. There was something gangling and adolescent about its long legs and slightly too-big paws.

Never taking her eyes off the hellhound, Ivy shrank back into her human skin. She jerked her gloves off the instant she had hands again, showing the cringing hellhound the venom glistening on her palms.

"Don't get any ideas," she warned. "I can kill you just as easily in this shape. Now shift so that we can talk."

The coal-black shape shimmered, shrinking down into an ebony-skinned girl, her hair braided into close cornrows. White dust from the gravel marked her black motorbike leathers. Her hands shook as she raised them above her head in surrender, but her full mouth was set in determination.

"You!" Ivy recognized her—it was the girl who'd been watching Hugh's house, the one Hope had claimed was her friend. "You're...Betsy?"

"Betty." The girl's voice quavered, but her hazel eyes met Ivy's without flinching. "Though only Hope calls me that. I'm Jezebeth Black. Don't kill me, I'm here to help you!"

"Like hell you are." Ivy didn't lower her hands. "You're the one who lured Hope into Gaze's clutches in the first place."

Betty's shoulders hunched in her leather jacket. "No, I never meant—I didn't know he was going to—please, there isn't *time* for this! You just have to trust me!"

Acid filled her throat. "Give me one good reason."

"Hope's my...that is, I think she's..." Betty squirmed, her voice dropping to a reluctant, sullen mutter. "Look, I'm pretty sure Hope's my mate, okay?"

Ivy stared at her.

Betty glared back, her jaw setting in teenage stubbornness. "Don't you *dare* tell her."

The girl's clear mortification convinced Ivy more than any fervent declaration of love ever could have. Shifters usually couldn't recognize their true mates until they were full adults, but there was a hardened maturity in Betty's direct gaze that Ivy recognized. She'd seen it in the mirror when *she'd* been seventeen. Betty might be young, but life had clearly made her grow up fast.

Ivy dropped her hands at last, straightening from her combat crouch. Part of her was gibbering in denial—*Hope's* seventeen! *She can't have a mate! She's supposed to be focusing on her studies, not dating!*—but there wasn't time to freak out about that now.

"Okay," she said. "We'll uh, talk about that later. Do you know where Gaze is taking Hope and Hugh?"

Betty nodded eagerly, pulling a cellphone out of her pocket. "Gaze doesn't know about me and Hope. I was real careful to constantly complain about having to hang out with her, so that he wouldn't suspect the truth. Anyway, I was able to find out his plan, and get a place with the group that was assigned to distract you. He's taking them back to his most secure location. It's an old warehouse on the outskirts of London. Here, look."

Ivy swore under her breath as she studied the map on Betty's phone. The marked address was a long way from Brighton, and Gaze had the advantage of a head start. Even flying at top speed, there was no way Alpha Team would be able to get there in time.

But no one was faster in the air than a wyvern.

CHAPTER 21

Hope squirmed as Gaze's thug slung her over his shoulder. Her legs were paralyzed, but her upper body and core muscles were strong thanks to years of hauling herself around. She managed to get in a solid head-butt, although it left her own ears ringing.

The thug grunted in pain and annoyance, but didn't pause. "Stop thrashing, kid. You'll only make things harder on yourself."

Naturally, this only made Hope redouble her efforts. But with her arms handcuffed behind her back and her mouth gagged, it was difficult to do anything to resist as the Gaze's henchman carried her after his boss.

"Here we are," Gaze said, as warmly as if welcoming them to another Christmas party. "Please don't consider trying anything foolish, Hugh, or our young friend here will regret it."

The world spun about her head as the thug dumped her onto the cold ground. He snapped a chain onto her handcuffs with a quick, practiced motion. The other end was secured to an iron ring set into the concrete floor.

Rolling onto her side, Hope managed to prop herself up enough to look around. A chill ran down her spine.

Large steel hooks hung from thick chains above their heads, half-visible in the gloom. The concrete underneath them was marked by old, rusty splotches. A gutter ran down the middle of the long room. It must have once been some sort of abattoir or meat-processing plant, but now the air smelled of mold and dust.

There was new thing that was clean and new, though. It gleamed in the middle of the dimly lit space, stark and ominous.

A cage.

"In you go." Gaze shoved Hugh into the cage, still smiling brightly. "I apologize if it's a little small. I had to guess at the dimensions."

Hugh straightened. Despite Gaze's words, there was plenty of room in the cage even for his tall, broad-shouldered form. It could have held a large animal like a horse or a bull.

Hugh looked around at the bars with the jaded air of a business traveler confronted with yet another bland hotel suite. "Charming. I'm sure I'll be very comfortable."

"I'm afraid not." Gaze glanced at the henchman still standing guard over Hope. "Wait outside. Don't let anyone in. And don't come in again yourself. No matter what you hear."

The goon nodded, his craggy face not betraying a hint of curiosity. "Yes boss."

"You shouldn't listen to him," Hugh called as the man headed for the door. "He's cheating you out of a fortune. I can pay you far more than he is."

"Yeah." The henchman didn't even pause. "They all say that."

The thick steel door slammed shut, leaving the two of them alone with Gaze in the gloom. It was the best chance they were ever likely to have. Hope wracked her brain, staring frantically around at the rusted equipment in search of inspiration.

There has to be some way I can hurt him. Or at least delay him. Ivy's on her way, I know she is, she has to be...

"Well now." Gaze strolled over to a wheeled metal table placed next to the cage. Hope was too low down to see what was on top of it, but given that it bore a suspicious resemblance to a surgical trolley, she was betting it wasn't anything good. "Shall we begin?"

Hugh folded his arms, looking bored. "You still can't force me to shift. You don't have any leverage."

That's right, Hugh, Hope silently urged him. She didn't know if he could use his mythic shifter telepathy to pick her thoughts out of her mind, but it was worth a try. *Keep stalling him. Don't worry about me.*

She still couldn't help flinching as Gaze gestured in her direction. He had some kind of surgical tool in his hand. It looked something like a power drill, except that it had a serrated saw blade sticking out the front.

"Oh, I think I have all the leverage I need." The saw blade whined into a lethal blur for a second as Gaze idly pressed a button. "You know, I've often wondered how the torment of being trapped in my stare compares to more traditional forms of persuasion. Shall we find out?"

Hugh's fingers dug into his biceps, but his haughty expression didn't waver. "Seems to me that there's nothing stopping you from hurting Hope anyway, once I'm out of the way. So I might as well make sure you don't get what you want."

"Now you're the one who isn't thinking things through." Gaze's tone was light and pleasant, as if this was a perfectly civil conversation. "I do want to live to enjoy my new treasure, after all. That means I need insurance against a certain vengeful little wyvern. Even after I've killed you, Ivy won't dare to come after me as long as I'm holding her sister. I'll keep Hope safe and secret, never fear."

Hugh's eyes flicked from Gaze to Hope. She shook her head frantically at him, willing him not to listen to the basilisk shifter.

"You're insane if you think you can get away with this," Hugh said to Gaze. "Ivy isn't the only one you need to worry about."

"You mean the Phoenix? Your erstwhile friends on Alpha Team?" Gaze's smile stretched wider. "Seems they can't be such good friends after all, given how fast you were to abandon *them*. I'll take my chances. Now, are you really going to put your young friend here through some very unpleasant experiences, just to spite me?"

Hugh gripped the bars of the cage, all ironic detachment abandoned. "Don't you dare touch her."

"Then do what I want." The basilisk too had lost all fake civility, his tone hard as steel. "Last chance, Hugh Argent. Shift."

Hugh's knuckles whitened. For a moment, he matched stares with the basilisk shifter, cold blue eyes locked with hidden crimson ones.

Hugh looked away first. Bowing his head, he leaned on the bars, drawing in a deep, shuddering breath.

"Hope," he said, very softly. "I'm sorry."

She thought for a moment that he was refusing, and her heart gave a weird lurch of combined terror and triumph—*yes, hold out, I can take it, oh God this can't be happening*—but then he stepped back into the center of the cage. His form shimmered.

No! she wanted to shout, as he shifted. And then, when she saw what he was: *Oh, no.*

The unicorn's silver light shone through the cage, striping the concrete floor with stark black shadows. The enclosure had been plenty big enough for a man, but the steel bars pressed cruelly into that gleaming white hide.

The great muscles bunched. Sparks flew as silver hooves struck steel, and Hope caught her breath. Surely no mere cage could contain all that shining power, surely the walls would buckle and fall away under the force of his kicks...

But there just wasn't any room. No matter how the unicorn twisted, he didn't have space to lash out with his full strength. He couldn't even turn his head. The long silver horn stuck out the front of the cage, trapped between the bars.

"Oh, you beauty," Gaze breathed.

The unicorn bared his teeth, ears flattening as Gaze reached for him. One of the huge hooves stamped, shaking the floor. His horn rattled against the bars of the cage...but the unicorn couldn't pull back as the basilisk shifter ran a possessive hand down the spiraling, gleaming length.

"Eternal life," Gaze whispered. "Or as good as eternal. I shall restore myself to youth and health again and again. Everything I've built so far will be insignificant compared to the power I will hold."

Forgotten, Hope flopped to her side. She writhed her upper body, dragging her limp legs over the concrete regardless of how the rough surface abraded her skin. If she could get close enough, she could bite Gaze in the ankle, or drag him down, or, or *something*. Anything.

Anything to stop what she was certain was going to happen next.

"Close your eyes if you want," Gaze said, taking off his glasses. He tucked them into his jacket pocket. "Though I suggest you let me hold you still for this part. It'll only be worse for you if I don't."

Hope squeezed her own eyes shut. Partly out of fear of catching the edge of the basilisk shifter's stare. Partly because she couldn't bear to watch.

Ivy, Ivy, Ivy! she shrieked helplessly in her mind, over and over. Her sister had to be coming, she had to be almost here, she couldn't let this happen…*IVY!*

She heard the saw blade whine. She heard the desperate clatter of hooves.

She heard a terrible, inhuman scream.

Hope's eyes jerked open again at the stench of acid-burned metal—just in time to see Ivy explode through the front wall in a storm of teeth and fury. Gaze flung himself to the side, taking cover from the wyvern's deadly breath behind the cage. An instant later, Ivy's scorpion-barbed tail smashed into the concrete where he'd been standing.

Hope was distracted from the battle by something hot and wet slurping against her ear. She shrieked through her gag as a huge black dog appeared out of nowhere, straddling her prone form. She beat at its gaping maw with her bound hands, futilely trying to push the animal away from her face.

"No, it's me, it's me!" Suddenly it was human hands pulling away the soggy remnants of the gag rather than a dog's slobbering jaws.

"*Betty?*" Hope gasped in shock.

Betty jerked at the chain binding Hope's wrists, trying futilely to break it. "Hold still. I can bite through this, but I have to—"

She broke off abruptly, pushing Hope down to the ground and covering her with her own leather-clad body. Hope hid her face in Betty's shoulder as a shower of steel fragments blasted over them.

"NO!" Gaze howled.

Peeking out from under Betty, Hope saw Ivy lunge for Gaze again. The basilisk shifter dodged, his form shifting and elongating.

The world went dark as Betty's hands clamped over Hope's eyes. "Hey!" she protested.

"Don't look!" Betty raised her voice, yelling across the room. "Ivy, Hugh, *shut your eyes!* He can kill instantly when he's shifted!"

Heart hammering, Hope could only huddle against Betty, trying to interpret the sounds coming from the battle. Snarls of anger, the crash of teeth against scales, a chilling hiss of triumph—

Light blazed through her closed eyelids. Not the pure white light of the unicorn, but a wilder, red-orange blaze.

"Close your eyes, basilisk," said a voice as cold as death. "Or I will burn them from your head."

Instinctive panic filled Hope as heat licked at her bare shoulders. Betty tightened her grip, holding her still despite the firestorm raging all around.

"It's all right," Betty whispered in her ear. "It's the Phoenix."

"Aye, he has it under control," said a different voice, in a familiar, reassuring Scottish burr. "It's safe now, lassies. You can look."

"Griff?" Opening her eyes, Hope saw the griffin shifter smiling down at them both. "It is you! What are you doing here?"

"Thank your sister and this brave lass here." Griff nodded at Betty, who'd shifted back into hellhound form in order to bite through the handcuffs. "They told us where to come. Afraid there wasn't time to collect a wheelchair. I'll have to carry you for a wee bit, if you don't mind."

Hope leaned on his broad shoulder, limp with relief. Behind Griff, the flames were dying down, revealing a struggling Gaze being forced to his knees by John Doe and Chase. The basilisk shifter was back in human form, a black bag over his head hiding his deadly eyes. Dai, in red dragon form, guarded the hole in the wall, growling.

No, Hope realized, the savage snarls filling the air weren't coming from the red dragon outside. Ivy was still in wyvern form, her green eyes savage and empty of any human thought. Her snakelike body curled possessively around the wreckage of the steel cage, half-spread wings hiding the contents from view.

"Ivy." Fire Commander Ash stood in front of the snarling wyvern, face calm despite the acid dripping from her jaws. The concrete floor behind him was scorched black in the shape of wide, feathered wings. "Ivy, you have to shift back. You have to let us see him."

The Phoenix took a step toward the wyvern. Ivy's growl increased, like a chainsaw revving up. She drew her wings closer around the cage.

"Griff," Hope said, tugging at his shirt. "Take me over there. I can talk to her."

A little half-whine, half-yelp of protest burst from Betty's fiery throat. The animal sound turned into words as the hellhound shimmered back into human form. "Hope, no! She's lost to her animal at the moment, it's too dangerous!"

"Ivy won't ever hurt me. I'm her sister. *Please*, Griff. I'm the only one who can get through to her."

The griffin shifter blew out his breath, but carried her over. Betty dogged his heels. When he stopped, the hellhound planted herself in between Hope and Ivy like a bodyguard. Despite everything, Hope couldn't help feeling a warm glow in her chest as Betty squared off against the furious wyvern.

She came to save me. She's worried about me. Maybe she really does like me...

But this was hardly the moment to think about such things. Hope looked past Betty to Ivy, focusing on her sister.

"Ivy," she said. "Ivy, it's okay. These are friends. They're here to help."

The wyvern's snarls ground down into a low, uneasy whine. Her head still wove from side to side like a snake about to strike, but the bristling spines down her back flattened. Her spread wings quivered uncertainly.

"You have to let them help, Ivy," Hope said, keeping her voice as low and calm as if she was trying to soothe a distressed dog. "I know you're just trying to protect Hugh's secret, but he needs their help now. You have to let them see."

With a final agonized whimper, Ivy folded her wings at last.

Hope's heart gave a great bound of relief. Hugh was still in unicorn form. He stood splay-legged, sides heaving, but at least he was alive. Livid marks striped his white coat where he'd flung himself against the bars.

Painfully, slowly, he raised his head.

Griff swore under his breath. The shocked exclamation was echoed by Chase and John, still restraining Gaze behind them. Outside, the red dragon hissed. Ash said nothing, but his fist clenched.

"Oh no," Hope whispered.

Thick white light oozed like blood from a deep cut at the base of the unicorn's darkened horn.

CHAPTER 22

"I'm *all right*," Hugh said again. Even though he was as white as a ghost in the strobing lights of the emergency vehicles, he still mustered an impressive glare. "For the last time, will you all please stop fretting?"

Ivy tugged at his hand, trying to urge him forward. "Hugh, you have to go to the hospital. You're hurt."

"I don't want to go to the hospital." Hugh cast a withering look at his colleagues. "And yes, I'm fully aware of the irony. Shut up."

Dai and John Doe, who hadn't said anything, exchanged glances. Ivy was pretty sure the two hulking dragon shifters were conferring telepathically about whether to bodily pick Hugh up and *stuff* him into the waiting ambulance.

Hope had already left in another ambulance, Betty at her side. The hellhound had nearly bitten a paramedic who'd tried to tell her that she couldn't ride along since she wasn't a family member. Ivy had expected her wyvern to object, but her beast had been oddly calm about the arrangement.

She is her treasure too, Ivy's wyvern had muttered, albeit with a hint of grudging reluctance. *We can share. We suppose.*

Ash was busy talking to the police, while Chase and Griff kept hold of

Gaze. The Phoenix had called some kind of secret emergency line, so the officers who'd arrived were all shifters who knew how to deal with this sort of special case. Ivy wondered what they would do with the basilisk.

We should have killed him, her wyvern snarled. *Still could.*

Ivy shivered, pushing her inner beast back down. Gaze wasn't her problem now. And no matter what her wyvern thought, she was glad not to have blood on her hands. After all, Hope and Hugh were all right. That was all that mattered.

Hugh *was* going to be all right. She clung onto that thought, as tightly as she clung onto his hand, and tried not to think about the terrible sight of that grey, lightless horn.

"Hugh, be reasonable," Dai said, his soft Welsh voice soothing. He took a step toward the swaying paramedic. "Come on, you have to—"

"*Don't touch me!*"

Heads turned across the parking lot at Hugh's shout. Ivy stumbled, jerked off-balance as Hugh recoiled from Dai. He flattened himself against the wall as if the dragon shifter had lunged at him with every claw bared.

Dai halted, holding up his hands in uncertain surrender. "I wasn't going to touch you. I'm nowhere near you, Hugh."

Hugh's breath hissed between his teeth. "Don't come any closer. None of you come any closer. Stay away!"

Dai and John both obediently backed off, though they were already well out of arms'-reach. Ivy started to pull away too, but Hugh's fingers tightened on hers.

"Not you." His voice was a bare whisper, pitched for her ears alone. "You don't hurt me. Please, Ivy. Just take me home. Brighton, not my parents' place. I have to go home. *Please*."

There was no arguing with the raw desperation in his voice. "Okay," Ivy said, letting go of his hand. "Wait here a sec. I'll go talk to Ash."

He slid down the wall into a huddled sitting position, fists clenched at his temples. "Hurry."

Worry stabbed through her gut. She was suddenly as desperate as

Hugh to get away from all the questions and concerns, the uniforms and sirens and flashing lights. Her wyvern instincts howled that she needed to carry her treasure away from all this.

She could feel her palms going clammy with deadly venom, her wyvern rousing in response to her distress. Despite her pounding heart, she forced herself to take a moment to check that her gloves were still safely in place before hurrying over to Ash and the other firefighters.

"I'm taking Hugh home," she said, deliberately phrasing it as a statement rather than a request for permission. "It'll be fastest for me to fly him back to Brighton. Griff, can you stay with Hope?"

"Of course, lass," Griff said, though his blond eyebrows drew down, brow furrowing. "But shouldn't Hugh go to the hospital too? There'll be doctors there who know how to treat shifters."

"He doesn't want to," Ivy said. "That's good enough for me. Tell Hope I'll come get her tomorrow, okay?"

"No need for that. I'll bring her and her friend back myself." Griff glanced over at Hugh, his golden eyes betraying his deep concern. "You just look after him, aye?"

Ash inclined his head slightly in agreement. "Do not worry about matters here, Ms. Viverna. I shall personally deal with everything that is required."

Ivy shifted her weight awkwardly, forcing herself to meet the Phoenix's eyes. It was hard to look into those dark, enigmatic depths for long. He was so disconcertingly *still*, with an unwavering focus that made her feel like a bug under a magnifying glass.

"Thanks," she said, awkwardly. "For, you know. Everything."

Her skin prickled as the penetrating power behind those dark eyes scrutinized her for a long, silent moment.

Then the Phoenix held out his hand to her.

"No," he said. "Thank *you*."

"We're here, Hugh," Ivy whispered, hurrying to support him the instant she shifted back into human form. "We're home."

Hugh didn't respond. He'd seemed barely conscious during the flight to Brighton. Ivy had been terrified that he was about to slide off her neck at any moment. Now he stumbled like a drunk man up the road, his arm heavy across her shoulders. The fact that he was letting her take some of his weight scared her even more.

Ivy was pretty sure that Hugh wasn't carrying his Brighton house keys in the pockets of his crumpled and stained formalwear, so she didn't waste time patting him down. Instead, she spat on the door lock.

"Sorry," she said, as her acid quickly ate away the mechanism. "Unhygienic, but it works."

"Just get me inside." His voice was low and hoarse.

Kicking open the weakened door, Ivy steered Hugh into the dark hallway. She'd hoped that he'd gain some comfort from being back in his own territory, but he stared around blankly, as if he didn't recognize his surroundings.

"Door," he rasped.

It took some effort to force the twisted door closed again. By the time Ivy had finally bludgeoned it back into its frame, Hugh had disappeared.

"Hugh?" she called, her pulse picking up with anxiety. She hurried down the corridor, glancing into the empty kitchen and dark lounge along the way. "Hugh?"

She found him leaning against the door down to the basement, one hand fumbling with the latch. "Hugh, what are you doing? Do you want to shift?"

He flinched as though she'd fired a pistol past his ear. "No. No. Just need to find somewhere quiet."

She blinked at him. Even to her own shifter-acute hearing, the house was dead silent. "It isn't quiet enough here?"

He swung his head in an emphatic arc. "Can still feel them."

"Who?"

He flashed a shadow of his edged, sardonic smile, though his eyes were haunted. "Everyone."

Is he delirious? There was a pallor to his face and a feverish jerkiness about his movements that made her deeply uneasy. *Maybe I should have forced him to the hospital.*

"Well, I can't carry you in human form, and if you try to go down those steps in this state, you're going to break your neck," she said, firmly taking his arm. "Come on, Hugh. Come and lie down and... maybe you'll feel better."

He let out a short, hollow laugh, but let her steer him away from the basement. There was no way she could haul his much bigger and heavier body up the stairs while in human shape, so she guided him to the couch in the living room.

"You're hurt," he said suddenly, as she knelt to take off his shoes.

Looking down, Ivy realized that her torn jacket and top had slipped, exposing her shoulder. A deep purple bruise from Gaze's bludgeoning tail was blooming below her collarbone. The basilisk hadn't dared to sink his fangs into her for fear of her poisonous blood, but he'd still managed to knock her around before Ash had arrived.

"It's nothing," she said, rolling her aching shoulder. "Don't worry. It'll heal in no time."

Hugh pulled her clothing away from her shoulder. Before she'd realized what he intended to do, he put his palm flat against the bruise.

She didn't feel anything—but a wordless, animal scream of pain tore from Hugh's throat. Snatching his hand away, he curled over, burying his head in his arms as if warding off a blow.

"Hugh!" She grabbed his shoulders, holding him tight as he shook. "What is it? What's wrong?"

"I can't heal," he said. "Ivy, *I can't heal.*"

That deep, ugly gash at the base of his horn. She arrived before Gaze had been able to finish the job, but he'd still half-severed it. Silver light had poured from the wound, the shining length draining to dull, dead grey...

"It's your horn, isn't it," she said, her throat dry. "You can't heal because he damaged your horn."

He nodded, face still hidden in his hands. "I can't focus my power. It builds up in my head, but I can't let it out."

"But it'll get better, right?" she asked. "With time?"

He uncurled at last. The utter despair in his eyes froze her heart.

"No," he said, simply. "It won't."

I was too late.

Ten seconds earlier, and I would have saved him.

I was too late.

"I'll never be able to heal again." He stared down at his curled hands. "I'm useless. Worse than useless. You want to know what the worst part is?"

She took his hand, silently. His fingers were cold as ice in hers.

"The worst part," he said, his voice low and savage with self-loathing, "is that losing my power *isn't* the worst part. All the people I won't be able to help anymore, and all I can think about is myself. Because it *hurts*, Ivy. The wound in my horn...I can't let my energy out, but everyone else's energies are coming in. I can't block them out at all anymore."

That's why he'd flinched away from Dai, why he'd been so desperate to escape the crowd at the crime scene. "Oh God. Your sensitivity is worse?"

"A thousand times worse. Even Ash felt like a knife in my skull, and he's been celibate for decades." He turned his head, staring blindly through the wall. "And I'm picking up on energies from much further away. Even now, I can still feel the people in the houses nearby scratching at my mind...I feel like I've been flayed. Like my skin's been turned inside out."

"Then—then we'll go somewhere else." She had to find a way to ease his suffering, she *had* to. "Somewhere there aren't any people. We'll go right now."

She tried to stand up, but he pulled her back down again. His expression was hollow and defeated, drained of all hope.

"What's the use?" he said. "Even if we go to the ends of the earth, what's the point? I can't heal, I can't be your mate…I can't do anything for you. And this is never going to get any better."

Her breath caught.

Because there *was* something that she could do for him.

"Hugh." She took his bowed head in her hands, turning him to look at her. "It can get better."

"My unicorn knows we can't heal from this, Ivy. Don't cling to false hope."

"I'm not. There *is* a way to take away the pain, Hugh." His eyes widened as she leaned in. "And you know what it is."

Her lips met his.

She closed her eyes, tears welling up at the sweet heat of his touch. His mouth opened, and she deepened the kiss, fiercely, stifling his half-formed words.

What she needed to tell him now couldn't be said with words. With her lips and tongue and hands, she needed to show him how much she loved him. How much his touch still healed her, despite the loss of his power. How much she needed him.

How much she needed him to accept this gift.

He made a low, despairing sound deep in his throat. His hands tangled in her hair as he kissed her back, his mouth hungry and desperate—but then he broke off, turning his head to one side.

He drew in a deep, shuddering breath. "Ivy, no. If I—if I do lose my unicorn, I won't be immune to your venom anymore. I won't be able to touch you."

"We can't touch *now*." She straddled his lap. His muscled thighs tensed underneath her own, but he didn't push her away. "This might not even work, if your dad is right. But in that case, at least we can be together, somewhere far away from anyone else."

His hands clenched into fists as though he was having to prevent himself from reaching for her. "But if he isn't right—"

"Don't worry about it." She pulled his shirt out from his dress trousers. "I have a plan."

She *did* have a plan, albeit a desperate, last-ditch one. Hugh would never agree if he knew about it. To distract him from asking more questions, she ran her palms among the smooth, rippling lines of his abs, under his shirt. His muscles hardened under her hands, his eyes going wide and dark.

"You can't go on like this, Hugh," she said softly, bending down to him. "*We* can't go on like this. Whatever happens, it has to be better than the way things are now."

He captured her mouth again, tongue thrusting past her lips in desperate need. Now *she* was the one making noises, gasping as desire pulsed between her thighs.

Blindly, she jerked his shirt apart, craving the feel of his hot skin against her own. She dug her fingernails into the hard planes of his chest, claiming his body even as he claimed her mouth. More, she needed more. There were far too many clothes still between them.

As if reading her mind, he ripped her jacket from her shoulders. She sat up, fumbling to pull off her layered tops. She got briefly stuck in the layered garments, but Hugh freed her, impatiently tossing the torn clothing aside.

She threw back her head as he bit at her bared throat. He worked his way down, feverishly kissing her collarbone and the soft curve of her breast.

When his hot mouth closed over her nipple, through the thin cotton fabric of her bra, she lost all control. She clutched at the back of his neck, pushing her breast further into his hungry mouth. Helplessly, she ground herself against his rigid length as he sucked and licked.

He broke off, pulling back. Cold air teased her nipple through the wet fabric of her bra. She made a brief, wordless sound of disappointment—but he'd only stopped in order to undo the catch. He caught her nipple again in his mouth as her bra fell free, and oh, if it had been good before, it was nothing compared to the sheer heaven of his touch now.

"Hugh," she cried out, as each swirl of his tongue pulled her helplessly closer to the brink. "Wait, slow down, too much!"

Rather than stop, he sucked harder. His agile hands popped open the button of her jeans. One long finger slid through her slick folds.

"Hugh!" Her hips jerked as he found just the right spot. "Hugh, stop, I'm going to—!"

She felt his lips curve in a smile against her breast as she exploded. She held tight onto his tattooed shoulders, lost to everything except him. Pulsing waves of pleasure swirled through her, more intense than she'd ever experienced.

He gasped. She froze, her afterglow quenched by sudden cold fear. She'd come, and he still hadn't.

"Oh no." Pulling back, she anxiously scrutinized his face, searching for any sign of pain. "Do *I* hurt you now?"

"No." His blue eyes were soft with wonder. He brushed her hair back from her face, fingertips light and tender on her skin. "You don't. There's no difference." His expression twisted in sudden dismay. "Shit. Did I do it wrong?"

"Oh *God* no." She was still trembling, lightning-jolts of pleasure shooting through her from the intensity of the experience. "That was —that was amazing. And also not what we were meant to be doing. This is supposed to be about you, remember?"

His eyes heated again. "That *was* for me. Watching you...nothing could be better."

His cock was an iron bar between them. He sucked in his breath as she reached down, stroking him through his pants.

"That sounds like a challenge," she said, grinning at him. Then her smile faded a little. "So...if I'm still not setting off your unicorn, does that mean that your father is right? I *can't* take your animal?"

"I don't know." His jaw had gone tight, the tendons on the side of his neck standing out as she continued to rub her palm against his hidden length. "But if you keep doing that, we're going to find out."

Her thighs trembled at the thought, but she made herself pause. "Hugh...do you really want to do this?"

He went still under her. His eyes met hers for a long, long moment.

Then, "Yes," he said softly.

With shaking hands, she undid his belt. The sound of his zip sliding down sounded shockingly loud in the silence. He lifted his hips to let her pull his clothes down. And then he was free, bare to her at last.

She couldn't look away from that hard, proud shaft. A little tentatively, she closed her hand around him. The unexpected softness of his skin there made her draw in a soft, surprised breath. He let out a low groan from his throat in response. Heart beating fast, she tightened her fingers, and was rewarded with another moan and a jerk of his hips.

"Ivy," he gasped. "I'm not going to last long either."

A pearl of liquid was beading at his tip. She leaned in close, licking at it. The salt-sweet taste was another surprise, and one that brought an answering rush of heat between her own thighs. She wanted more, needed more.

"Ivy!" He grabbed at her hair, holding her back as she tried to take him into her mouth. "If you do that, I won't be able to help myself."

"That's the idea." She squeezed him, marveling at the contrast of soft and hard. "If you do lose your unicorn…we can't risk you being inside me. We don't know how quickly my venom would affect you. This is the safest way, Hugh."

His eyes were dark. Primal desire had stripped away his usual control, his need for her clear in every line of his body. "This isn't—I didn't want—I'm sorry. You're right. But I wish we could do this properly."

"Shh." She pushed him back down again. "Next time."

Though she wasn't sure if she hoped there would be a next time. If she couldn't take his unicorn, he'd still be in agony.

No. She had to focus on the present rather than worrying over the future. This was Hugh's first time too. She had to make it as good for him as he had for her.

She slid her mouth down over his shaft. He swore, thighs taut under her hands as she explored his hard length. The merest flick of her tongue over a certain spot on the underside made him thrust helplessly into her mouth, his fingers digging into her shoulders.

Now she understood what he'd meant when he'd said that her pleasure earlier had been as much for him as for her. Every one of his gasps and moans stoked her own fire. To be the one making him writhe and buck, to be the one taking him higher, to be able to taste the effect she had on him—it was almost better than her own release.

Mate him! Her wyvern's animal lust swept through her, nearly burning away all other thought. *Mate! Now!*

Despite her wyvern instinct and her own desire, Ivy held onto control by her fingernails. She worked him harder, channeling all her own desperate longing into giving him pleasure.

He was her mate. She wanted to do this for him. It was the one thing that she *could* do for him.

"Ivy!" he cried out, arcing up. "Ivy!"

CHAPTER 23

Goodbye, whispered his unicorn.

CHAPTER 24

It was so quiet.

Hugh couldn't get used to the echoing silence in his own head. He'd always thought of his unicorn as a quiet presence, but now...now he knew the difference between *quiet* and *nothing*. He kept holding his breath, listening for a whisper that would never come again.

"Hugh?"

He jumped, coming back to himself. "Sorry. Keep zoning out. This is damned peculiar."

From the expressions on his fellow firefighters' faces, *damned peculiar* were not the words that they would have chosen. Dai and John were both staring at him as if he'd misplaced a limb. Griff didn't seem able to look at him at all. Chase had his back pressed into the corner, all his usual laughter drained from his face. Only Ash was as expressionless as always.

It was strange, seeing them all crowded into his kitchen. It was even stranger to just see...*them*. They all seemed oddly different now that he could only see their physical forms. No hint of the powerful energies hidden underneath their skins; no subtle brush of their minds against his. He couldn't even sense that they were shifters.

They could have been any ordinary group of humans, for all he could tell.

And they didn't hurt. There wasn't even the faintest trace of pain, despite their proximity. He'd never truly realized how omnipresent his headaches had been. Now, instead of the familiar dull ache, there was...nothing.

It was so *quiet*.

Chase cleared his throat. "Uh, Hugh? You still with us?"

Damn it, he'd drifted off again. "Right. Sorry. What was I saying?"

"You were explaining," Dai said very carefully, as if he thought Hugh might have lost the ability to understand simple English along with his unicorn, "why this is a good thing. Again."

"Yes. That was it. Anyway, I know it's going to be hard for you to understand, but—what do you mean, again?"

The rest of Alpha Team exchanged glances. He wondered if they were talking to each other telepathically. He didn't have the foggiest clue anymore, of course.

"Shield-brother." John Doe stumbled on the name, the faint melody of his sea-dragon accent more pronounced than usual. "You have now told us how this loss is actually a blessing three times, by my count. There is no need to repeat the chorus. If this is truly what your heart desires, then we...we rejoice with you."

"No, we don't!" Chase burst out. The pegasus shifter gestured at Hugh, his mouth twisting with distress. "How can you look at him and say this is right?"

"This *is* right," Hugh said firmly. "And you're all going to be happy for me."

Chase raked a hand through his black curly hair, making it stand on end. "But you've lost your animal. You're not—this can't have been what you wanted. Did that damn wyvern talk you into it?"

"Ivy did exactly what I wanted," Hugh said icily. He hoped that Ivy —who was in the front room explaining things to Hope separately— couldn't overhear any of this. "And don't any of you *dare* make her feel worse. She's having a hard enough time as it is."

The way that she'd jerked away from him, the terrible look on her face when she'd realized what had happened...that had been the worst part of losing his unicorn.

He'd tried to reassure her that it *was* all right. That everything was fine. That for the first time in his life he was without pain. He didn't think she'd even heard his words. She'd just stared at him, eyes blank with shock and horror, as if she could see some wound that he didn't even feel.

He didn't know why she'd reacted like that. This had been her idea in the first place. This was what she'd *wanted*, wasn't it? Why was she now creeping around as if it hurt to look at him?

Perhaps she was just feeling guilty at having taken his animal, but in the silence of his soul, he feared that it was more than that. Was there something wrong with their bond now? Something he could no longer sense himself?

He waited for his unicorn's reassurance that they were still her mate, as she was theirs...but none came. No whispered comment. No subtle pressure. No wordless nudge.

Nothing.

It was so quiet.

"See?" Chase flung up his hands, entreating the ceiling to bear witness. "There you go again! And yet you still insist that this, this maiming is a good thing?"

"I'm afraid this is going to take some getting used to, Hugh." Dai was still squinting at him as if he might be able to uncover Hugh's missing beast if he just found the right angle. "Most of us didn't even know you were a unicorn, and now we have to wrap our heads around you *not* being a unicorn? You insist this is better, but I can't imagine anyone being happy to lose their animal."

Ivy unfortunately picked that moment to come back into the kitchen. Catching the dragon shifter's last few words, she flinched.

"It *is* a good thing," Hugh said sharply. "Believe me, this is much better. I was in pain, and Ivy healed me. Griff, tell them I'm not lying."

The griffin shifter's golden eyes flickered over him, but jerked quickly away. "He's telling the truth. He honestly prefers his state now to how he was...before."

Chase sank down onto a kitchen chair, scowling. "Well, I don't. And what's this going to do to the case against Gaze, anyway?"

"That is a good point," John said, his brow furrowing. "We cannot bring the evil-doer to full justice, if there is no evidence that his greatest crime was ever committed."

"He'll go down for assault and kidnapping." Hugh shrugged. "That's good enough to put him away for a long time. I was never going to stand up and publicly accuse him of trying to saw off my horn, after all."

"He *should* be charged with murder," Chase muttered. From the dark look he threw at Ivy, he didn't think the basilisk was the only one.

Ash spoke before Hugh could snarl at the pegasus shifter. "Hugh, while you may not have been intending to reveal your true nature, I fear that the same is not true of Gaze. There is a very real risk that he will announce what you are during his trial."

"Oh, perfect." The sheer irony of it made him laugh out loud. "So now that I'm not a unicorn anymore, everyone is going to think I *am* one. Wonderful."

From Ivy's pale face, she hadn't thought of this either. "Is there any way to convince him not to talk? Make a deal?"

"There's an idea," Chase said, straightening. "I know where he's being held—the police brought him back to a secret shifter detention center not too far from here. We could go pay him a visit. Persuade him to hold his tongue."

John Doe drew back as if Chase had wafted garbage under his nose. "One does not negotiate with honorless pondscum."

Chase cracked his knuckles meaningfully. "I was thinking of a different sort of persuasion."

"Leaving aside the legality of such action," Ash said, looking rather pained, "I fear that it would be futile. We have no leverage. Apart from a certain amount of short-term discomfort, we have no way to threaten Gaze. He is already facing life imprisonment for his crimes. We have no power to either increase or reduce that sentence."

"And he has every reason to want to reveal Hugh's nature," Griff said grimly. "Once Hugh's secret is out, he'll be a tempting target for other criminals. Not everyone is going to believe that he's truly lost his animal. Someone might decide to see if he can be 'persuaded' to rediscover his unicorn. If Gaze goes down for life, that'll be the only way he can get revenge on Hugh."

"Damn it." Hugh glared around at them all, his anger at his own helplessness spilling over. "Why couldn't one of you have just killed the bastard when you had the chance?"

He regretted his outburst instantly as Ivy winced, looking stricken. Reflexively, he reached out to her, but she recoiled.

It made his heart hurt worse than his head ever had. She was in pain, and he couldn't do anything about it.

She hadn't let him near her since last night. She wouldn't let him touch her, not even fully clothed. She'd insisted that they had to wait until she'd done...whatever it was she was planning. He still didn't know how she intended to get around the problem of her venom.

He let his hand drop again, though it went against every instinct not to touch her. "Sorry," he muttered, looking round at the rest of Alpha Team. "That was unfair."

"But not wrong," Chase said, his own fists clenching. The pegasus shifter looked as frustrated and helpless as he himself felt. "Damn it, there has to be *something* we can do."

"There is," John Doe said. He drew himself up to his full seven-foot height, chin lifting. "We can let it be known far and wide that any miscreant who thinks to threaten our shield-brother will very quickly regret it."

"Right. If anyone comes after you, they'll have to get through us," Dai said, to general murmurs of agreement.

The unanimous show of support brought an unaccustomed tightness to his throat. He'd lied to them all for so long, about so much, and yet they still had his back. They'd forgiven him so easily, it was like they didn't even think there was anything to forgive.

He was lost for words...but he had more than words available to him now. Reaching out, he clasped John's forearm, in the sea dragon gesture of one warrior thanking another.

John gripped his arm in return, his indigo eyes softening. It was strange, so strange, to feel nothing but warmth and comradeship in his touch.

Releasing the sea dragon, Hugh turned to Chase next. He'd intended to just shake his hand, but the pegasus shifter sprang up, instead pulling him into a bone-crushing hug. And then they were all around him, clapping him on the back or clasping his shoulder. Their friendship and support surrounded him.

And for the first time, he could accept it without flinching.

Out of the corner of his eye, he noticed Ivy circling the room, being careful to stay as far away from everyone as possible. She sidled over to Ash, who also still stood a little apart from the group.

"Can I talk to you for a sec?" Ivy muttered to Ash. "Privately?"

"Ivy," Hugh said, concerned by the way her gloved hands were twisting together. He broke away from his friends, stepping toward her. "What's the matter?"

"Nothing." Ivy looked up at Ash, her face set and pale. Hugh couldn't interpret her expression. "But I need to talk to the Phoenix."

CHAPTER 25

Ivy made herself wait until they'd walked a little way up the street, away from prying ears. Hugh didn't have shifter hearing any more, but his friends' senses were as acute as ever. She didn't want any of them overhearing this conversation. They might tell Hugh...and then he would do everything in his power to convince her not to go through with this.

But she had to. It was their only remaining option.

Steeling her nerve, she turned to Ash.

"You have to burn away my wyvern," she said.

The Phoenix looked at her with those dark, ageless eyes. His face was never exactly expressive, but now it turned as blank and forbidding as a fortress. Her wyvern cringed at the sense of a much greater power looming over them.

"You have asked this of me before," he said. "The answer is still the same. No."

"Things are different now." It took all of Ivy's strength to stand her ground. "You *have* to. For Hugh's sake. I have to be able to touch him."

"I sympathize with your predicament," Ash said. Despite his expressionless face, Ivy had an odd certainty that he genuinely *did*. "I understand all too well what it is to be so close and yet so far from one's mate. But destroying your wyvern would not help Hugh."

"You don't understand. He needs me—"

"Precisely," Ash interrupted. "He needs *you*. Not a burned-out husk that looks like you. Ivy, our animals are intertwined through our souls. If I burned away your beast, you would no longer be Hugh's mate."

"But Hugh lost his unicorn, and he's still *my* mate."

"Yes." Ash's eyebrows drew down a little, his tone turning thoughtful. "That surprises me. When I take a shifter's animal, the destruction is total, like burning a tree to the ground. Hugh…is more like a tree that has been split by lightning. The trunk may be shattered and hollow, but the roots are still strong. The leaves will grow again."

Ivy's breath caught. "Are you saying his unicorn is still there?"

Ash shook his head, killing her tiny seed of hope. "No. I have no sense of his animal. But *Hugh* is still there. He is still the same person. Ivy, if I took your wyvern, *you* would not be the same person as you are now. You might be content, because you would not know that you had ever been otherwise, but Hugh would know. It would be the worst thing either of us could do to him."

"Don't be so sure," Ivy said bleakly. "I met Hugh's father. He lost his unicorn too. He told me that ex-unicorns need sex to stay sane. But Hugh can't touch me. And if, if he has to get what he needs elsewhere, I'll go mad. I can't bear to think of him with someone else."

The Phoenix's controlled expression cracked at last, revealing a hint of true, human pity. "It is bad enough to be unable to be with one's mate. If someone else was with her…well. I am grateful beyond words that the situation has never arisen for me. But in any case, you do not need to fear that Hugh will be unfaithful. You are his true mate, as much as he is yours."

"Then *he'll* go mad. Hugh's father tried to be abstinent, and he said it nearly killed him. He's forced to do things he doesn't want at all, just to cling onto sanity."

Ash's mouth tightened. "Hugh has one of the strongest wills I've ever encountered. He will not be forced into anything. Not even out of self-preservation."

"Exactly! I'm so scared that he'll destroy himself. *Please*, Ash. You have to take my wyvern. No matter what it does to me. Can't you see that it's better for Hugh to at least have some version of his mate rather than nothing at all?"

Ash drew in a deep breath through his nose, and let it out again, slowly. "No. It is not. I will not burn your wyvern."

"I'll *make* you do it," Ivy vowed, meaning it with all her heart. "I know you sometimes punish criminals by taking their animals. I'll, I'll burn down a house. I'll burn down *your* house."

"I do not have a house," Ash murmured. "And please refrain from burning down my fire station. It would be immensely embarrassing if you succeeded."

Ash rubbed his forehead, suddenly looking old and tired. He usually projected such an aura of calm that he seemed as eternal as a mountain, but for the first time Ivy noticed the silver streaked through his brown hair and the weathered lines around his eyes. She wondered just how old the Phoenix actually was.

"You are a very determined young woman," he said, dropping his hand again. "As strong-willed as Hugh, in fact. If I do not assist you, then I have no doubt you will devise some even worse solution."

Ivy's heart thumped against your ribs. "So you'll do it?"

"I will not burn your wyvern. I cannot do that to either Hugh or yourself. But there is another way I could free you both from this trap. I swore I would never do it again, but…I can see no other way out." His jaw clenched for a moment. "Though I will only do it if Hugh agrees to it as well. If I do this, it must be completely, not just to one of you. *That* mistake, I will not repeat."

"I'll persuade him," Ivy said, though she had no idea how. "If it's the only way for us to be together, I'll *have* to persuade him."

"It is not a way for you to be together." Ash's fathomless eyes were strangely human for once, the fiery power in them overshadowed by some old, deep pain. "It is a way for you to be able to be apart. Ivy, if you both wish it…I can burn the connection between you, your love, your very memories of each other. You would no longer be each other's true mate."

CHAPTER 26

Betty shook her head, her jaw set in the stubborn expression that Hope found both exasperating and ridiculously adorable. "I still don't like it. He's not right."

"Hugh's been through a lot," Hope argued. "You can't expect him to be all sunshine and smiles straight away. He's still a good guy."

They were sitting at Hugh's kitchen table, ostensibly catching up on the homework that they'd both missed over the past few days. In reality, Hope hadn't actually read so much as a word of the biology textbook spread open between them. She kept getting distracted by the sweep of Betty's long eyelashes, the taut line of her neck, the full curves of her—

"What?" Betty said.

Hope jerked her eyes back to the textbook. "Nothing. Just —nothing."

Mitochondria. Cell wall. Hope tried to concentrate on the words, instead of the thought of Betty's soft, full lips. *So kissable. No, bad brain! Mustn't think of that sort of thing!*

If Betty *had* had those sort of feelings for her, surely the ideal moment to have confessed them would have been just after the hellhound had so dramatically—not to mention romantically—saved Hope's life. But she hadn't. So Hope couldn't say anything either.

After all, Betty was a shifter. Surely she could sense how Hope's pulse raced whenever they were together, how her fingers shook whenever they accidentally bumped hands reaching for the same pen. And if they were meant for each other, Betty would have *known*. The fact that she hadn't said anything…meant that they weren't.

Sometimes, Hope really wished that *she* was a shifter. It must be nice, never falling for the wrong person.

"Anyway, I still don't like you staying here, in his house," Betty said, continuing the argument. "Especially with your sister. It's not safe. What if there was an accident?"

"I've lived with Ivy my whole life, and her venom hasn't killed me yet," Hope said, both annoyed and touched by Betty's concern. "There's nothing different there."

Betty pursed her lips in a way that made Hope earnestly stare at her cell diagram again. "Yeah, but…there is. *She's* not all there either. I mean, I don't blame her from being preoccupied. If my m-mate—" she stumbled a little on the word, "was hurt like Hugh, I wouldn't be able to think of anything else either. But I worry that means Ivy might get careless when it comes to keeping you safe."

"Ivy will never hurt me," Hope said, with complete certainty. "She's never careless. So stop worrying."

Betty blew out her breath, looking frustrated. "I can't. I can't help it. I think about what could happen, and—if there was an accident, it's not like Hugh could heal you any more."

Hope couldn't help flinching a little at the brutal statement, even though it was only the truth. She'd been very carefully trying not to think about Hugh's healing powers…or, more specifically, his half-complete cure.

She had no way of knowing how much of the venom in her body he'd managed to neutralize before he lost his powers. She still felt better than she had in years, but was this just a temporary reprieve? Would she wake up tomorrow or next week or next year with the familiar pain biting at her, paralysis slowly creeping further up her body?

It had almost been better when she'd *known* that she wouldn't live to see her thirtieth birthday.

Betty must have caught her reaction, because she flinched as well, looking stricken. "Sorry. I didn't mean to remind you of—you know."

Hope pasted a smile onto her face, the familiar one that she usually deployed to reassure Ivy. "It's okay. Don't worry about me. If nothing else, I'm still pain-free. I'm grateful just for that."

Betty eyed her sidelong without speaking for a moment. There was something unusually hesitant about her manner. She was usually so bold and direct, it unnerved Hope to see the shifter clearly searching for words.

"You know," the hellhound said tentatively, "it's okay to be upset, or mad, or whatever you feel. You lost your chance of a cure for your illness. That's a big thing too."

Hope could feel the corners of her mouth wanting to wobble. She smiled harder, forcing brightness into her tone. "Oh, I never expected to live a normal lifespan anyway. I haven't lost anything really. Not compared to poor Hugh."

Betty put her hand on top of Hope's, resting on the table. The hellhound's skin was hot, so hot. Hope burned at the touch, a strange wave of heat prickling over her entire body.

"You have," Betty said, very quietly. "And you don't have to pretend you haven't. Not with me."

They sprang apart guiltily as Ivy came into the kitchen. Hope was certain that her shifter sister would instantly pick up on the electric tension in the air, but Ivy didn't make any comment. She just gave them a preoccupied nod on her way to the sink.

Betty's right, Hope realized with a twinge of concern as she watched Ivy take one of her special, red-banded cups out of the Box o' Death. *She's not herself.*

Her sister might not be going literally catatonic, but her eyes held a hint of the same haunted, thousand-yard stare as Hugh's did whenever he blanked out. She'd been distant ever since she'd talked to Fire

Commander Ash a few days ago. Hope didn't know what they'd discussed, but it was clearly still preying on Ivy's mind.

"Hey, where were you last night?" Hope asked, hoping to fish for clues as to what was going on inside her sister's head. "I didn't hear you come in."

"Went back to our apartment," Ivy muttered as she filled her glass at the sink. "I'm sleeping there at the moment."

Hope exchanged a startled look with Betty. "Really? Why?"

"Just...keeping an eye on it. Don't want anyone breaking in and trashing the place."

"I could house-sit for you," Betty volunteered, to Hope's surprise. "I could look after Hope there too. So you and your mate could be alone together here."

Ivy choked on her water. "No! Uh, that is, thanks. But no."

"Why not?" Hope demanded.

Inwardly, her mind was doing backflips. And her stomach. Had Betty actually just proposed that they *move in* together? Even if it was just as roommates...

"It's a brilliant idea! You could concentrate on Hugh, and we wouldn't have to worry about keeping all our dishes and laundry and stuff separate, and it would solve so many problems." Words tumbled uncontrollably out of her mouth, as if she could change Ivy's mind if she just talked fast enough. "We're paid up until the end of the month, so it's just sitting empty. And Betty needs a place to stay, and—"

"You do?" Ivy interrupted, turning to Betty. "Why? I thought you had a place, at that special home for orphaned shifters."

The hellhound squirmed in her seat, shooting Hope an accusing glare. "I thought we weren't going to tell her about this. You said she had enough to deal with already."

Hope dismissed this with an airy wave. "That was when it was a problem without a solution. Go on, tell her."

"The home might not be open for much longer," Betty said reluctantly. "It was almost entirely funded through Gaze's charity. He genuinely did put a lot of money into it—he grew up on the streets himself. With him out of the picture, well..." She shrugged. "There aren't a lot of shifter foster families to start with. Let alone ones eager to take in hellhounds and other monsters."

"You're not a monster," Hope and Ivy said together.

Betty flashed a grin. "Thanks, but you guys are biased. Anyway, if you aren't going to be using your old place, I could sublet it from you. I can pay," she added quickly, as Ivy opened her mouth. "I've got an evening job, and I'm gonna look for another. And as soon as I finish school, I can work more."

"No, then you'll be going to university on full scholarship, like me," Hope said firmly, ignoring Betty's expressive eye-roll. "I have it all planned out. So you just need a place to stay for a year. Come on, Ivy. Say yes. It's perfect."

"I'll...think about it." Ivy's head suddenly jerked up, and an alarmed expression flashed across her face.

"What is it?" Hope asked, and then heard the footsteps moving around upstairs herself. "Oh, Hugh's up. Do you think that means he's—"

"I gotta go," Ivy interrupted, abandoning her half-finished glass of water on the kitchen counter. "Tell him—tell him I've gone out to work."

"But-" Hope started, but Ivy had already disappeared out the back door. She exchanged a puzzled look with Betty.

"Is it just me," Betty asked in an undertone, "or was that really weird?"

"Was what really weird?" Hugh had come into the room, barefoot. He wore jeans, a plain white T-shirt, and a rather groggy expression. His hair stuck up in unruly spikes on one side, tousled from bed.

"Nothing," Hope said quickly. "Hey, you're up early today!"

Hugh blinked blearily at the clock. "It's nearly eleven."

"Yeah, but the past few days we haven't seen you before one," Hope pointed out. "Are you feeling better?"

Hugh stopped in the middle of reaching for a cupboard. Hope's heart sank as the by-now familiar blank look crept across his face, his mouth going slack.

A soft growl escaped Betty's mouth. The hellhound's eyes were fixed on the motionless Hugh, her lips wrinkling back to expose her teeth.

"Stop it, Betty!" Hope hissed. Then, louder but more gently: "Hugh? Hello?"

He started, his outstretched hand dropping back to his side. "Sorry. Just...listening. Yes, I'm feeling better." A hint of the lost look crept into his pale eyes. "I think."

"Well, that's good!" Hope said brightly. Under the table, she poked Betty. "Isn't that good, Betty?"

The hellhound finally managed to choke off her growling, though she was still physically drawn back in her chair as if Hugh was a particularly large spider. "Yeah. Great. Uh, listen, I just remembered, I have a...thing."

Hope narrowed her eyes at her. "No, you don't."

Hugh let out a soft huff of sardonic laughter. "It's fine, Hope. Let Betty go and do her...thing."

The hellhound didn't need to be invited twice. With an apologetic glance at Hope, she grabbed her bag and made a dash for the door.

"*Rude*," Hope muttered. She started stacking up the discarded homework. "I'm so sorry, Hugh. I don't know what's gotten into her."

"That's because you aren't a shifter," he said, rather dryly. He opened a cupboard. "Speaking of which, where's Ivy?"

"She, uh, had to go out."

"Oh." Hugh closed the cupboard again without taking anything out, and moved on to the next one. "Is that 'had to go out' as in the same way that Betty had to go do 'a thing'?"

"Um." Hope wasn't sure whether to be glad or dismayed by this unexpected flash of his previous sarcasm. "Yes."

His mouth twisted a little. "Thought so."

Hope bit her lip, watching him for a few minutes. He kept opening cupboards and drawers, staring at the contents blankly, and then closing them...only to reopen them again a moment later.

"Hugh?" she ventured, about the third time he randomly inspected his plates. "What are you looking for?"

He stilled. "I'm...not sure. Nothing, actually."

Nonetheless, he took out a glass, and poured himself some water. Drink in hand, he leaned back against the kitchen counter, shooting her a slight, strained smile.

"I'm a mess, aren't I?" he said. "No wonder Ivy's avoiding me."

Reversing out from behind the table, Hope wheeled herself closer to him. "Things aren't okay with you guys, are they."

He shook his head, looking weary. "Things are about as far from okay as it is possible to be. Whatever she talked to Ash about—and I have a horrible suspicion that I know what it was—it clearly didn't go the way that she wanted. And now she doesn't even want to be in the same room as me."

"What *did* she talk to Ash about?" Hope asked.

He took a long drink of his water before answering. "I think she asked him to burn out her wyvern."

"What, again?" Hope frowned, puzzled. "Why?"

Hugh made a sweeping hand gesture at himself. "Because of me. So that we can touch."

Hope shook her head, still not getting it. "Why would she need to lose her wyvern for that? You're her true mate."

Hugh stared at her. She stared back, in a moment of mutual confusion.

"I think," Hugh said at last, putting down his glass, "that you'd better explain why you think that's relevant."

"Well, she's venomous all the time because of her animal, right? Her wyvern is scared of everything, so it's always on the defensive. But it's not scared of *you*." Hope shrugged. "So you should be able to touch her."

Why was he still staring at her like that? Wasn't all this painfully obvious?

"Haven't you even tried?" she asked.

"Ivy won't let me near her. She said the thought of hurting me made her so nervous, her venom would be strong enough to kill on contact. You really think that I'm still immune?"

"Well, not exactly immune. I mean, you shouldn't be sharing gloves or anything—her venom would still affect you if you came into contact with it. But don't you get it? You *won't* come into contact with it by touching her directly. Her wyvern won't want to hurt you, so if you get close to her, it will *have* to settle down."

"So she wouldn't be venomous at all," Hugh said slowly. "Not only to me, but to everyone."

"Exactly! And once she's turned off her venom once, maybe she'll learn how to do it whenever she wants, even when you're not around. You can help her relax enough to control it." Excited, Hope wheeled right up to him, tugging at his arm. "You have to go after her, Hugh. Right now! You have to make her listen to you."

Hugh let her pull him upright, but balked as she tried to urge him toward the door. "What if your theory is wrong?"

"It's not my theory," Hope said. "It was our mom's. She was always searching for *her* true mate. She wasn't as venomous as Ivy, but she was still always a bit toxic. She was certain that if she could just find her mate, her wyvern would finally learn to chill out."

Hugh ran a hand over his face, his expression so closed it was impossible to tell what he was thinking. "Does Ivy know about this?"

"Of course." Hope hesitated, wrinkling her nose. "But I don't think she believes it. She doesn't exactly have a great relationship with our mom. And Ivy's always preferred to expect the worst possible outcome. That way she can't be disappointed."

"She's scared to even try," he said softly.

"Right! But you have to make her try, Hugh. Don't let her push you away. Just, just sweep her off her feet and kiss her!"

"Damn it, that's a tempting thought," Hugh muttered. He picked up his glass of water, shaking his head slightly. "I don't know, Hope. I rushed into one irreversible decision, and look where it got me. I need to think about this."

Hope opened her mouth to argue further…and then saw the red ring around the bottom of Hugh's glass.

It wasn't his glass.

Ivy's never careless, she'd told Betty…but she had been. And now Hugh, oblivious, was raising her venom-contaminated drink to his mouth.

"Hugh, no!" Hope flung herself forward, with one hard, frantic push of her wheels. "Stop!"

The edge of her wheelchair crashed into his thighs, knocking him off-balance. Ivy's glass slipped from his hand. As if in slow motion, Hope saw it tumble, glittering water droplets scattering outward in a deadly arc.

Straight into her own face.

CHAPTER 27

Ivy came out of the emergency care ward to find Hugh sitting alone in the waiting room, his head in his hands. He sprang up as she entered, face pale and every muscle tense.

"Is she...?" He left the sentence hanging in midair, looking near-sick with worry.

"She's going to be all right," Ivy said, and her own tight chest eased a little at the sight of the relief that washed over his face. "She's still unconscious, but she's breathing on her own again now. I left Betty watching over her. She'll let us know when she wakes up."

Hugh closed his eyes for a moment, his lips moving soundlessly in prayer. Then his expression tightened, relief turning to self-recrimination. He sank back down into the plastic chair.

"She got hurt because of me. Because of my carelessness." He leaned his forehead against his clenched fists, elbows braced against his knees. "I couldn't even do anything to help her."

None of that was true. It was *Ivy's* fault, her own carelessness, that had nearly killed her sister. Hugh had saved Hope's life, by performing CPR until the ambulance arrived.

She ached to tell him that. She wanted to wrap words of love around him, embracing him with her voice as she couldn't with her arms. To take away the burden of guilt that slumped his shoulders.

But she didn't.

Our mate hurts! Her wyvern pushed at her, urging her forward. *He needs us, now!*

It was the hardest thing she'd ever done, but Ivy set her feet, even though every instinct screamed to go to him. No matter how much she wanted to comfort him and be comforted in return, she couldn't.

If she was going to save him from worse pain later...she couldn't ease his agony now.

In fact, she had to make it worse.

NO! Her wyvern reared up in her mind, spitting acid. *He is our mate! We can never hurt him!*

Ivy ignored her agitated animal. "Hugh, this shouldn't have happened. It *wouldn't* have happened if you still had your unicorn."

He jerked as if she'd slapped him in the face. "You think I don't know that?"

"I think you're desperately trying to pretend that nothing's changed. But it has, Hugh."

"I know. I do know, Ivy. I'm trying to get better."

"But you aren't. You *won't*. The way you are now? That's the way it's always going to be. And I can't cope."

Finally she understood why all the other firefighters of Alpha Team had rejected her, why they hadn't been able to stand to have her in the same room as their mates. Because now that Hugh wasn't immune to her venom, she felt exactly the same way. *She* couldn't stand to have her mate in the same room as herself.

Even now, her awareness of the deadly venom slicking her palms made her want to bolt out the door. Her very presence put her mate in danger.

No shifter could stand that.

Hugh was staring at her, motionless. All the color had drained from his face. "Ivy, what are you saying?"

"I can't go through this again." She gestured around at the ER waiting room. "I can't be constantly watching you, making sure no one gets hurt."

Hugh dropped his gaze in shame. He rubbed his right bicep in an unconscious, habitual gesture, and she knew that he was thinking of the dead leaves tattooed there. Thinking of how close he'd come to having to ink another failure onto his skin.

"I'm sorry," he said quietly. "Not that it makes any difference. If...if you don't want me around Hope any more, you two could move out. I could make sure I only see you alone, when she isn't around."

"It's not just about Hope. It's about *you*, Hugh." Taking a deep breath, she told him the truth. "I'm so scared of hurting you. It's all I can think about, every second that we're together. And I can't live like this any more."

"But you don't have to!" He shot to his feet, as fierce and desperate as her wyvern. "Hope told me about your mother, how she thought she wouldn't be toxic around her true mate. What if that's true? What if you *can't* hurt me?"

"I *did* hurt you, Hugh!" How could he even think of clinging onto this false hope? "I took your unicorn! Your father was wrong, and now you want to trust my mother, the woman who's in jail for *murder*? Haven't we learned by now that being true mates isn't some magic get-out clause that solves everything?"

He hesitated for a second, the bitter truth of the words clearly hitting home. Then he shook his head stubbornly.

"We have to at least try. And this is the perfect opportunity, while we're in the hospital, so if anything *does* go wrong, help is close at hand." He took a step toward her, reaching out. "Please, Ivy, we have to—"

"*Don't touch me!*"

He froze at her shriek. She scrabbled away from him, pressing her back against the far wall. She was sweating, terror of hurting him making her skin slick with venom. She had to stop him from trying again.

"I don't want you to touch me," she lied.

If he'd still been a shifter, she would never have gotten away with it. He would have sensed the truth in his soul, felt the way every part of her cried out with yearning.

But he wasn't a shifter.

He physically staggered, as if the words had knocked all the breath out of him. The back of his knees hit one of the chairs, and he collapsed into it.

She kept speaking, although her wyvern clawed at her mind trying to silence her. "You must have noticed how every shifter looks at you now, Hugh. How they react to you. *I'm* a shifter. What do you think *I* see, when I look at you?"

His throat worked convulsively. He stared at her as if she'd suddenly turned into a stranger.

"They only see what's missing," he said at last. "But I hoped that you saw what still remained."

Life had taught her how to hide her feelings. She used every brutal lesson now to forcing her own face into a hard, unyielding mask.

"It isn't enough," she said.

She'd seen him bloody and staggering, light running from his wounded horn. She'd seen him curled over, trying to shut out the world. She'd seen his unicorn die behind his eyes.

None of them compared to the look on his face now.

"I can't be with you any more," she said, which was true. A monster like her didn't deserve a man like him. "You have to set me free."

Hugh's face went slack for a second—but then his eyes focused again. It was the first time since he'd lost his unicorn that she'd seen him pull himself out of that strange, blank state. He clenched one fist, fingernails digging into his palm as though he was trying to physically hold onto the present moment.

"But we're mates," he said. "Nothing can change that."

"Ash can. He told me he can burn away the connection between us. You won't even remember it ever existed."

"You *want* that?" he whispered, barely audible.

"Yes," she said, even as her wyvern howled *no, no!* "Promise me you'll let Ash do it, Hugh."

Slowly, his head bowed. He didn't say yes…but he didn't say no, either.

"I'm going now." She had to leave, right now, or else she would crack and undo everything. "Please, let Ash help you. Don't suffer pointlessly."

He spoke just as she was stepping out the door. "Where are you going?"

"To the only person who can help me." She kept her back to him, so that he couldn't see the betraying tears streaking her face. "Goodbye, Hugh."

CHAPTER 28

He'd zoned out. At the worst possible time, right when he should have been chasing Ivy and begging—no, *demanding*—that she stay. He should have run after her, grabbed her in the corridor, shown her that she was worrying about nothing.

But instead, he'd been frozen, not even aware of time passing. Turned inward, listening futilely. Waiting for his unicorn to guide him. Waiting to be told how he could win back his mate.

When he'd finally resurfaced from the void within, he was alone. Ivy was long gone.

He could only pray that it wasn't already too late.

He lengthened his stride, barging past other pedestrians regardless of their startled glares and muttered comments. He didn't need to look down to know exactly where to put his feet. He'd run down this road many times, heart laboring in his chest, knowing that a few seconds delay could mean the difference between life or death.

This time, however, it wasn't a patient's life that hung in the balance.

The imposing bulk of the fire station dominated the corner of the intersection. The old brick building loomed three floors high, above the massive red-doored bays that held the fire engines and other appliances.

Please let them be out on call, please let them not be here!

But all the fire engines were slumbering peacefully behind their red doors. Evidently no emergencies were in progress at the moment. The on-duty shift would all be at the station.

Hugh didn't waste time on a useless curse. Instead, he ran full-tilt through the staff entrance.

"Hugh!" Chase's eyes widened at his abrupt appearance. From the greasy rag in the pegasus shifter's oil-stained hands, he'd been cleaning his beloved fire engine. "Speak of the devil. What are you—"

"Where's Ash?" Hugh interrupted, panting.

"Upstairs. But, listen, I need to—hey!"

"No time!" Hugh hurled over his shoulder as he took the stairs three at a time.

He crashed through Ash's office door so hard he literally tore it off its hinges. The Phoenix glanced up from his paperwork, unfazed as always.

"Ah," he said, as if he'd been expecting the intrusion. "I take it Ivy spoke to you."

"How could you—" Hugh's chest heaved, his words coming in short, gasping breaths. It wasn't just the physical exertion. He was furious, more furious than he ever had been in his life. "How could you offer—how could you dare—*am I too late?*"

"If you are asking whether I have already burned Ivy's feelings for you, the answer is no." One of Ash's eyebrows rose very slightly. "Believe me, you would have known if I had."

The wave of relief that rushed over Hugh was so strong, he had to grip the back of the chair opposite Ash's desk in order to stay on his feet. He'd beaten Ivy here. He was still her mate.

"Why the hell did you even offer to do such an appalling thing?" he demanded. "Damn it, Ash! You won't burn someone's animal, but you'd do *this*? Why?"

The Phoenix put down his pen, carefully. He steepled his fingers in front of him.

"Because I know exactly how painful it is to be unable to be with one's mate," he said quietly. "And if someone could do something to take that burden away from me, I would welcome it."

"Well, I don't!" Hugh glared at him. "Don't you ever, *ever* use your power on me, understand?"

Ash's shoulders stiffened. "I told Ivy I would not do it without your consent."

"I don't consent. I will never consent. If I ever think you've burned so much as one second of my memories, the tiniest bit of my pain, then I will bloody *end* you."

Ash did not comment on the likelihood of this. Which was just as well, since Hugh was one wrong word away from hauling back and punching the most powerful shifter in Europe square in the face.

"I will never affect any part of your mind or soul without your express permission," Ash said, with utmost formality. "As the Phoenix Eternal, I swear it."

Hugh let out a long, shaking breath, some of the tightness draining away from his own shoulders at last. "Good. We're clear on that, then."

"Very." Ash studied him for a moment. "Would you have me make a similar vow regarding Ivy?"

Hugh opened his mouth to say *yes*…but hesitated.

It's not enough, she'd said.

Ivy creeping about the house, finding any excuse to leave a room the instant that he entered. The way she flinched whenever she looked at him. Like he was a severed limb. A useless remnant, a gruesome relic of past trauma. Something better off burned and buried.

"Hugh?"

He twitched, pulling back from that echoing, silent space inside. There was no voice there to insist that he still had a purpose, that his mate still needed him.

Ivy didn't need him. She needed to heal.

"No." He sank down into the chair opposite Ash, weary in every part of his body. "No, don't promise that."

"It is irrelevant anyway." Ash straightened the paperwork on the desk, precisely aligning the corners of the pages. "As I told Ivy, I will not do it to only one of you."

"Yes. You will."

Ash looked up sharply. "I beg your pardon?"

Hugh took a deep breath, bracing himself. "Ivy's going to come see you soon. She'll ask you to burn her side of our connection. I want you to do it."

"No," Ash said without hesitation. "You do not know what you are asking."

"I do. I know exactly what it's like to have something, and then lose it utterly. I wouldn't ever want to forget my unicorn. I don't ever want to forget Ivy either. But she needs to forget me, if she's going to heal."

"Hugh, you cannot ask me to do this to a friend. If I give her the comfort of forgetting, it will only increase your own suffering."

"I'm asking you to do it *as* your friend. I want her to be happy, Ash." He leaned forward, bracing his hands on the desk. "Let me take her pain as well as mine. I'd rather carry that burden than forget a single second we spent together."

Ash sat absolutely motionless for a moment. Hugh couldn't guess what was going on behind the Phoenix's impenetrable eyes.

"I must warn you that the loss does not get better," Ash said at last, softly. "The grief does not pass."

He held the Phoenix's gaze, unflinching. "If it hurts for the rest of my life...it will still have been worth it."

An unexpected, heartfelt, and utterly obscene curse from the hallway made them both turn. A second later, Chase slunk sheepishly into view.

"Sorry," he said. "The door was, uh, destroyed. I couldn't help overhearing."

"Indeed," Ash said, his tone notably cooler. "Perhaps that would have been more easily avoided if you had been at your assigned post."

Chase winced, but stayed put. "I need to talk to Hugh. I should have done it earlier, I should have called you—damn it, I should never have told her in the first place! But she was so insistent, so certain it would help you, and I thought you couldn't still feel the mate-connection since you weren't a shifter anymore, so it truly seemed best—oh, I'm an idiot. An utter idiot. You're going to want to break every bone in my body. You *should* break every bone in my body."

"Chase," Hugh said, finally managing to insert a word into the torrent of remorse. "What are you babbling about?"

"Ivy *was* here earlier. But she didn't come to see Ash. She came to see me." Chase scrubbed a hand over his face, looking sickened. "And I've made a terrible mistake."

CHAPTER 29

Rear cell block, top floor, third window from the right.

That was what Chase had told her. Perched in an old oak tree outside the prison walls, Ivy narrowed her eyes. Despite the distance and the darkening evening, her keen wyvern vision easily picked out the right cell. Now she just had to wait.

She was only going to get one shot at this.

This prison wasn't a top-security facility, but she had no doubt that she'd trip some sort of alarm the instant she flew over the high concrete outer wall. She'd only have a few minutes at best.

But a few minutes were all she needed. The cell block walls were steel-reinforced and designed to withstand even a dragon...but nothing was stronger than wyvern acid. One blast at the barred window, and she'd be inside.

And then she'd help Hugh the only way she could.

Tell me where the police are holding Gaze, she'd said to Chase. *And you'll never have to see me again.*

She hadn't dared explain much more than that. After she was caught—and she *would* be caught—she didn't want anyone to be able to accuse the pegasus shifter of colluding with her.

Still, Chase was no fool. She'd known from the way that his

simmering hostility had turned to unease that he'd worked out what she intended to do with the information. He already thought of her as a dangerous assassin, after all.

But, as she'd hoped, his fierce loyalty and protectiveness had worked in her favor for once. He wanted to help Hugh nearly as much as she herself did. Add in the fact that it also meant that Chase would be rid of *her* for once and for all, and it was just too good a bargain for him to turn down.

Chase had told her where to come. Now she just had to wait for the right moment to strike.

Yes, her wyvern hissed in bloodthirsty approval. *Spit. Strike. Kill. Destroy all threats to our mate!*

For once she didn't attempt to hold back her beast's murderous instincts. Acid burned at the base of her throat, more potent and concentrated than ever before. With one act, one breath, she would forever silence Gaze. Hugh's secret would be safe.

And *he* would be safe. Not just from potential hunters, but from a far more dangerous threat.

Herself.

She had to be locked up, to protect him. She wasn't strong enough to just leave him. Plus, there was always the risk that Hugh might track her down—even after the terrible things she'd said.

The only way to be absolutely sure that he'd be safe, that he'd never come into contact with her venom, was to put impenetrable walls between them. Walls that neither of them would be able to breach, even if one or both of them was tempted.

She wouldn't be locked up in a pleasant, airy prison like this one, open to the wind and sky. No, she would be put away in a maximum-security facility, deep underground, like her own mother. Monsters belonged in dungeons.

I'm sorry, Hope.

But her sister had Betty to look out for her now, and Griff, and all her other friends. None of *them* would ever accidentally put her in a coma due to a moment of carelessness. Hope was better off without her.

Everyone was better off without her.

A dark shape moved behind the cell window. Ivy snaked her neck out, straining to see through the dusky twilight. She had to be absolutely certain that she had the right target.

The man in the window turned his head, his profile silhouetted by the harsh cell light. There was something on his face—something far too bulky to be mere glasses. Some sort of visor was strapped to his head, completely covering his eyes.

Only one person could be wearing *that*.

Heart hammering, Ivy spread her wings. Her talons flexed on the tree branch. It was time.

Time to save her mate.

"IVY!"

Hugh's shout shocked her so badly, she lost her grip on her branch. She fell out of the tree in a shower of twigs and snapped branches, too off-balance to be able to twist in mid-air and take flight. Her back hit the ground with a crash that knocked all the breath out of her.

She struggled to her feet just as four black hooves touched down in front of her. Hugh slid off the pegasus's back, his hair and clothes windswept. He stepped toward her, holding out his hands.

Ivy recoiled, scrabbling awkwardly backward on her hind legs and clawed wing joints. She hissed in frantic warning.

Hugh stopped, though his hands stayed outstretched, as if he was trying to calm a wild beast. "I know what you're planning, Ivy. You can't go through with this. You aren't a killer."

Acid dripped from her jaws, scorching smoking black holes in the leaf litter. He was wrong. She was *made* for killing, from her deadly breath to her venomous tail. She'd fought her monstrous nature all her life, but now she was finally willing to embrace it.

"I know you're trying to protect me," Hugh said. His expression was intent and focused, his eyes fixed on her as if nothing else existed in the world. "The fact that you're willing to do this proves that you were lying before, at the hospital. You said you didn't want to be my mate, but we both know that isn't true."

Unable to speak mind-to-mind with him, Ivy could only swing her head from side to side in mute denial. She *didn't* want to be his mate. She had brought him nothing but pain.

She could never undo the damage that she'd caused, but she could at least stop him from getting hurt again in the future.

Chase still had his black-feathered wings spread, blocking her way, and the oak branches above her head prevented her from simply leaping into the air. Although she was faster than the pegasus in flight, he was much more nimble on the ground. She'd never be able to get past him in this form.

She shifted. The moment that she was back in her human skin, she attempted to dodge around Hugh, but he was faster. She had to skip backward to avoid touching him.

"Please, Hugh." She circled, trying to keep a wary eye on both him and Chase. "Let me go."

"No." His arms were spread wide, ready to catch her if she tried to make a break for it. "You can't do this, Ivy. You don't *have* to do this."

"I do!" She jerked off her gloves, throwing them carelessly to the ground. She put up her hands, not in surrender, but to show him the venom slicking her skin. "Now get out of my way, or else!"

He stepped forward again. "You won't hurt me."

"I will!" she cried, her voice breaking in desperation. "If you don't let me do this, I *will* hurt you, Hugh! Sooner or later, I'll slip up, or I'll give into temptation, and I'll touch you!"

"Good," he said softly. "Because you can. *We* can."

"You don't know that!"

"I feel it." Hugh touched his heart. "Right here."

She shook her head in denial. "You don't. You can't. You're not a shifter, you don't have an inner animal-"

"I don't need an animal to know that I love you." His mouth quirked. "And to know that you love me, for all that you try to deny it. Trust that love, Ivy. Trust yourself."

"That's not the problem!" Ivy stumbled backward, hands still upraised defensively. "I don't trust my animal!"

No, her wyvern said, unexpectedly. *You do not trust* him.

She'd never before heard her inner animal speak of itself in the singular before. Always, always it said *we* or *us*. But now she had a sense of it pulling away from her. The ever-present burning core of rage at the bottom of her soul faded into nothing.

I will always protect you, her wyvern said to her. Its mental words came slowly, haltingly, as if it found it unnatural to refer to the two of them as separate beings. *But you must stop being afraid now. You are hurting our mate.*

She could almost *see* it standing behind Hugh. He glanced up, looking startled, as if he too felt the shadow of emerald wings closing over him.

He trusts us, her wyvern said, very gently. *Trust him in return. He will never hurt us. He will always treasure us, always defend us, as we treasure and defend him. You don't have to be afraid anymore.*

In the strange silence of her wyvern's withdrawal, she could finally feel what its anger had always masked. Her own deep, terrible fear.

Not the fear of hurting others, but the fear of being hurt herself.

Letting other people get close, letting them in, meant that they could hurt you. Deep down, she'd wanted to keep the world at arm's length, to never be vulnerable. Her wyvern had only been trying to protect her.

But she didn't need to be protected from Hugh.

He was still standing in front of her, head cocked and a slight frown on his face, as if trying to catch a conversation right on the edge of hearing. His eyes widened a little as she stepped forward, but he didn't flinch. He held her gaze, and there was nothing but love and faith in his own.

She let go of fear…and took his hand.

His fingers folded over hers, warm and strong. He smiled down at her.

"Let's go home," he said.

CHAPTER 30

Ivy's phone beeped as they arrived back at their house. Hugh's whole body thirsted to stay in contact with her, but he reluctantly relinquished her hand so that she could answer it. The brief separation was worth it though, for the way her expression changed into a relieved, thankful smile as she listened to the voicemail message.

"That was Betty," Ivy said, lowering the phone again. "Apparently Hope woke up, demanded one of everything from the vending machine, and is currently asleep in a pile of empty cans and chocolate bar wrappers."

"Sounds like she's going to be fine," he said, smiling back. "Do you want us to go pick her up?"

Ivy shook her head. "Betty says the doctors still want to keep her in under observation for a while."

He reclaimed her hand. He never, ever wanted to be parted from her for a second longer than was strictly necessary. A deep, quiet joy filled him as her strong fingers intertwined through his.

"Then we have the house to ourselves tonight," he said, drawing her up the stairs.

Ivy's lips parted a little, her breath coming faster. Nonetheless, she hesitated in the doorway to the bedroom.

He paused too. A part of him—a very specific part—wanted to pull her straight into bed. But even more than that, he wanted this to be right for her. That meant that she had to come to him whole-heartedly, without reservations or fear.

"Are you still nervous?" he asked.

She dropped her gaze, peeked up at him shyly through her dark lashes. "A little."

He raised their joined hands to his lips. She drew in her breath as he gently kissed the tips of her fingers, lingering over each one.

"You won't hurt me," he murmured.

"I know." Her cheeks flushed a delicious pink as she made a vague, embarrassed gesture at his crotch. "But, uh, I've seen how big you are. And this is my first time like this."

He let out a low chuckle, relief sweeping over him as he realized the true reason for her hesitation. "Oh. Don't worry, Ivy. *I* won't hurt *you*. I'll make sure of that."

She raised her eyebrows at him, a naughty smile tugging at her mouth. "But this is your first time too. Are you sure you know what you're doing?"

"Trust me," he said, pulling her into his arms. "I'm a doctor."

She let out a giggle, which turned into a startled laugh as he twirled her around and flung her onto the bed. He covered her body with his own, stretching her arms above her head, their hands still intertwined. She arced up eagerly to him as he bent his head down to claim her mouth.

Oh, it was even better than he'd remembered. He kissed her leisurely, deeply, and she opened like a flower to him. Nothing holding them back from each other. Nothing coming between them.

Except, of course, far too many clothes.

Despite the impatience singing through his blood, he made himself take his time. He savored the sweetness of her lips, the heat of her mouth, every little breathy sound of pleasure she made.

She kissed him back with equal fervor, exploring him in return.

Together, they learned the shape of each other's desire, until they were both gasping, their interlocked fingers clenched tight with the effort of holding back.

Breaking away from her mouth, he kissed his way along her jaw to her ear. "How do wyverns mate?" he murmured.

"I—ah!" Her hips jerked underneath him as he nibbled at her earlobe. "I have—no idea. Don't stop."

He laughed under his breath. "Wasn't planning to." He nipped gently at her neck, and was rewarded with another one of those delicious, helpless moans. "Well in that case, we'll just do whatever feels right."

What felt right to *him* at the moment was to get rid of these increasingly irritating clothes. Drawing back, he pulled her upright, off the bed. She was as eager as him, undoing his shirt buttons even as he unfastened her jeans. There was a mutually awkward, impatient moment of tangled limbs and cloth…and then they were both bare to each other at last.

All the breath left his lungs at the sight of her glorious, naked curves. He had to close his eyes for a moment, fighting for control.

He very nearly lost it again as Ivy's hot mouth closed over his own nipple. His cock jerked, seeping helplessly in response to her slow, circling tongue. It was all he could do not to throw her onto her back and thrust into her there and there.

She made a smug little sound of delight, deep in her throat. Her hands stroked over his clenched abs, exploring every line, then traced the sharp lines of his hipbones. Every light touch seared him like fire. It was a glorious agony, all-consuming yet leaving him desperate for more.

He caught her wrists, forcing her away. "My turn now," he said, his voice hoarse with desire. "Please."

She pouted a little, but allowed him to push her back down onto the bed. He knelt down on the floor, between her parted knees. Her soft thighs trembled as he gently urged them further apart.

Finally, *finally* she was revealed to him, in all her magnificent splendor. Her plump, pink folds were wet for him, eager and welcoming. With both thumbs, he spread her even further, adoring the way she gasped and arced into his touch. Her scent beckoned to him.

He dipped his head, finally able to do what he'd dreamed of doing, every night since they'd first met. Slowly, savoring every second, he ran his tongue up her slick folds.

From the first taste, he was lost—addicted to her forevermore. He devoured her more deeply, his fingers digging into her hips to pull her more firmly to his mouth.

Ivy's thighs clenching around his head, her fingers tangling in his hair. Her release burst in a wave of sweetness, the pulsing waves of her pleasure throbbing against his tongue. The blood pounded in his cock in answer, so hard that for a moment he teetered on coming there and then.

"Now." Ivy tugged at his hair, pulling him up with insistent urgency. "Now, Hugh, oh please, now!"

He couldn't hold back any longer. He joined her on the bed, sliding his hands under the stunning curves of her ass. Kneeling between her legs, he supported her hips, getting just the right angle.

Slow, slow, slow. He had to be slow, no matter how she writhed and thrust in desperation.

Teeth gritting, he held her back, making her take him slowly. Inch by inch, she enveloped him, and *God*, it was better than dreams.

The faintest hint of resistance, and he made himself stop—but Ivy whined, her legs wrapping round him with irresistible force. There was nothing but drunk, dazed pleasure in her face as she pushed onto him. And at last, *at last* he was fully there, joined to her at last.

Her silken depths enfolded him, driving all other sensation away. He was blind to everything but her. Urgent instinct gripped him, setting a fierce, insistent rhythm. He drove into her again and again, each stroke better than the last as she tightened around him.

"Hugh!" Ivy clawed at his back, her eyes wide and dark with animal need. Her arms wrapped around his neck, straining to pull him closer to her bared teeth. "I want—I need—"

He knew what she wanted. As he made one last, deep thrust, he pulled her close to him, giving her his throat. Her teeth bit deep into the side of his neck.

Ecstasy exploded through him. He emptied endlessly into her, pouring himself out in hard, shuddering pulses. Even as he did, he felt her mind pour into his. As their bodies united, so did their souls.

My mate, he cried out silently, knowing that she could hear him again now. *My mate!*

My mate, she echoed, her own mental voice soft with wonder.

No, said a different voice.

It was almost Ivy's, but not quite—harsher, wilder, with a core of utter certainty. Emerald eyes flashed in his mind, staring into his soul with the merciless focus of a hunting predator.

We will have all of you, Ivy's wyvern snarled. *How dare you hide? All of you is ours, always, forever. You are our mate, and we claim you, NOW!*

A storm of wings and fury struck through him, even more intense than orgasm. The wyvern dove into the void at his core without hesitation, disappearing into the darkness.

And then—

CHAPTER 31

She'd killed him.

For five agonizing seconds—the longest five seconds of her life—she was certain that something had gone terribly wrong. Hugh's head snapped back, his whole body seizing as if in a fit. He jerked apart from her, toppling off the bed with a crash.

"*Hugh!*" she shrieked, all of her afterglow extinguished by stark terror.

A blinding flash of light made her instinctively throw an arm across her face, shielding her eyes. A gust of wind blew back her hair. She tasted the scent of fresh rain and bruised greenery in the air, like a forest in the wake of a thunderstorm.

Her wyvern slammed back into her soul with the force of a comet. She'd dimly been aware of it separating from her during the overwhelming ecstasy of mating, but now it was back in its accustomed place in her mind, green-scaled sides heaving with exertion.

There, it said, sounding tired, smug, and not in the least concerned.

The eye-searing blaze faded to a shimmering glow. She dropped her arm, blinking in the sudden soft, golden light.

The unicorn staggered to his feet, uncertain as a newborn fawn.

He stared at her with wide, sapphire eyes, looking even more astonished than she was.

"Hugh," she whispered. And then, louder, a shout of pure joy: *"Hugh!"*

Hugh's ears flicked back and forth, as if he was still trying to work out what had happened. His shining horn scythed the bedside lamp off the side table as he swung his head round to inspect his own white flanks. He lifted each front hoof in turn, stamping horseshoe dents into the bedroom carpet.

What the devil? he said in her mind, sounding utterly dumbfounded.

"You're back." She scrambled off the bed, flinging her arms around his shining neck. His fur was soft as velvet against her naked skin. "Oh, Hugh, you're back!"

Fingers trembling, she brushed his sweeping mane back from his forehead. His horn was no longer only silver. Now, a gleaming line of pure gold spiraled up the long length, shining bright as the rising sun.

She traced the gleaming path, feeling how it thickened a bit near the base, where Gaze had cut him. There was no sign of that dreadful wound now. His horn shone from base to tip. Where once it had shimmered with faint, firefly motes, now it glittered with white-gold sparks.

"You're healed," she said, tears streaking her cheeks. "Hugh, your horn. It's healed."

He went cross-eyed, as if trying to see his own forehead. Even on a unicorn, it was an undignified look. Ivy broke into giggles, her legs giving way underneath her. She collapsed back onto the bed, shaking with laughter and gratitude and sheer disbelief.

Hugh blurred, shifting back into human form. He stood there, naked, looking down at his own hands with a lopsided, bemused grin. Still gasping for breath, Ivy pulled him down next to her. She wound arms and legs around him, kissing him indiscriminately over lips and jaw and neck.

"But how did this happen?" she asked, breaking off for a moment. "You didn't suspect this *could* happen, did you?"

"Not in the slightest." He traced a circle over her heart with one finger. "I think it was your wyvern. I felt her go...into me, somehow. And she pulled out my unicorn."

He was hiding. Her wyvern yawned, flipping its wings as though it hadn't done anything extraordinary. *We didn't like that. We wanted* all *our mate. All of him, ours, always.*

"Did you hear that?" Ivy asked him, curious. "Can you still hear my animal?"

He shook his head. "No, she's gone back to you. I can only hear my own now." A soft, wondering look came into his eyes. "It isn't quiet anymore."

She snuggled into his shoulder, idly tracing the lines of his tattoos. "What does your unicorn say? Where was it?"

"It doesn't really know. It remembers going, and then...it was back." He was silent for a long moment, his fingers running lightly up and down the length of her spine. "I think it was always still there. Just lost. It was driven down into some deep, dark place by the sexual energy we created."

She stiffened in sudden alarm. "Oh no. Does that mean we can't—"

He cut off her words with a passionate kiss, his tongue sliding between her lips. She closed her eyes, surrendering to pleasure.

"We can do anything," he murmured into her mouth. His hand slid over her breast, making her gasp and press against him. "Everything. My unicorn's stronger now. That sort of energy won't hurt it anymore."

"No more headaches?" she breathed, as his fingers teased and caressed.

"No more headaches." His mouth turned up in a wicked smile. "I think that calls for a celebration, don't you?"

He ducked his head, kissing along her collarbone. She squirmed in delightful anticipation as he worked his way down to her eager nipple.

"Wait," she said, another cold thought breaking her out of the moment. "What about Gaze?"

Hugh made a muffled, impatient sound. "What about him?"

From the way Hugh's rock-hard length was pressing against her thigh, he had far more interesting matters on his mind at the moment. Nonetheless, she tugged at his hair, pulling him up.

"Well, you're a unicorn again," she said, worried. "And Gaze is still free to talk. How are we going to hide your secret?"

His expression tightened, brow creasing. He looked away, eyes going distant, as if he was having some internal dialogue with his animal.

"Secrecy didn't keep me safe," he said at last. "It just distanced me from people who could have helped, if I'd let them. Maybe…maybe it's time to stop hiding."

He flashed a grin at her. "After all, I've got a rather powerful mate to watch my back now. Only a fool tries to stand in the way of a wyvern."

Yes, her wyvern said, pleased and smug. *Good mate. Trusts us. We will never let anyone hurt him.*

Ivy wasn't sure she shared her animal's confidence. "Are you sure, Hugh?"

He kissed her forehead, very gently.

"You were brave enough to let go of your fear," he said. "Now I need to let go of mine."

EPILOGUE

"Hughnicorn!"

Hugh scowled as Chase enfolded him in a welcoming hug. "How many times do I have to tell you not to call me that?"

"As many times as you want. I'm still going to do it." Chase released him, turning to Ivy and Hope with a broad grin. "Lovely ladies! Merry Christmas!"

Hugh's irritation melted away as Chase embraced Ivy without the slightest hint of hesitation. It was probably just a typically exuberant, spontaneous gesture, but Chase couldn't have picked a better time or place.

The Full Moon pub was packed with celebrating shifters. Rose always relaxed the pub's 'adults only' rule on Christmas Eve. Toddlers tumbled amidst the bar tables on four legs or two, overcome by excited anticipation. Older children were on their best behavior, wide-eyed with the thrill of being allowed into the usually forbidden territory and determined not to do anything that might put them on Santa's Naughty List at the last minute.

Although word had slowly been getting round the shifter community over the past few weeks that Ivy could now control her venom,

Hugh had noticed more than one parent stiffen at their arrival. Chase's casual acceptance went a long way to soothe the lingering wisps of suspicion.

Chase let go of Ivy, turning back to Hugh. "So, how does it feel to be a National Treasure?"

Hugh grimaced. "Very odd. And if you start calling me *that*, then I swear to God I will hit you."

When Hugh had told his parents of his intent to stop hiding his nature, he'd been expecting to be disinherited. He'd at least expected his father to be incandescently angry.

What he *hadn't* expected was for his father to use his position as the Earl of Hereford to seek a private audience with the Queen.

Hugh was rather glad not to have been involved in *that* discussion. But whatever his father had said to the monarch, it had been effective. The Queen had declared the whole Silver family to be National Treasures, under her direct protection. Harming them was now tantamount to stealing from the Queen herself.

And no one was going to mess with the most powerful dragon shifter in Great Britain.

Chase's teasing smile widened. "So if you're officially part of the Royal Hoard now, does that mean you're technically owned by the Queen?"

Hugh put his arm over Ivy's shoulders. "There's only one person I belong to."

"On the topic of mates," Chase said. His chest swelled, pride clear in his face as he beckoned to someone in the crowd. "Ivy, Hope, there's someone I've been wanting you to meet. *My* mate, Connie."

Ivy's smile turned rather fixed. Hugh felt her alarm flash down the mate bond. The pegasus shifter might have forgiven her for what she'd done to him and his mate, but Hugh knew Ivy still hadn't forgiven herself.

He sent a wave of love and reassurance to her. *It's all right*, he said in her mind. *Chase wouldn't introduce you if there was still any bad feeling.*

And indeed, Connie reached out to shake Ivy's hand firmly. The short, curvy pilot looked Ivy in the eye.

"It's good to meet you properly at last," Connie said, her tone sincere. "We're both so grateful for what you've done for Hugh."

"I'm sorry I wrecked your plane!" Ivy blurted out, looking stricken.

Connie grinned, her smile as easy and welcoming as Chase's. "Ah, it's all fixed now. And if you hadn't, Chase and I would never have become mates. I can thank you for that."

Despite these words, Ivy still looked rather worried. "At least let me repay you for the damage I did."

A slightly strangled cough escaped Hugh. He was certain that Ivy hadn't the faintest idea just how rare and valuable Connie's Spitfire actually was, or she'd never have made the offer. And in any event, Chase was the only son of a billionaire. He could afford to buy—and did buy—any plane that Connie fancied.

"No need for that," Chase said, with a rather amused sideways glance at Hugh. His expression brightened, a reckless gleam entering his eye. "But if you really want to make amends, perhaps we could have a little wager. We still haven't determined who's *really* fastest in the air."

Hope raised her eyebrows at him. "From what Ivy told me, the last time she left you in the dust."

Connie chuckled. "That's not the way Chase tells that story. We *should* have a race to settle the matter for once and all. But just for fun." She poked Chase in the side, throwing a mock-glare at him. "No gambling."

A tentative smile broke across Ivy's face. "Pegasus versus wyvern versus airplane?"

"You're on." Connie grinned at both Ivy and Chase. "Prepare to eat my slipstream."

"Don't think I'm going to let you win just because you're my mate," Chase warned. "Pegasus honor is at stake here."

"Ivy is gonna thrash you both," Hope declared.

"We'll see," Ivy said, though Hugh could sense her secret confidence. "Well, if you won't let me pay for the plane, at least let me buy you a drink."

"Ooh, thanks," Hope said. "I'll have a mulled wine."

"You're *seventeen*," Ivy and Hugh said together.

Hope shrugged unrepentantly. "It was worth a try. Hey, there's Betty! Catch you all later."

"I'll come to the bar with you," Chase said to Ivy as Hope wheeled off through the crowd. He turned to his mate. "Mulled wine for you, my love?"

Connie shook her head. "Soft drink. Just in case."

Chase's merry expression sobered a bit. He planted a swift, soft kiss on his mate's forehead before following Ivy to the bar.

From the way Connie's hand drifted down to rest on her stomach, Hugh could guess what was going on. For a week every month, Connie would have that hopeful, nervous air. And then, every month, she would be disappointed. No matter how hard she and Chase tried, they just couldn't get pregnant.

His unicorn nudged him. *We should do something about that.*

Hugh slapped his own forehead. "I'm an idiot. Connie, may I touch you?"

"Yes, of course," she said, although she flashed him a puzzled look. "But it's okay, Hugh. I know you can't do anything to help."

"I *couldn't* do anything to help," he said. "Before."

Keeping his touch professionally neutral, Hugh slid his hand under Connie's shirt, resting his palm against the soft curve of her stomach. He closed his eyes, concentrating.

The energies involved in reproduction were strong...but he was stronger now himself. Now that his unicorn no longer flinched away from sexual energies, his questing mind could navigate the powerful forces surging within Connie's abdomen.

There *was* a tiny spark of potential there. It struggled to cling on, to put out roots that would allow it to grow. But the environment that should have supported it was slightly off. A little tilt in the hormonal balance...easily shifted back again...

"Hugh, what are you doing?" Chase said, in a not entirely friendly tone.

Hugh started, coming out of the healing trance. Chase and Ivy had returned with drinks. They both wore matching tight, fixed expressions of barely-controlled jealousy. Shifters didn't cope well with other people touching their mates.

"Oh, don't look at me like that, both of you. This is strictly for medical reasons." Hugh withdrew his hand, flexing his fingers to shake out the tingle of using his healing powers. "I'm just helping Connie stay pregnant."

A glass slipped from Chase's hand. "Did you say...*stay pregnant?*"

Hugh tried not to look *too* smug. "Allow me to be the first to congratulate you both."

"We're going to have a baby?" Chase breathed. He seized his mate, hugging her one-armed. "We're going to have a baby!"

Connie looked like she didn't dare to believe it. "We can't celebrate yet—it's still too early, anything could go wrong."

"I'm fairly certain it won't." To Hugh's senses, that tiny spark of potential was now beating strongly, shining with vibrant life.

In fact...

"Ah," he said, rubbing his chin. "Hmm. Chase, you said that you wanted three children, right?"

"One would be a miracle," Connie said quickly. "Don't worry about more. If you can only help us just this once, that'll still be more than enough."

"Yes, but you wouldn't be *upset* to have three babies, would you?" Hugh said cautiously. "Like, oh, just hypothetically speaking...identical triplets?"

Chase dropped the other glass.

"*Triplets?*" Connie squawked.

"I may have slightly overdone it," Hugh admitted.

～

"Triplets." Hugh's mother shook her head in amusement. "Well, it seems Hugh could have a lucrative career as a fertility consultant, should he ever tire of being a paramedic."

"I wouldn't hold your breath on that one," Ivy said, smiling. "He loves what he does too much to ever give up Alpha Team. Just look at them."

Across the room, the firefighters of Alpha Team were gathered at their usual corner booth. Broad-shouldered Dai, so gentle and soft-spoken despite the fiery dragon in his soul. Kind-hearted Griff, laughing as his three boys clambered all over him. Swift Chase, his black eyes lit up with exuberant joy. Towering John Doe, solemn and severe but with a gleam of wry humor hidden under his knightly discipline. Ash, quiet and contained, at the heart of the group and yet somehow still apart.

And Hugh, her Hugh. He sat in their midst, relaxed and at ease. He didn't flinch away now from the press of Dai's elbow against his, or Chase's open, spontaneous backslaps. He might still growl and glare at his friends, but his sharp-tongued banter concealed true, brotherly love. Ivy knew he would have died for any one of them, as they would for him.

Lady Hereford's face softened as she watched the group. "I cannot tell you how much it means to me to see that he has found a true home here. Much as I might selfishly wish for him to come back to the estate." She hesitated, casting Ivy a sidelong glance. "Though he will inherit one day, you realize."

"I know. We'll deal with that when it happens. But for now, we're staying in Brighton." Ivy made a face. "Which means I really need to work out what I'm going to do. Hugh's not that happy with me continuing to scrub toilets."

"I had a suggestion on that, if you would indulge me," Lady Hereford said, sounding uncharacteristically tentative. "I was talking earlier with Hope's delightful young friend Betty. What she told me of Gaze's charity piqued my interest. I would very much like to start a new organization, with similar aims. Wyverns and hellhounds aren't the only ones who face discrimination from other shifters."

"I think that's a wonderful idea," Ivy said warmly. "I don't want vulnerable shifter kids like Betty to get scooped up by some other crime boss now that Gaze is out of the picture. So you want me to find you some contacts to get started?"

"No." Lady Hereford took a sip of her mulled wine. "I was hoping that you would run it."

Ivy stared at her, slack-jawed. "Me? I don't know the first thing about running a charity!"

"I can teach you that. But I can't teach anyone else what you already know. You have the experience of what it's like to grow up outcast from shifter society. And who better than a wyvern to mentor surly, defensive teens who've been taught to think of themselves as monsters?" Lady Hereford leaned forward, touching the back of Ivy's hand. "Think about it, won't you?"

Ivy's heart beat faster as she began to imagine the possibilities. Not a job done at night, solitary and invisible, but a real career helping people. Helping people like herself.

"Okay," she said. "I'll need to talk it over with Hugh, though."

"Of course," said Lady Hereford. "You are mates, after all."

Ivy noticed the way her voice dropped a little on the word 'mates.' A slight sadness passed across Lady Hereford's usually serene face, but Ivy didn't think it was anything to do with her and Hugh.

"So where's the Earl?" she asked, guessing at the real reason for Lady Hereford's sudden melancholy. "I thought you were both going to come down for Christmas."

"Oh, he's here, upstairs in the private room," Lady Hereford reassured her. "I'm sure he'd be delighted if you went up to share a drink with him later. But...well, tonight is a party for shifters and their families. He escorted me here, but felt it best to stay away from the festivities himself."

Ivy couldn't blame the Earl for that. The loss of his unicorn was old, but it was still deeply disconcerting for any shifter to see that grotesque scar in his soul. And perhaps it was also difficult for the Earl to be around people who still had their own animals.

"Uh...is it going to be hard for him to be around Hugh tomorrow?" Ivy asked, belatedly realizing that this might be a more fraught family Christmas than she'd thought.

"No," Lady Hereford said, without hesitation. "It meant more to him than you can imagine—certainly more than he'll ever say—that

Hugh invited us both. Thank you for finally telling Hugh the truth about his father, by the way."

Ivy shrugged. "It just didn't feel right to keep that secret from him anymore. I'm glad that he and Hugh might finally be able to mend some fences. But are you sure it doesn't upset him that Hugh's got his unicorn back, when he doesn't himself?"

Lady Hereford shook her head firmly. "He's overjoyed that Hugh regained his animal. You don't need to worry about that."

Despite Hugh's mother's words, there was a crease in her brow that spoke of some hidden concern. But if it wasn't about her husband...what could it be?

A flash of insight came to her. "Is it hard for *you* to be around Hugh now?"

Lady Hereford dropped her gaze, toying with her wineglass. "I am happy for him, of course. But now that we know a true mate's love can restore a unicorn...well. I have to think about what that means for me and my husband."

Ivy sucked in her breath. She's assumed that Hugh's parents would finally be able to be together fully, as husband and wife, now that Hugh was no longer sensitive to sexual activity. But it seemed her own happiness had only made his parents' situation worse.

"The Earl doesn't want to leave you, does he?" she asked, dismayed and guilty.

"Oh, no." Lady Hereford smiled sadly. "His honor would never allow it. He would never abandon me, nor even breathe a word of his true feelings. But I know how much your animals mean to you shifters. I know how he still walks the house in the small hours of the morning, unconsciously searching for something he lost long ago. I love him too much to allow him to live in such pain. I think you understand."

Ivy did. Her heart bled to think of Hugh's kind mother being in a similar impossible position.

"Are you sure *you* aren't his true mate?" she asked. "I mean, you could be, right? Maybe he just wouldn't know, not being a shifter anymore."

Lady Hereford's slim shoulders rose and fell in a sigh. "I cannot cling to that false hope. We were...intimate, before Hugh was born. And his unicorn never came back. No. I am not his true mate."

A slight cough made them both look round. Rose, who was serving drinks behind the bar, had drifted nearer during the conversation. The middle-aged pub owner regarded them both thoughtfully as she pulled a pint of beer.

"Pardon me," Rose said, "but I couldn't help overhearing. I can assure you, your husband very much *is* your true mate."

Lady Hereford's expression iced over a little, as if she was suspecting some sort of scam. "May I ask how you are so certain?"

"I'm a swan shifter," Rose said, deftly sliding the full pint down the bar. "I can sense mate bonds."

The crease between Lady Hereford's eyebrows deepened. "Your kind are renowned for always being able to find their true mates. I know that swans go on a quest when they reach adulthood, with their inner animal leading them unerringly to their other half. But as far as I am aware, swans can only sense the location of their *own* true mate, not other people's."

An old sadness shadowed Rose's calm eyes. "I'm not like other swans. When I was younger, I *could* sense my true mate calling to me. I even set off on my quest to find him. But one day, in the middle of my journey, I woke up and couldn't feel him anymore. Perhaps my mate died before I could meet him. Anyway, for some reason losing my own heart's desire made me sensitive to other people's hearts. So now I help other people find *their* mates. And I am absolutely certain that your mate is right upstairs at this very minute."

A bright hope kindled in Lady Hereford's face...and swiftly died. "But in that case, I should have brought back his unicorn on our wedding day."

"But you weren't truly open to each other then!" Ivy exclaimed, remembering her first ever conversation with the Earl. "Because he never told you about his unicorn, not until Hugh's powers started developing. Even though he loved you, he was holding back, not trusting you fully with his secrets. You didn't even know there was something you could be doing. But now you do!"

Lady Hereford caught her breath. "Do you—do you truly think that a non-shifter could do what you did?"

Doesn't take claws or wings. Just determination, her wyvern commented. Its jaw dropped in a serpentine smile. *And our mate didn't get his stubbornness from his sire.*

"My wyvern says you can do it," Ivy told Hugh's mother. "You can restore the Earl's unicorn, Lady Hereford!"

Rose's mouth twitched up. "This seems an excellent time to mention that there's a guest room upstairs. With a bed. And a lock on the door."

Lady Hereford blushed like a schoolgirl. Draining the rest of her wine in one swallow, she stood up. With a parting nod, she hastened through the crowd, heading for the back stairs.

Rose let out a deep, satisfied sigh. "I do love being able to set people on the right path."

"I'm sorry about your mate, though," Ivy said, feeling a twinge of pity. "Maybe there's hope for you too, somehow."

"Ah, well." Rose went back to making drinks. "Not everyone gets the fairytale."

"I've never believed in fairytales." Ivy shrugged. "Still don't. I think if you want a happy ending, you have to make it yourself."

The swan shifter's busy hands stilled. Her head raised, but it wasn't to look at Ivy. Her thoughtful gaze was turned on the corner where Alpha Team still sat, deep in conversation.

"Yes," Rose said softly, her eyes resting on Ash. "Maybe you're right."

∾

Thank you for a Christmas miracle. Perhaps Hugh knows a good place to shift near the city?

Hugh, who was busy lighting the log fire in the grate, cast her an inquiring glance over his shoulder. "Good news?"

"Just a text from your mother," Ivy said, trying to sound casual. "They're looking forward to coming over later. And your father wants to go out for a run after dinner."

Hugh's eyebrows drew down. "My father hates jogging. Come to think of it, so do I. What the devil is he thinking? Some sort of ghastly father-son bonding experience?"

"Something like that." It was hard to keep a straight face. "Come on, humor him. He's trying to make up for lost time."

Hugh snorted, going back to messing around with matches. "If he tries to drag me out fishing, I'm pushing him overboard. Come on, you bastard thing, light."

"You're not very good at that," Hope observed cheerfully, from under her blanket of cats. Most of Hugh's whole horde was piled onto her lap, squabbling over the last bits of buttery croissant from breakfast.

"I put out fires, not start them," Hugh growled. "Where's Ash when you need him?"

"Well, hurry up." Scattering cats, Hope wheeled closer to the glittering Christmas tree dominating their lounge. "I want to do presents!"

"I thought you were seventeen, not seven." Ivy slipped her phone back into her pocket. "But okay. You want to unwrap yours first?"

To her surprise, Hope shook her head. "Nope. I want to give you your one from me first."

"Wait," Hugh said. Abandoning his futile fire-making efforts, he rose, turning. "I don't want to miss this. I did help you work on it, after all."

That slightly eased Ivy's fears of being presented with some Pinterest disaster. She knelt down next to the Christmas tree, reaching for the pile of wrapped presents. "Okay, which one is it?"

"Hang on." Hope pushed Mr. Mittens off her lap, standing up. "I'll get it for you."

Hope did it so casually, it took Ivy a second to even register what her sister had just done. Ivy froze, staring in stunned disbelief at Hope's bare toes, wiggling on the carpet. Slowly, her gaze tracked up, past her sister's straight knees, up, up, to her wide, brilliant grin.

"You can walk," Ivy whispered. She leaped to her own feet, an answering smile splitting her own face. "You can *walk!*"

She nearly threw her arms around her sister in pure joy—but jerked back at the last minute. Even though she could control her venom now, she still hadn't dared to touch Hope. Her sister was still deathly sensitive to wyvern venom, after all. It wasn't worth taking the risk.

She turned to hug Hugh instead, squeezing his torso tight. "You said you didn't think you'd be able to reverse her paralysis, even after you neutralized the venom!"

"I kinda made him say that," Hope said. She took a step forward with a dramatic flourish, like a magician revealing a trick. "I wanted to surprise you."

"It's the best surprise ever," Ivy said fervently. "The best Christmas present ever."

Hope's grin widened even further. "Oh, this isn't your Christmas present."

Without a hint of weakness, she strode forward. Before Ivy knew what was happening, Hope's strong arms encircled her from behind.

"*This* is your Christmas present," Hope whispered in her ear, her cheek warm against Ivy's.

Stunned, still with her own arms around Hugh, Ivy looked up into his face. He smiled down at her, his blue eyes soft and gentle.

"I also healed her sensitivity," he said. "She's not allergic to your venom anymore."

Slowly, she released her mate. And, for the first time in her entire life, she turned around and hugged her sister.

"Okay," Ivy said, when she could finally speak through her tears. "Now I feel kinda terrible that I only got you a laptop."

Hope let out a shriek that nearly split Ivy's eardrum. "You didn't! Oh my God, thank you thank you thank you! Where is it?"

Hugh laughed as Hope flung herself at the presents under the tree, sorting eagerly through them. "And so the true spirit of Christmas appears at last. Well, before we descend into rampant consumerism, I want to—"

"No," Hope interrupted, not looking up from unwrapping her present. "Not yet. Ivy, give Hugh his present next."

Even though she'd prepared for this, Ivy's heart skipped a beat. Hugh's present felt hot as a coal in the back pocket of her jeans. She swallowed, mouth dry.

"I, uh," she stammered. "Didn't really know what to get you."

Hugh cocked his head, looking a little baffled. From the sudden surge of worry down the mate bond, she knew he must have sensed her own tension.

"You didn't have to get me anything," he said. "You've already given me everything."

Damn it, she'd *practiced* this. But all her carefully planned words had flown out of her head. All she could do was sink to one knee, pulling the small velvet box out of her pocket.

"Well, I was hoping you might let me give you this too," she said, showing him the simple silver ring inside. "Hugh, will you marry me?"

For a second, he just stared down at her, looking completely nonplussed.

Then he swore, which was not entirely the reaction she'd been hoping for.

"Oh, hellfire and damnation," he said, pulling a matching velvet box out of *his* back pocket. "You beat me to it."

Ivy stared at the emerald and diamond band. Then she looked over her shoulder at Hope, who'd fallen into helpless hysterics amidst crumpled wrapping paper.

"Did you know about this?" she asked her sister.

Hope nodded, shaking with hiccuping laughter. "He swore me to secrecy too. You both planned beautiful speeches, by the way. Pity neither of you actually remembered them."

"Well, apparently we can just ask you to recite them for us later," Hugh said. He still looked somewhat exasperated, but through it shone deep, profound joy. "Ivy, may I assume this means that your answer is yes?"

"If *yours* is," Ivy said, happy tears streaming down her face again.

She slid the silver ring onto his finger, as he put the emerald one on hers. She turned her hand, dazzled by the way the brilliant green stone sparkled in the Christmas lights.

"Wow, I'm really being outdone in the present stakes," she said weakly. "I'm gonna have to go all out next year."

Hugh tilted her chin up with one finger. "Like I said," he breathed, bending down to her, "you've already given me everything."

"Ugh," Hope called as they kissed. "Get a room."

Ivy flipped off her sister behind Hugh's back. She closed her eyes, her whole body melting against his at the miracle of his mouth on hers. No matter how long she lived, she would never, ever take that simple touch for granted.

"Ten more seconds and I start Instagramming this," Hope announced. "Come *on*, guys. I want to give Hugh my present."

Ivy broke off, reluctantly. "Brace yourself, Hugh. She's a terror with a hot glue gun and glitter."

"Well, I didn't have time to make anything this year, what with killer basilisks and nearly dying and then having to learn how to walk. Also, I'm very broke." Hope bounced to her feet, clutching her new laptop possessively to her chest. "So instead I will give you the greatest gift of all."

Hugh's eyebrow rose. "Oh?"

"Time," Hope said beatifically. "In particular, time without me. I'm gonna go to Betty's for the rest of the morning. By my reckoning, that gives you four hours alone before Hugh's parents arrive. I'm sure you'll find something to do."

Hugh chuckled, his arms tightening around Ivy's waist. "I'm sure we will. You want a lift?"

"Nope," Hope said, with deep satisfaction. "I'll walk."

With a cheery wave, she departed, a hopeful line of cats following her out. Ivy nestled against Hugh's chest, sliding one finger teasingly between his shirt buttons.

"You didn't come to bed until after I was asleep last night," she murmured. "I hope you're planning to make that up to me now."

"Oh, I will." He caught her wrist, stopping her from undoing the top button of his shirt. "I have another present for you."

She pressed her hips against his, heat rising at the feel of his hard, ready shaft. "So I can tell."

He snorted. "Not that. Something else."

There wasn't anything else Ivy wanted at the moment, but she released him. She didn't want to spoil another surprise.

"So what did you get me?" she asked, stepping back.

His eyes gleamed. "A tattoo."

Ivy blinked at him. "I'm pretty sure I would have noticed getting a tattoo."

"It's for you, not *on* you." His mouth quirked. "And it's been bloody difficult hiding it from you for the past two days, so allow me a dramatic reveal."

Holding her gaze, he flicked open the top button of his shirt. Ivy's breath caught as he slowly undid each one, revealing an enticing sliver of his torso. The snake tattooed in the center of his chest winked at her, its sinuous body drawing her eye down to the groove between his abs.

Hugh shrugged his shirt off his shoulders, and Ivy jerked her gaze back up. There were the familiar twining vines...but the design was no longer unbalanced.

She could barely make out the original dry, curled leaves on his right arm. Now they were hidden amidst a riot of new growth. His left arm too no longer had any bare vines remaining. Every inch of twining stem now sprouted intricate leaves.

But not just any leaves.

Ivy leaves.

Speechless, Ivy ran her finger over the fresh black ink. So *that* was where he'd been the day before yesterday. The new tattoos were already healed, indelibly part of his skin, thanks to his unicorn powers.

"No more keeping score?" she breathed.

He shook his head. "I don't need to anymore."

She kissed one of the three-pointed leaves, feeling his breath catch. "Because you'll always be able to heal."

He cupped the side of her face, his fingers sliding along the line of her jaw. His palm was warm against her cheek.

"No," he said. "Because you healed me."

<<<<>>>>

Printed in Great Britain
by Amazon